D.P. Hart-Davis

THE STALKING PARTY

A FIELDSPORTS THRILLER

Merlin Unwin Books

First published by Merlin Unwin Books, 2015
Text © D.P. Hart-Davis, 2015

Merlin Unwin Books Limited
Palmers' House, 7 Corve Street,
Ludlow, Shropshire, SY8 1DB
www.merlinunwin.co.uk

A CIP record of this book is available from the British Library.

Printed and bound by TJ International, Padstow, England
ISBN 978-1-910723-04-3

Dedicated with love to all the friends
who have shared stalking with us at:

Achnacarry
Ardtornish
Black Mount
Conaglen
Fealar
Corrour
Glenaladale
Glenetive
Glenfeshie
Glenkinglass
Knoydart
Loch Choire
Strathossian

and to the stalkers and ghillies
who made every day on the hill
unforgettable

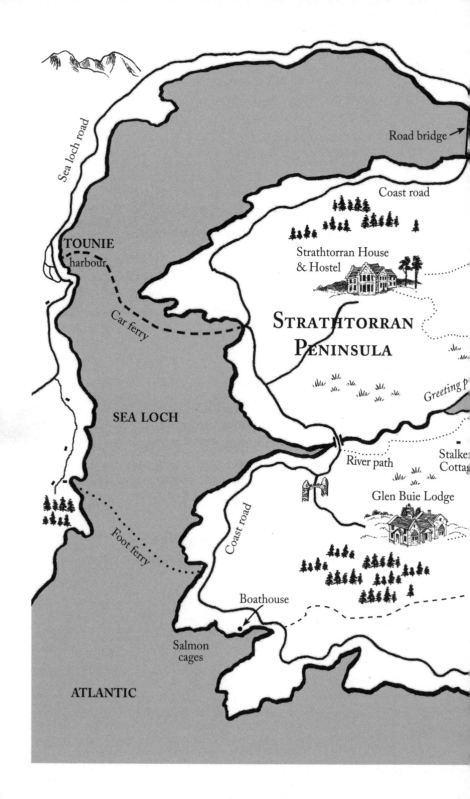

PRINCIPAL CHARACTERS

The Glen Buie house-party
Sir Archibald Hanbury, half-owner of Glen Buie deer forest
Gwendolyn Hanbury, his second wife
Nicholas Hanbury, his son by his first wife
Marjorie Forbes, his widowed sister
John Forbes, Marjorie's elder son
Benjamin Forbes, Marjorie's younger son
Everard Cooper, tycoon
Lady Priscilla Cooper, Everard's wife
Astrid (Ashy) Macleod, Lady Priscilla's daughter by her first husband
Maya Forrester, widow of Gwendolyn Hanbury's son Alec, who has inherited his half-share in Glen Buie
Beverley Tanner, Nicholas Hanbury's guest
Joss and Cynthia Page, guests at Glen Buie

Staff at Glen Buie Lodge
Sandy McNichol, head stalker
Mary Grant, cook
Duncan Grant, butler and gardener
Fergus Grant, their son, the second stalker
Catriona McNichol, Sandy's mother
Elspeth, the cook's teenage niece
Ishbel, parlourmaid
Kirsty, Sandy's girlfriend

The Strathtorran family
Torquil, Earl of Strathtorran
Janie, his wife
Ian McNeil, his widowed brother

Police
Detective Inspector Robb
Det. Sergeant Winter
Constable McTavish

Others
Hector Logie, retired schoolmaster and birdwatcher
Jock Taggart, landlord
Donny, pony-boy and ghillie

Chapter One

HIGH ABOVE THE narrow neck of the sea loch known as the Sound of Gash, the stag stood motionless in the moonlight, every sense alert, every fibre in his heavy muscular body tensed for action. Steam rose from his peat-blackened coat, and drifted in twin jets from his nostrils, while the wide trumpets of his ears strained forward to catch the sound that had jerked him from fidgety, desultory grazing into full vigilance: the challenging roar of a rival.

Behind him his twelve-strong harem, by no means enough for a handsome ten-pointer in his prime, stamped and jostled nervously, cloven hoofs crunching in the first frost of autumn. The mating-call of another dominant male drew them like a powerful magnet, yet with their present lord's eye upon them, none of his hinds dared shift her ground.

On the fringes of the little herd the few young males still tolerated at this early stage in the rut – a couple of two-year-old 'knobbers' and a stunted four-year-old with the unbranched antlers known as a switch head – used the opportunity of the stag's distraction to edge privily nearer to the tantalising oestrogen-scented forbidden zone.

Another roar, distinctly closer: the big ten-pointer grunted in response and, with a burst of irritable energy, forced his hinds into a closer bunch then drove through the middle, scattering them, and rounded them up once more, freezing them, daring them to defy his authority while he trotted away to confront the intruder.

Again the young stags drifted closer.

Thirty yards apart, in a natural arena of peat-hag, the rivals stopped to paw the ground and assess one another. Evenly matched, eight points to ten, fourteen stone to fifteen, each head bearing similar wide antlers with well-defined points – brow, bey, and trey – with cups at the top which could well have come from the same gene-pool. Brothers, maybe, who had spent the summer months grazing and cudding in amity, now super-charged with testosterone and inflamed into murderous rivalry.

Like saluting duellists, they raised and lowered their armed heads and then, by common accord, swung broadside on and began to pace parallel tracks across the peat, back and forth, back and forth, at each turn narrowing the gap until they were jostling shoulder to shoulder.

Suddenly, as if at a signal, the two heads clashed together, their lean haunches pivoted sharply, and with locked antlers and straining backs they fought for the advantage of the slope. They broke free, charged, and clashed again, grunting and wrestling in ferocious combat that belonged to a different world from that of the twinkling necklace of headlights circling the loch road a thousand feet below, or the glowing blue screens in holiday chalets along the foreshore of the Sound, that separated them from the Strathtorran peninsula.

Ten-points was heavier, Eight-points younger and more agile, but soon weight began to tell. Step by step the challenger gave ground until, with blood streaming from a gash in his shoulder, he turned abruptly and fled downhill with the older stag in hot pursuit.

Bounding over rocks and tussocks, the beaten challenger leapt white-water runnels and jinked through peat-hags in his efforts to shake off his pursuer. In a matter of minutes they descended two hundred precipitous feet, galloping full tilt across a landslip of huge jumbled boulders as easily as if it had been smooth lawn. Twice Ten-points drew close enough to deliver slashing blows to his fleeing opponent's haunches, but each time a desperate swerve saved his life, and after galloping the best part of a mile from the scene of their encounter, the victor abruptly tired of the chase.

With heaving sides and outstretched neck, he watched his rival out of sight, and his roar of triumph echoed across the bleak hillside. Then he waded into a wallow and rolled, urinated, rolled again and, silvered with sweat and dripping peat, trotted back towards his hinds.

They were gone.

The corrie was empty, silent apart from the sharp yap of a hunting fox, but as he stood there snuffing the frosty air, a freakish eddy of wind stealing round the hill told the stag what had happened as plainly as if the theft had taken place in full view. Head upflung, powerful hocks driving him forward like pistons, his nostrils recognised the scent of treachery, and he trotted smartly in pursuit.

Tucked away in a sheltered grassy bowl at the top of sheer cliffs, he came on them like an avenging fury. Hinds and calves scattered at his approach, but he paid them no heed, his concentrated rage targeted wholly on the runty switch engaged in mounting his most favoured hind, the pearl of the harem.

The first the ravisher knew of his peril was a vicious sideways swipe which knocked him off his hind legs, swiftly followed by a series of short, fierce jabs at his unprotected belly. With a squirm and a bound, the switch regained his feet and lowered his head more in submission than provocation, but it was too little, too late to deflect the mature stag's furious charge. Weight, strength, and rage of battle were all in Ten-points' favour. The frontal impact of those mighty antlers was enough to break the switch's neck, but instead of standing up to the charge, the youngster feinted sideways, so that the left-hand point of his own unbranched antlers ripped his attacker from shoulder to flank and, driven deep by the force of his charge, slid in to pierce Ten-points' intestines.

An assassin's stroke from an assassin's weapon, but the switch's involuntary blow was to be his last. Wrenching free, the big stag charged again, catching the youngster off balance and hurling him over the lip of the cliff to perish far below, while the hinds briefly raised their slim necks to watch, then returned to the serious business of grazing.

High on adrenalin, the stag paced to and fro across the cliff's edge, sometimes swinging his head round to nose at his flank. Presently the sweat dried and the fire of battle ebbed. He lay down, rose and circled, then lay down again, and deep in his belly the wound began to burn. Still grazing, his hinds moved away, but he did not follow.

Dawn found him stumbling alone through the mossy, overgrown wood that clothed the loch's steep sides, his antlers draped in bracken caught up in his many falls, shiny loops of intestine pushing through the ugly gash in his flank. When he reached the semi-circle of yellow shingle, he lowered his head to lip at the water, then slowly waded in until the blessed cold numbed his burning belly into insensibility.

The red sun rose over the high, frost-glittering hills, and touched the rippling wavelets with gold, and still he stood chest-deep, watched and noted by ravens commuting across the Sound, and golden eagles wheeling in wide sweeps from shore to shore. Noted, too, by the powerful tripod-mounted telescope belonging to the birdwatching retired schoolmaster whose croft commanded the finest view on the Strathtorran peninsula.

'A braw heid,' muttered Hector Logie, who lived alone and was in the habit of talking aloud. Minutely he adjusted the focus to count the points. 'What ails him now, I wonder?'

Thrice while cooking breakfast he left his porridge to splutter unstirred in the pan while he returned to his telescope, and on each occasion it seemed to him that the stag had moved deeper into the water. Hinds and calves were coming down from the hills, dipping muzzles in the shallows to drink, but they ignored the stag and he, in turn, took no notice of them.

'Wounded sair, poor bugger,' diagnosed Logie, 'though whether by his brethren or mine, and how long it'll tak' him tae die, the Dear only knows.'

It occurred to him that someone else might also know. Dumping mug and porringer in the sink, he dialled the cottage of Sandy McNichol, head stalker of Glen Buie forest.

'Is that you, Kirsty?' he asked when a woman's voice answered. 'Can ye tell me now, did Sandy lose a beast in the Glas Corrie yestreen? The boat came down the loch wi' nae stag in it that I could see.'

He held the receiver away from his ear as she shouted shrilly above the squalling of the bairn, and presently Sandy himself came on the line.

'A wounded beast? Ten points? Not ours, but I'd best give him a bullet tae end his suffering. Where is he, Hector? Aye. Aye. I ken the spot. He'll have been fighting, for sure. Keep your glass on him now, man, and I'll be wi' ye right away.'

Ten minutes passed before Logie saw the green Land Rover swing out of the Glen Buie lodge drive and speed along the loch road, and when he looked back at the stag, only his branching head was still visible above the water.

As Sandy's burly form emerged from the vehicle, slipping a rifle from its canvas sleeve, the wounded stag gathered the last of his strength and struck out into the raging white-capped waters of the Sound.

Chapter Two

SIR ARCHIBALD HANBURY had spent too long in City boardrooms to allow his square, blunt-featured, good-humoured face to reflect his feelings, but as he finished carving the haunch of venison and took his place at the head of the long table, his heart sank.

Oh, my darling, my best beloved! he appealed silently to his wife Gwendolyn, stately and serene at the other end of the shining expanse of mahogany, What have I done to deserve this?

But Gwennie was beyond eye-contact, talking to her own neighbours, as remote as if she was on another planet. He could hardly blame her for allocating him the most recent arrivals among his female guests as his dinner companions, but as his practised eye surveyed the two young women between whom he was inescapably planted, he felt isolated and depressed by the thought of the conversational spadework ahead.

On his right sat his son Nicky's addition to the guest-list, though whether she rated as girlfriend, guru, or simply business colleague he had yet to find out. A thoroughly modern miss, or more likely ms, thought Sir Archie despondently: skinny, dark, intense, with an uncompromisingly cropped head and, unless he was very much mistaken, an outsize chip on her shoulder.

Still, he mustn't complain. If entertaining this particular visitor was the price he had to pay for Nicky's return to the fold, he would put the best face he could on it. There had been times in the past three years when he feared that his efforts to interest Nicky in what should eventually become his inheritance had merely served to alienate him. This long-sought rapprochement was a delicate plant, and must be protected from the slightest chill.

Prospects for conversation looked only slightly easier on his left. Maya Forrester, widow of his stepson Alec, was another unknown quantity, born and bred to a different kind of life. She was twenty-four years old, stunningly attractive, daughter of a Tennessee judge and a history professor, and black as your hat.

Shouldn't say that, he chided himself. Shouldn't even think it. A good horse is never a bad colour. But why, oh why couldn't Alec have married a country-loving tweeds-and-pearls English girl, instead of leaving this exotic flower as part-owner of Glen Buie?

Being a fair man, he wouldn't dream of holding Maya responsible for Alec's death, but there was no doubt in his mind that marrying her had been the mistake that precipitated the tragedy. Head over ears in love, Alec had thrown up his steady job in a merchant bank, and ploughed a ridiculous sum of money into a deep-sea fishing venture.

We'll fly over next summer, Mum, when the boat is laid up, he had written to Gwennie. *I want to take Maya to the hill, and show her Glen Buie. She'll love it, I know...*

Alec had never been a great communicator, and the long silence that followed had scarcely worried them. It had been Judge Paulson, Maya's father, who eventually telephoned, his deep voice choking, to tell them the *Jenny B* had been lost with all hands.

This was no time to rake up such memories. Sir Archie shook them off, turning his attention determinedly to the girl on his right. Now, what the hell what her name? He had been so taken aback when Nicky arrived with her in tow that he had failed to listen properly when she was introduced.

He tried to sneak a look at her place-card, but it was half hidden by a plate. All he could see was LEY, and that struck no chord. There was something odd about the condition of her plate, too. Meat and gravy had been scraped off and deposited on her side plate, leaving only a brownish smear among the main-course vegetables.

I might have guessed, he thought.

'Is that enough for you, my dear?' he asked kindly. 'I can ring for some cheese, if you like, or an egg?'

'I wouldn't put you to the trouble.'

'No trouble, my dear. Can't have you starving.' He pressed the bell with his foot, feeling her bristle at the two *'My dears'* and searching his mind for the missing name. One of those odd, unisex affairs: a place he knew quite well. Henley? Berkeley?

'Some cheese for Miss ... er ...' he mumbled to Duncan Grant, gardener-cum-butler, attentive at his elbow.

'My name is Beverley,' said the girl sharply, 'and I said I didn't want any cheese.'

'Oh! Sorry. Just as you like. Thank you, Duncan. No cheese.'

'Verra guid, Sir Archibald.' Duncan cat-footed away.

'Nicky should have told us you are vegetarian,' said Sir Archie, hoping he sounded friendly, not patronising – heaven forbid!

'I'm not.'

'Er ... then why?'

'Your cook told me what you were going to eat tonight.'

'Venison?' He looked at his plate and laughed. 'Don't worry, it isn't high. And you don't get your ears cropped for eating it, nowadays.'

'How can you joke about it?' she demanded fiercely.

'Joke? My dear girl ...' He caught the note of patronage, smothered it, started again. 'I'm not joking, far from it. Feeding this household is a serious business. We have to live off the land as far as we can. No supermarket, no delicatessen, only the boat three times a week to bring the grocery order.'

'How can you be so cruel? Killing beautiful wild creatures for sport?'

'It would be a damned sight more cruel if we didn't,' he said bluntly, disliking her, yet determined to be fair. She didn't understand how a deer-forest was managed – how could she, unless Nicky had explained? She probably expected it to be some kind of wildlife park, complete with notices explaining the ecology of the region and warnings about slippery bridges.

'If we didn't keep numbers down to a sustainable level and shoot out the surplus beasts, the place would soon be overrun with deer and half of them would starve. No natural predators, you see. No wolves, coyotes, hyenas, wild dogs.'

'So you play God?'

'We manage very poor resources in the most humane way we can.'

'How can you say that?' she exclaimed angrily.

'It happens to be true.'

Beverley made a disgusted sound and began to cut up her vegetables, then laid the knife on the side of the plate, transferring the fork to her right hand. 'Why can't you let the poor creatures live their lives as Nature intended?'

'Nature never intended deer to live on a barren mountaintop.' His tone was dry. 'They're woodland animals. They need shelter, leaves to browse, decent grazing. Do you know that if you take a 15-stone stag from here and release him in his proper environment, somewhere like Thetford Chase, for instance, his progeny may grow to weigh thirty stone? It's only through miracles of adaptation that deer can survive here, in the last wild corners we humans have left for them.'

'There's lots of grass along the river,' she said defensively.

Sir Archie shook his head. 'Precious little feeding value in that stuff. Besides, the deer don't come down to the river at this time of year. Too many midges. Too many damned people walking along the river path.'

'Are you implying that I shouldn't have gone there?' she snapped.

God! She was quick on the draw, he thought. 'No, no,' he

said wearily. 'The deer are on the high tops in this weather. Stick to the paths and you won't bother them. You'll be safe enough.'

Her eyebrows drew together. 'Safe? Isn't it safe off the paths?'

'Not really. Not when deer are being culled. A rifle bullet can travel over two miles – if it doesn't hit something, that is.'

There was a pause while she digested this, then she said in a combative tone, 'There's no law of trespass in Scotland. Ramblers have the right to go where they please.'

'True enough, but all the same they stick to the paths if they know what's good for them. We put up warning notices during the cull, as a precaution against accidents.'

'Have there been accidents?'

Under the table, his fingers tapped wood secretly. 'No shooting accidents, thank God. One can't be too careful.'

'But other kinds?'

'Oh, nothing serious. Broken legs, people getting lost, fishermen wading in too deep... that kind of thing.' Again his fingers sought wood. 'It's not a dangerous place, exactly, but it is untamed. That's what I like about it. You have to keep your wits about you and recognise the power of natural forces. Wind, cold, water, precipices. You have to remember that if you get into difficulties, there may not be anyone around to help you.'

She wasn't listening. 'I still think it's cruel,' she said.

Sir Archie sighed. Useless to ask how she would dispose of hundreds of surplus beasts, or feed the ones who survived the long, bitter winter in these remote glens. Useless to speak of blood-stinking abattoirs, or half-stunned turkeys struggling on conveyor-belts. Her mind was closed. She didn't want to see things as they were, but how she would like them to be.

He chewed steadily at his meat, reluctant to admit that her accusatory stare was spoiling his pleasure in it. She was good-looking, in a sharp, hawkish way, but her very glance offered a challenge born of...what? Insecurity? Fear? A genuine disgust at the spectacle of the rich at play? If the last, why the hell had Nicky brought her here? He must have known she'd hate it.

'Have you known Nicholas long?' he asked, carefully neutral.

'Two years, I suppose. A friend brought him to one of our meetings.'

'A political meeting?'

'No.' She looked down the table to where Nicky was talking animatedly to his solid, grey-chignoned aunt, Marjorie Forbes. 'I run a charity called *Home from Home*. You won't have heard of it.'

Statement, not question. In her book, bloated capitalists like him knew nothing about charity work. If he mentioned his firm's vast annual donations, she wouldn't believe him, and in any case his mental alarm bells were already ringing. Trust Nicky to have got himself mixed up with a dodgy charity.

'Interesting. What exactly do you do?' he asked, though he could make a fair guess.

She said glibly, as if she had answered the question a hundred times, 'We act as a safety net for people who don't qualify for help from official social services. People with emotional or financial crises, who have no one to turn to.'

'Teenagers on the loose? Battered wives?'

'We try not to categorise. We assess each case on its merits. We offer victims a roof over their heads, counselling, support until they can pull their lives together.'

'It sounds expensive.' He wished she would talk instead of lecturing.

'We do a great deal of fund-raising. Nicky is our Financial Director.'

'My God!' he said, startled. 'I hope someone checks his figures.'

She frowned. 'Why do you say that?'

'Two re-sits of GCSE Maths, you know.'

'Oh, there's a girl to take care of all of that,' she said dismissively. 'Nicky just advises us on who to approach.'

That boy is every kind of fool, thought his father in silent fury. Duns my friends, no doubt. God, what a mess! An explanation for her presence here at Glen Buie struck him with a jolt. No, he thought. I'm damned if I will. Even if I have to sell, she's not getting her hands on this place and filling it with down-and-outs.

Duncan was making his rounds, offering second helpings. Sir Archie rubbed his jaw, planning the week ahead. His difficulty nowadays was finding friends who were still fit enough for a week's intensive exercise. It had been easy enough when they were all in their forties, but desk-bound lawyers and bankers and captains of industry developed aches and creaks in their fifties, and their wives – if they still had them – were mostly struggling against fat or arthritis, menopause or hysterectomy, none of which helped on the hill.

Over recent years, he had relied more and more on his stepson's friends to provide youthful stamina and muscle-power, as well as high spirits; but now Alec was dead, and the people his own son hung out with were not interested in stalking deer.

There was no ducking the fact that it was a tough sport. However carefully he stage-managed, it was impossible to guarantee an easy day. Even on the low ground which he privately termed 'the Liberian Ambassador's beat,' it could take three hours' walking to come up with a shootable beast, and the irony was that the more inferior stags he culled, the more difficult it became to find one that he didn't consider too good to shoot.

He had begun the policy of conserving beasts with out-standing antlers, instead of shooting them for trophies, as Continental sportsmen did. A quarter of a century later, you often had a long climb to find a mature stag with fewer than eight points. That was why Everard Cooper, the sleek-haired paper-manufacturing fat-cat booming away fruitily two places to his left, was so keen to get his hands on Glen Buie. As his expense-account paunch indicated, he spent much of his time and energy buttering up foreign bigwigs, and would jump at the chance of being able to offer them deer-stalking on a famous forest. Merely imagining what he would do to the place made Sir Archie shudder.

Certainly the solid, spacious, mock-Gothic Victorian lodge would get a new roof, which would be no bad thing, but modern baths and showers would oust the 7-foot cast-iron monsters in which guests loved to soak out the day's exertions, and very likely bidets would further vulgarise the bathing arrangements. An up-to-date fitted kitchen, full of machines and gadgets, would replace the stone-flagged cavern with its Belfast sinks and huge, scrubbed table at which Mary Grant, the cook, wove her culinary spells.

That would be for starters. When it came to the sporting side – the side that really mattered – Sir Archie could all too easily predict Everard Cooper's pattern of behaviour. No true businessman could happily contemplate pouring money indefinitely into a bottomless hole. Once Glen Buie belonged to him, phrases like 'eating its head off,' and 'not earning its keep,' would crop up in Everard's conversation. Next would come references to 'the bottom line,' 'breaking even,' and the dreaded 'rationalisation.'

From that point, it was but a short step to the 'Sporting Lets' columns, which would unleash the international fraternity of what Sir Archie called the four-letter men – Frogs, Huns, Wops, Yanks, and very probably Nips as well – on to Glen Buie. The sort of trophy-hunters who shot polar bears from helicopters and gazelle from sand-bikes.

Sir Archie shuddered. The deer-forest which he and his father had cherished would be plundered and despoiled. And then when his enthusiasm waned or his legs packed up, Everard would probably sell out to some giant leisure group. Chalets would mushroom in the glen. Hikers in fluorescent anoraks would drop coke-cans and plastic bags in the heather, and by sheer human pressure drive out the deer. *Black rain will fall, and the deer will leave the hills.* Four hundred years ago, the Braham Seer had foretold the destruction of the Highlands, and in the first years of the twenty-first century his prophecy seemed likely to be fulfilled. Black snow was common nowadays, when pollution-laden clouds dropped their acid burden.

If he sold Glen Buie to Everard Cooper, he would contribute his own mite to the destruction.

There must be some other way.

Beverley had turned to her other side. It was time he did his duty and talked to his stepson's young widow, though too much shooting without ear defenders had damaged his left ear, and he was gloomily certain he wouldn't catch a quarter of what she said.

To his relief, he saw that Everard Cooper was giving her a crash-course in Highland social history, to which she was listening with no open signs of boredom. Rapidly the monologue, delivered *fortissimo,* touched upon crofting, the Clearances, and arrived at the Victorian passion for deer-stalking, which had led to the building of Glen Buie Lodge.

'The original house was at Strathtorran – still is, of course, but in a very delapidated condition,' boomed Cooper. 'The McNeils are an old family, but most of them had the sense to keep their noses out of politics, so the earldom of Strathtorran survived, along with most of their land, until very recently. Then the Auld Laird, as they still call him – Torquil Strathtorran's father – got into deep water in the 1950s, and sold this house and more than half the deer-forest to Archie and your late father-in-law, Hamish Forrester, fifty-fifty. The old house is just across the river. Wonderful view. I walked over to look at it last Sunday.'

Did you just? thought Sir Archie, pouring cream over his treacle tart in defiance of Gwenny's censorious eye. Dreaming of adding Strathtorran to your spoils, I shouldn't wonder.

'Been empty for years,' Everard went on, 'but now young Torquil has gone and turned the outbuildings and barn into a hostel. Awful idea, but he needs the money. Unless you can get a job at the fish-farm or with the Forestry Commission, there's precious little hope of finding work here, despite all the millions we taxpayers pour into the Scottish economy.' He raised his voice still more. 'How do you feel about it, Archie? A lot of Outward Bounders on your doorstep, eh?'

'Oh, we rub along,' said Sir Archie, deliberately neutral. 'No one can deny that coming here has done Torquil Strathtorran a power of good physically. Remember how seedy he was as a boy?'

'Ah, but has it done *you* a power of good?'

Sir Archie shrugged. 'No harm, anyway. He's keen to get the place in order – works like a... ' He caught the word 'black' and hastily substituted, 'galley slave, and looks very well on it.'

'What about his brother? Ian – or is it Euan? Roughish diamond, I gather.'

'Oh, well, we all have our crosses. Ghastly tragedy to lose his wife like that. Lovely girl, too. A real cracker.'

'But hardly the sort of work-horse needed up here,' put in Lady Priscilla Cooper, Everard's wife, listening from across the table. 'I never thought Eliza McNeil looked at home in oilskins.'

'Thoroughbred between the shafts,' Everard agreed, and on Sir Archie's right Beverley caught Nicky's eye and gave an impatient little snort.

Leaning towards Everard, Sir Archie said softly, 'How did young Benjamin get on today? You were with him, weren't you? I saw his stag in the larder: a good beast.' Rather too good, in fact. A handsome ten-pointer, the sort he preferred to see alive on the hill.

When Everard said nothing, Sir Archie called down the table to Benjamin Forbes, his teenage nephew. 'How was your stalk, Ben? I see you got a stag.'

'Wasn't it splendid?' broke in Marjorie Forbes, before her younger son could open his mouth. 'Fergus said it was a frightfully difficult crawl, right in the open.'

'Mum!' Benjamin looked agonised.

Why is the old bitch yapping so hard? Sir Archie wondered. Something must have gone wrong and she's trying to cover up. I should have sent the boy with Sandy McNichol. Fergus is too much of a chancer – but then Marje would have insisted on going with them. She can keep up with steady old Sandy. Nothing more likely to upset a boy's first stalk than having his mother breathing down his neck. I must find out what happened. The shot looked all right – perhaps a trifle too far back...

Pointedly he addressed himself to his nephew. 'Was it a long shot, Ben?'

'Not – not really, Uncle Archie. About a hundred yards. Only we were on such a steep slope, looking down. Almost straight down. I'm – I'm awfully sorry I made such a hash of it.'

'My dear boy, I don't call that a hash. You shot him clean enough; just a fraction too far back.'

'But it was the wrong stag.' Now Benjamin had got the confession off his chest, words poured out of him, his half-broken voice rising and falling in jerky sentences as he tried to justify his mistake. 'It was so different from shooting at the target. I hadn't realised. The light was tricky. The mist kept closing in, then melting away. Half the time I wasn't even sure the stags were there. There were four of them, but I could only see three. I thought I was looking at the one Fergus meant. He kept saying, "Are you seeing him?" and I said, "Yes", because I – I –'

'I know just what you mean,' said his uncle seriously. 'They move about, and the cloud comes and goes, and it's damned difficult to tell t'other from which.'

Ben took a deep breath and tried to speak calmly. 'We scrambled down through the rocks until we were a hundred yards above them on the ridge behind Tulloch Mhor. Where the burn flows in two directions, you know? The cloud was down, and we had to wait until it lifted, and just when we started moving closer, a whole party of hinds came round the shoulder of the hill.'

Most of the table had fallen silent to listen.

'They stopped and stamped and glared at us, but they hadn't got our wind. They kept moving on. The stags all jumped up, and Fergus said, "Quick, take him now!" but I wasn't in a good position. They were looking up, and the one I was aiming at was half hidden. Fergus said, "Go on, shoot, or they'll be off," but my stag still wasn't clear. Then he moved a couple of steps forward and I shot him, and – and Fergus said it was the wrong one.'

What Fergus had actually said as the ten-pointer crumpled into the peat hag, was 'God, boy! Ye've killed one o' Sandy's young feeders. Now the fat will be in the fire,' and Ben had felt ready to die of shame. It was done, and nothing could undo it. The wrong stag! How could he have made such a mistake?

All the way home, he had been rehearsing how he could tell his uncle. He was bound to hear of it sooner or later. On the hill, everything had been so different, so difficult. This morning, when he shot at the target and hit that circled spot every time, it had been easy. There was no rush. You wriggled into a firm position flat on your stomach, legs spread, wrist on someone's rolled coat, and all you had to do was line up the cross-hairs of the telescopic sight, hold your breath, and squeeze the trigger. Easy as falling off a log.

But on the hill, his heart had been hammering from the scramble through the rocks, and the strap of his binoculars kept getting caught under him. His hands had been stiff with cold, and the sight misted up when he tried to look through it. The stags were not neatly broadside on, as the pockmarked target was; nor was there a nice little circle to tell you where to aim.

Worst of all, instead of firing from his familiar prone position, Fergus had made him prop his back against a rock and shoot downhill between his own feet. It had felt awful – insecure and wobbly. For one ghastly moment, as the echoes thundered around the rocks, he thought he had missed completely. Perhaps it would have been better if he had.

Then the stag had given a great bound and stood swaying, looking vaguely round at the empty hill where his companions had vanished. He had put his head back, until the antlers lay along his neck, and crumpled among the rocks.

His uncle was staring at him. Ben wondered how many of the doubts and fears he had felt there on the hill it would be politic to express, and decided he had said enough.

'I'm sorry,' he repeated.

'Never mind, old boy, easily done. Can't be helped.' I must have a word with Fergus, thought Sir Archie. Tell him to be more careful, particularly with beginners. No sense in making a fuss now and putting the boy off stalking altogether. At least he had kept his nerve and shot accurately, even if he *had* killed the wrong stag.

Beverley's face was stiff with disapproval. 'It's disgusting. It shouldn't be allowed.'

'Why?'

'Because it's obviously a substitute for sex. Initiating boys into the customs of the tribe. Proving you're a man.'

Sir Archie considered this charge. There was a grain of truth in it, particularly the initiation aspect. As his own powers declined, nothing gave him more pleasure than seeing a youngster take to stalking with his own enthusiasm. Everard Cooper's son, Lucas, for instance: now *that* had been a turn-up for the books. Thickset and heavy-featured, with brutally shaven hair and a gold earring, young Lucas had looked unpromising material. You would have said his natural habitat was a street corner. His own father could hardly bear to be in the same room with him.

Yet he had taken to stalking like a duck to water. On the one occasion when Sir Archie had gone with him to the hill, he had been astounded by the change in Lucas – his keenness to learn, the way he got on with the stalkers, his instinctive understanding of wind conditions and how they would influence the deer.

Some of his own friends, who had been coming to stay at Glen Buie for years, had never learned to do more than follow the professional stalker and obey his instructions. Others, like Lucas, could have gone out on their own, once they knew the ground.

Over their lunchtime piece, looking down on the network of shining lochs and hills blending out towards the Western Isles, Lucas had haltingly confided his longing to be a gamekeeper, and his father's angry opposition. Sir Archie had promised to put in a word for him, but the last he had heard, Lucas was serving in the Marines.

Initiation to the tribe? Maybe. But surely stalking was not a substitute for sex? Not for him, at any rate. With guilty pleasure he remembered this very afternoon with luscious little Cynthia

Page, trophy-wife of his old friend and one-time brother officer Joss Page, on the sunny bank of the pool known as *Miss Hazelrigg's Catch*. Standing behind her, thigh-deep in water, while she played a salmon, he had slipped his hands under her quilted waistcoat and layers of wool and silk until his fingers cupped her full breasts.

'Archie, you brute! Stop it! You'll make me lose my fish!' She had wriggled ecstatically, firm and sleek-bodied as a puppy.

'Keep your rod point up!'

'Stop it! No, really, I mean it. Archie! You filthy old man!'

Her reel had screamed as the fish fled downstream. While she struggled to bring it to the bank, he had aroused her to such a frenzy of passion that the moment he had it safe in the net, she had flung down her rod and begun to tear off waders and breeks. They had made love on the little beach, getting very wet in the process.

Fishing offered excellent opportunities for sex during the drowsy afternoons when the fish lay deep and torpid, and now that dear Gwennie's interest had become so patchy, why turn down sporting invitations?

Sex while stalking was another matter entirely. Difficult, he would have said, if not downright dangerous. You might die of exposure. Even if you were left for an hour in a peat-hag with a willing woman, the cold and the clothes were against you. Easier for Scots, of course, but only an idiot took off his boots on the hill. The thought of copulation wearing Hogg of Fife's stubborn brogues made him smile. Besides, who could tell when the advance party might not crawl silently back and catch you at it?

'Speaking from a purely personal viewpoint,' he said judiciously to Beverley, 'I can't see stalking as a substitute for sex. No way.'

'Well, you can't deny that it's cruel.'

'Oh, I do!' he said with vigour. 'I deny it absolutely. It's far less cruel than so-called humane killing in an abattoir. Take Ben's stag today. He wouldn't have had any idea what hit him, or that it was going to. No anticipation. No stress, no fear, no pain. One minute he was chewing the cud, surrounded by his mates. The next – bingo! Stone dead. What's cruel about that?'

'It's barbaric.'

'Let me suggest an experiment,' he said, with heroic disregard of self. 'I may stalk tomorrow. Why not come with us? You can judge for yourself whether or not it involves any cruelty.'

'I couldn't possibly.'

'Afraid to put theory to the test?'

Beverley said angrily, 'I couldn't bear to watch anything so horrible.'

'Come on, my dear,' he goaded. 'Try anything once.' Except incest and Morris dancing, he added with an inward smile, and for a moment thought she was going to accept the challenge.

Then she said edgily, 'I have no intention of lending my support to a cruel and despicable activity.'

'I'm not asking for your support. You're entitled to your opinion, but it ought to be an informed opinion, not just prejudice. Come as an observer. Watch what happens from start to finish, then form your own judgement. Isn't that fair?'

Maya had turned to listen. A tinge of pink flared in Beverley's cheeks, but she said, 'No, thanks. I didn't come here to murder animals.'

He wanted to ask why she *had* come, but bit it back. Pudding plates had been cleared, and cheese was making its rounds. Everard trimmed a cigar and, as usual at this stage of the meal, people glanced expectantly towards their host.

Sir Archie tapped his tumbler and, as silence fell, he said, 'Well, it's been a good day all round. A fine first stag: well done, Ben. First of many, I hope. Also a nasty little switch shot by Joss. Better off the hill.'

'What about my fish?' Cynthia flashed him a look from under her eyelashes. 'Aren't you going to congratulate me?'

'Oh, that was the most remarkable catch of the week,' he said, grinning. 'I insist that you take it home to remember us by.'

'That's very decent of you, old man,' said Joss, always on the scrounge for a free meal. 'Sure you don't need it to feed the troops?'

'No, no. Yours by right of conquest, eh, Cynthie? I don't have to tell you how sorry we are to lose you tomorrow.' He paused, cleared his throat, began afresh. 'Right, now. Plans for the rest of the week. Twelve stags to get, if we can, to keep up our numbers while the weather lasts. Tomorrow's first rifle is Ashy, right?'

He smiled at his god-daughter, Astrid Macleod, Lady Priscilla's daughter from her first marriage, and his spirits rose as always at the sight of her: tall, blonde, athletic, with long flaxen plaits wound into a crown to give her the look of a Norse goddess. Now *that* would have been a match to gladden his heart. He wondered what had gone wrong between her and Nicky, and thought the reason was probably sitting beside him.

Ashy smiled back, her teeth very white and even. 'Lovely!'

'You go with Sandy to the Black Corrie tomorrow. All right?'

'Very all right.'

'Everard will take the second rifle – '

'Hang on, old boy,' said Cooper quickly. 'I meant to tell you before dinner that I'd like a day off, if it's all the same to you. I've got the devil of a blister after yesterday's death-march, and I can't say I'm happy about my rifle. I want to take it down to the target again. It was firing all over the place yesterday.'

Ashy looked down to hide a smile, but Sir Archie said seriously, 'In that case, of course you must sort it out before you use it again. Let's see...' He looked round the table. 'Johnny? I gather you're driving your mother over to the McPhails?'

John Forbes, Marjorie's elder son, looked up keenly. He was a rangy, craggy-featured young man with a thatch of dark hair and an air of can-do enthusiasm which contrasted sharply with his cousin Nicky's languid manner. 'Oh, we can do that another day, can't we, Mum?'

'No, we can't,' said Marjorie firmly. 'Sadie's expecting us for lunch, and I want to see her arboretum before the gales ruin the leaves. I'm sorry, but that's the plan, and we will stick to it.'

John looked sulky. Sir Archie said quickly, 'Don't worry, I'll be happy to take the second rifle myself. All right, my love' – as Gwennie began to protest – 'we'll take it steadily, I promise.'

Though his tone was light, she recognised the order. He had made her swear to keep the doctor's verdict to herself. 'Just till I have things sorted out,' he had said, and she knew he meant, 'Until I've made up my mind what to do about Glen Buie.' As soon as his heart trouble became generally known, all the people who depended on the deer-forest for their livelihoods would begin to fret about the future, and the less time they had to do that, the better. He wanted to present them with a fait accompli, but first he had to decide his own course of action, and not even Gwennie could help him do that.

He turned directly to his son. 'I leave it to you to entertain your guest, Nicholas. I've tried and failed to persuade her to come stalking, so it's up to you to find something she'll enjoy.'

Nicky, who had been folding his place-card into ever smaller triangles while the sporting arrangements were made, looked up as if startled to find himself the centre of attention. He was thin, fair, and narrow-shouldered, with a mop of blond hair curling over his collar, and looked younger than his twenty-three years. His guileless blue eyes had an anxious, defensive look as he glanced across the table at Beverley.

'Oh! Well, we'll... we'll... ' he mumbled, and briskly Beverley took charge.

'Nicky will show me around the place,' she said firmly and added with a challenging look at Sir Archie. 'He'll see I don't wander into any *danger*.'

'Fine,' he said blandly, refusing to rise to the bait. 'That's all fixed, then. Oh, just one more thing, Nicky. Mary asked if she could have a word with you after dinner. She wants you to get her a nice young roebuck for the larder. She says the new plantation is fairly crawling with them.'

'OK, Pa. Don't worry, I'll see to that.'

With inward amusement Sir Archie registered Beverley's

look of shocked disgust, and thought she couldn't know Nicky very well after all. His gaze roved the table. 'All right, then? Everyone happy? Priscilla?'

Her long horse-face broke into a smile. 'I'm going on a tweed-hunt with Gwennie. There's a new shop on the road between Tounie and Fort Charles, and people tell me they've got wonderful handwoven stuff.'

Sir Archie shuddered. 'Chacun à son goût.' He turned to Maya. 'Would it amuse you to go with them?'

'I'd rather go hunt deer with you,' she said, and his heart sank a little.

'You think you'd enjoy it? We may have a long walk.'

'Sure. I've hunted quail with Alec. I won't hold you up.'

Sir Archie well remembered his own experience of shooting quail in Texas. The big Land Cruiser with its trunk full of food and cold drinks, negro boys to hold the pointers, the flat, dry, easy walking...

'You'll find this a bit different,' he warned.

'I know that,' said Maya easily. 'Alec told me it's a whole different ball game.'

On her own head be it, then. At least he would be there to see that she came to no harm, and once would probably be enough for her.

'According to the forecast, it's going to be wet. Have you got boots and a waterproof jacket?'

'Oh, sure. I brought the whole outfit – kammo vest, foul-weather gear, gloves. Alec told me it can get real cold up in those mountains.'

Why should it make him flinch every time she mentioned Alec? Sir Archie forced a smile. 'I'll ask Mary to put you up something to eat, then, and we'll leave here sharp at nine.'

Chapter Three

'THEY'RE GOING THROUGH.' Mary Grant the cook cocked an ear as the rumble of men's voices grew suddenly louder with the opening of the dining-room door. A whiff of cigar-smoke, rich and greasy, pervaded the corridor.

With one hand she stubbed out her own cigarette, and with the other sprinkled oatmeal into the big porridge-pot and set it on the back of the Aga. 'Shift yourself, Elspeth, ' she urged. 'Finish loading the machine and give Ishy a hand tae lay up breakfast, then awa' tae your beds with both of ye, or ye'll never be up for Early Tea.'

Slave-driver, thought Elspeth, making a face at her aunt's back. She was a slim, pert redhead, who found this holiday job a sight too much like hard work for her taste. The ritual of Early Tea, which involved carrying a heavy tray to the upper landing and distributing cups to a dozen sleepy, tousled guests, offended her free teenage spirit. She would have answered back, if she dared, but Auntie had a sharp tongue, and after Elspeth's fall from grace at the end of the summer term, she preferred to keep a low profile until time should have dimmed her father's memory of seeing his youngest daughter brought home drunk in a police car.

Although the hours were long and the work demeaning for a girl with ambitions for going to college, there were compensations, among them the chance to flirt with her handsome cousin Fergus, the second stalker, and squint-eyed Donny, the pony-boy, as they ate their meals at the Formica-topped table in the corner of the kitchen. Other bonuses were the gossip she heard among the guests, and the substantial tips they left in envelopes on their dressing-tables when they departed.

'Shift, lassie!' Duncan the gardener, who doubled as butler, set a tray of glasses on the draining-board and gave Elspeth a friendly shove, holding his palms against her haunches a fraction longer than was necessary. 'I'll finish in here. Has Ishbel set the trolley?'

He sauntered through the scullery door into the big, stone-flagged kitchen, untying his apron, and sat down at the table where Donny and Fergus were playing cards.

'What's the orders for the morn?' asked Fergus, glancing up. 'Do I take Ashy to Carn Beag?'

'Ye do not. Miss Ashy,' said his father with reproving emphasis, 'goes tae the Black Corrie with Sandy. Ye tak' the laird tae the hill, and mind ye get him a stag on the low ground, and don't go racing him up the top of Ben Shallachan, or her leddyship will have your blood.'

'There's nae beasts on the low ground,' said Fergus scornfully, 'as ye'd ken weel if ever ye took your nose out o' your damned tatties.' He had been looking forward to a day on the hill with Ashy, and was annoyed to hear she was to go with Sandy, the head stalker, who would hardly notice if it was a Page Three topless or an old cow lying beside him in the heather, so long as she fired when he told her to.

'I thought the laird wasna stalking this season, after the trouble last year,' he added with a frown.

'Why else would I tell ye to tak' good care of him? None of your seven-league boots, now, Fergus! It's good news for us all if he's changed his mind, for when a man gives up the hill, the next you know he's thinking about selling the forest. Now Mr Alec's dead, the laird is all that stands between us and those damned busybodies of conservationists, and don't ye forget it.'

'There's Mr Nicky,' objected Mary, pulling up a chair and

easing off her shoes. She was a lean, square-shouldered woman in her fifties, handsome in a battered way, with fine dark eyes, a bad skin, and an air of forceful confidence.

'His young leddy doesna hold wi' shooting puir beasties,' said Duncan, putting on a falsetto whine.

'She's no leddy,' snapped Mary. 'That's the stamp of lassie I canna abide. Sticking her nose into my kitchen and telling me I shouldna keep the rubbish bins by the sink. Where would she wish me tae keep them, I'd like tae know? And then she tells me she'd be happy tae see this big house full o' the homeless folk she takes off the London streets! Says there'd be jobs for local people if they turned the byre into a craft centre, and tarmacked the road through the glen so the towerists wouldna get mud on their boots.'

'She said that?'

'She did.'

'What's Mr Nicky thinking of, bringing that kind here?' demanded Duncan, bristling, and Mary shrugged and blew smoke at the ceiling.

'Whiles he's a strange laddie. D'ye mind the time he spent the night on the hill, sooner than tell the laird he'd lost a beast? And when the laird found him cleaning a salmon in my rubber gloves, and made him keep them on all through dinner? Poor Mr Nicky! It's my belief Sir Archibald is tae blame as much as he is.'

Fergus smoked and brooded as they reminisced. It made him impatient to hear his mother's 'Mr Nicky' and 'Miss Ashy.' To listen to her, you'd never think this was the twenty-first century, when all humans were equal. Like Sandy McNichol, Duncan and Mary had lived and worked on this forest all their lives, and ingrained habits of speech died hard.

He could only put up with it himself by pretending he was acting the part of a servant for two months of the year. Anyone could do it so long as he knew that release was just round the corner. From the third week in October until the third week of the following August, Sandy ruled this little kingdom of hill and loch; and he, Fergus, was the Crown Prince, the heir apparent.

With that well in mind, he could endure the short annual reign of Sir Archie and his Sassenach guests, and even laugh at their demands and complaints. He could hide his contempt for their physical flabbiness, and curb his tongue in response to their patronising remarks. But nothing gave him more pleasure than to watch the last of their shiny cars bump away slowly down the drive and over the cattle-grid, leaving Glen Buie to its true owners once more.

The threat of disruption to this pattern worried him.

'Fancy a job as a towerist guide?' asked Duncan with grim jocularity. 'Eco-towerism, they'll call it. Dinna harm the corbies and maggies. Dinna cull the deer. Dinna shoot the foxes. Let the bluidy towerists trample where they please.'

'They do that already,' said Fergus dourly. 'There's four camped bold as brass by the Sanctuary Burn the nicht, with two wee orange bivvies and a fire you can see for miles. There won't be a beast left on that face by morning, for all the wind's in the North, yet they claim they never disturb the forest! I'd a mind to put a couple of rounds over the tents, by way of a lullaby.'

'Now, Fergus,' reproved his mother. 'That talk wouldna please the laird. They're within their rights.'

Fergus grunted, and ground out his butt. 'I'll take out the dogs. Coming, Donny?'

Hunched over a well-thumbed comic, the boy shook his head. Fergus nodded to Mary and went out.

His three dogs lived in a wired-off section of the old coach-house, a rank and gloomy cavern into which the light of day barely penetrated. It was one of the stalking season's minor irritations that he had no time to exercise them properly, and he knew very well that if any of the guests – particularly the female guests – discovered their living quarters, he would get a lecture on cruelty to animals. That he could do without. All the same, he preferred to take them for a run after dinner, when chances of meeting the guests were minimal.

Hearing his step, the dogs whined and scrabbled at the wire. He called to them softly, 'Here, Dogger! Fisher! German Bight! Good lads!'

He unbolted the door and they rushed out, the terrier leaping in a vain effort to lick his face, the flatcoat rolling ecstatically, and the dark-tipped golden Alsatian circling him with ears flattened, lips grinning.

He moved off briskly towards the shrubbery, for Duncan complained if they emptied themselves on his smooth lawn, and carefully skirted round the house to avoid crunching on gravel.

Music and laughter and the clink of glass came from the drawing-room overlooking the loch, but the four long windows were closely curtained, and he could only imagine the scene within. Next door a crack in the billiard-room shutters gave him a glimpse of Sir Archie's firm profile bent over his cue, while velvet-clad backs and shawled shoulders watched.

The other ground-floor rooms were dark, apart from the dining-room where Ishbel and Elspeth had pulled back the curtains and thrown up the sash windows to dispel the lingering cigar-fumes. He could see the two girls hurrying to and fro, silent and preoccupied, laying breakfast. Cups, bowls, juice-glasses ranged on the sideboard. Side-plates, cutlery, table-mats on the broad mahogany table.

He considered jumping through the window and giving them a fright, but resisted the impulse. It was better to see without being seen, and they didn't look in the mood for jokes. Elspeth's expression was sullen as she scattered cutlery with a careless hand. Ishbel, wife of Big Ian the ferryman, moved with one hand pressed to the small of her back. Her thin face was pale: another mouth to feed was on its way.

Fergus padded on, keeping to the wall of the house as he crossed the patch of moonlight in the angle of two wings, where anyone looking down from a bedroom might see him. The dogs were hunting in the shrubbery; now the rabbit bolted across the lawn, white scut bobbing, with all three in silent pursuit.

He was about to whistle them back, when a voice close at hand startled him. A man's voice, deep and angry. 'Is that a threat?'

It came from the darkened library on the corner of the house. Fergus flattened against the wall, straining his ears. Who would dare threaten Everard Cooper?

Another voice spoke, too far away to identify, but Cooper's indignant response was clear enough.

'You dirty little slut! I'm damned if I will.'

Mutter, mutter went the second voice. Fergus tried to guess who it was. Mr Cooper's rudeness to his wife was legendary, but surely even he would not call Lady Priscilla a dirty little slut? Could it be Ashy, his stepdaughter? She often holed up with a book in the library after dinner.

Cooper growled, 'Tell him, then, and see what good it does you. It makes no odds to me. But I warn you, you're on thin ice. Don't do anything foolish, or you'll regret it.'

Footsteps stamped across the floor. A door slammed. Fergus longed to know who was standing by the window, looking out over the moonlit loch. Then the curtains swished across. Thoughtfully he whistled up the dogs and went on round the house.

*****

When Nicky had put his wet tweeds into the drying-room and up-ended his boots for Duncan to dubbin, he went into the kitchen to discuss Mary's needs, and spent half an hour chatting to her and Duncan as they cleared the last of the vegetable dishes and scoured the saucepans.

There was nothing modern or even hygienic about her cooking arrangements. No environmental health officer would have approved of the way the four-oven Aga backed on to the larder, which was made even hotter by two freezers in which fishing-bait, surplus salmon, chopped lights for the dogs, and hard-to-classify joints of meat were accommodated.

Along the wall whose windows overlooked the gravel drive, three stained Belfast sinks held a variety of cooking utensils at different stages of purification, and dishes wrongly shaped for the dishwasher, as well as a bucket full of muddy shooting-stockings. Beneath the sinks were black polythene bins labelled *Tins, Hens,* and *Burning.* The deal table, six-foot by four, dominated the middle of the room, and instead of fitted units with easy-wipe surfaces, a collection of oddly-shaped and rickety cupboards held Mary's dry stores, china, and serried ranks of tins.

Tea-trolleys and an untidy stack of trays were parked in one corner. The table at which the single men ate their meals was pushed against the wall by the scullery door, where the glaring fluorescent strip turned even hill-weathered complexions to a ghastly pallor.

Everard Cooper never entered this kitchen without a shudder, but for Nicky it was the most welcoming room in the house, and Mary a lifelong ally.

Tonight he noticed a coolness in her manner, and knew she did not approve of Beverley. He would have liked to spend the rest of the evening in the kitchen's shabby warmth, but after securing his promise to shoot a young roe for her larder before the weekend, she chased him back to the drawing-room.

'Be off wi' ye now. They'll be wondering where you are.'

He left reluctantly, pushing through the swing door that led from the uncarpeted kitchen wing to the polished boards of the serving-room and dining-room, with the great entrance hall on his left.

The party had split up. The click of balls from the billiard-room indicated that his father had accepted Benjamin's challenge to a return match. As he passed the door of the adjoining study, Nicky saw his cousin John Forbes at his father's desk, poring over the Game Book, with curvy Cynthia Page draped decoratively over the back of his chair.

In the drawing-room, the big bay windows were shuttered and curtained with the faded but still beautiful silk curtains made in Hong Kong in the 'Fifties. Black-lacquered Chinese cabinets acquired at the same time now held boxes full of indoor games: Halma, spillikins, backgammon, and numerous packs of cards.

His aunt Marjorie was at the piano, strumming from a heap of yellowing sheet-music, while Ashy sang snatches and turned the pages. Two black labradors, a spaniel and a whippet occupied the chairs and sofa, looking indulgently down on the humans crouched on the carpet to play Racing Demon.

'Come on, on, *on!*' urged Gwennie, fidgeting like an impatient child. 'Four of hearts. Four of hearts. Someone must have it!' Her hand, rings flashing, stretched out and pounced. 'Look, Maya, in your Demon. Staring you in the face.'

'Ten, Jack, Queen – '

'King!' Triumphantly Joss Page slapped the card face down on top of the suit.

'Cheat,' muttered Lady Priscilla, and he flushed.

'Nonsense.'

'I saw you. You're supposed to turn over in threes.'

Joss said in his prim, pained way: 'The rules clearly state that you can turn over the last three cards singly.'

'Stop arguing,' snapped Gwennie. 'Thank you, Joss, just what I needed. Four, five, six... wait for it. Seven, eight, black on red...and I'm out!'

She sat back on her heels, flushed and animated.

'You can't have shuffled properly. I've got six left in my Demon,' Joss complained. 'God! My legs are agony.' He turned to Maya. 'Do you see how it goes?'

'I guess so.'

'Right. Then we'll call that a trial round and begin properly now. Come on, draw to deal.'

They'll be at it for hours, thought Nicky, stepping carefully over their legs and sinking into an armchair near the window. Ashy left the piano and joined him.

'Where's Bev?' he asked quietly.

'God knows.' She surveyed him with a little smile. 'Tell me,

Nicks, do you think she's going to enjoy herself here?'

'She wanted to come,' he muttered. 'I told her what it would be like.'

'But *why* did she want to come?'

'For God's sake, Ashy, give me a break.'

'I'm curious, that's all. I'm wondering what she's going to do all day. Sit about the house and get in Mary's hair?'

He said with a touch of defiance, 'It's no skin off *your* nose if she does.'

'Oh, but it is. I can't bear to watch my friends being taken for a ride.'

'Nobody's taking me for a ride,' he said irritably.

'You're sure of that?' Her aquamarine eyes were mocking. 'Would you like to know where your girlfriend is now?'

'You said you didn't know.'

'I said, God knows. And so, as it happens, do I. And I know who's with her.'

'Who?'

'My beloved stepfather.'

'Oh, *God!*'

'Exactly. You should have warned her, Nicks.'

'I did.' He glanced over at Lady Priscilla, but she was absorbed in her game. 'I warned her about the whole damned lot of you.'

'Even little me?'

'Especially you. I told her she'd be bored and uncomfortable…'

'Yet she came all the same.' She rolled her eyes. 'Ah, the power of love!'

'It's not funny.'

'You still haven't said why you brought her. Why you let her push you around. Come on, Nicks: give. You can trust me.'

'I wish I knew who I *could* trust,' he said, pushing the hair off his forehead. 'Oh, Ashy, I'm in such a mess.'

'Tell me about it,' she coaxed. 'Trouble shared… You know me, Nick-knack. I can keep a secret.'

For a moment he looked her full in the face, considering. Seeing him waver, Ashy pressed her advantage. 'Did I snitch when you pulled up Jock Taggart's lobster-pots and sold the fish down the strath? Did I let on who knocked out those pitons and left the bird-nesters stuck on the ledge all night?'

' Served them right.' He grinned reminiscently. 'Anyway, how did you know? I heard you tell the rescuers that it must have been old Logie up to his tricks again.'

Ashy said seriously, 'I don't like to see my friends getting into trouble. If I can help them out of it, I will. So how about it, Nicks? Are you going to tell me what's up this time?'

For a long moment he hesitated, looking round the room as he weighed pros and cons, but finally shook his head. 'Not here,' he muttered. 'Not now. I … I just can't.'

Ashy's clearcut profile was suddenly hard as marble, her eyes chips of blue ice. 'All right, Nicks. If you can't, you can't.' She rose and stood looking down at him with a mixture of affection and contempt. 'Well, I'm off to bed. Sandy and I have to leave early. Remember, if you feel like coming, we'll be glad to have you along.'

He said nothing, and she turned and left the room.

*****

'Bloody cock-teasing dyke!' Everard crashed the bedroom door shut and stalked across the worn, pale-blue carpet to stand behind the dressing-table where his wife was brushing her hair.

In the mirror, she surveyed him warily, wondering how she had ever found him attractive. His big body was heavy now about the middle; his strong nose and jaw padded with good living. Though still thick, his hair was streaked badger-grey, and his burning chestnut eyes were meshed in wrinkles. All the same, he still exuded the strength of will and brute energy that had wrested her from courtly, indecisive Mike Macleod, her first husband. Now the quality that had attracted her seemed wholly repellent.

There was no need to ask whom he meant. An hour earlier she had seen him detach Nicky's girlfriend from the group about the billiard-table as expertly as a collie cuts out a ewe from the flock. By the time Gwennie finished pouring out coffee, they had vanished, and she had thought wryly that at least she would have the full width of the double bed to herself. Leggy, sexy, common as hell, Beverley was just the sort to appeal to Everard, especially if he could steal her from under the nose of a younger man.

Clearly the encounter had been a disappointment, and Everard meant to vent his temper on her. Let him try, she thought. If he starts to knock me around, I shall ask Gwennie to find me another room.

'What went wrong?' she asked coolly. 'I thought she looked rather your type.'

'Is that why you went and told her about the Mona Peat report? Thank you for nothing, *darling!* I should have thought even you would have more sense.'

'Mona Peat? Don't be absurd. Of course I didn't.'

'Then how the hell did the little bitch hear of it? We've been very careful to keep it out of the media.'

'I expect she heard you talking about it.'

'How could she, you daft cow?'

'You men are such gossips. Useless at keeping secrets,' said Lady Priscilla, beginning to enjoy herself. 'Who does your boardroom lunches, for instance?'

'What the hell has that got to do with it?'

'Quite a lot, I imagine. Who organises them?'

'I haven't the foggiest. Old Witherspoon deals with that kind of thing. I think he gets in a team of girls – you know – freelances. Cordon Bleus.' He paused. 'You don't mean …?'

'Perhaps he uses a firm called *Gentlemen's Relish*. I'm told they do a lot of boardroom meals. Eliza McNeil – Ian's wife – used to drum up business for them.' She smiled at him blandly. 'Waitresses aren't blind and deaf, you know.'

He said slowly, 'You mean this … this Beverley …'

'Was Eliza's partner, that's right.' She watched the information sink in, then added gently, 'I expect Beverley Tanner has enough dirt on you and your fellow tycoons to put half of you behind bars; or at least out of the running for a K.'

'Put a sock in it, you ugly bitch!' Her husband's hands were heavy on her shoulders, and abruptly she stopped enjoying herself. He said between his teeth, 'If she breathes so much as a word about that report to Archie, I'll do her in, I swear. And if you, my dear wife, try to …'

'Hush!'

He listened. Next door the bath water had stopped running.

'It's only Gwennie,' he said.

'Not unless she's taken to wearing *Brut*. What does it matter about the report? Won't it soon be common knowledge?'

Everard said with suppressed anger, 'It matters because if Archie gets wind of it, bang go my chances of buying this place. Don't you understand? If he thinks I'm involved in peat extraction, he'll refuse to sell, no matter what I offer.'

She met his eyes in the mirror. 'Surely you would never think of extracting peat here? Not if you owned it?

'That's beside the point.'

'Is it?'

He said furiously, 'That little bitch threatened to tell Archie. Can you beat it? A tuppeny-ha'penny tart like that trying to blackmail me?'

'What did she want?'

'What do you think? Ten grand to some blasted charity of hers. Some hope!'

He fiddled with the pots and tubes on the dressing-table, opening, sniffing, putting them down without their lids. She guessed he would pay up, all the same.

'If it's *Home from Home*, you might as well make your cheque out to Cash,' she said dryly.

'Isn't it on the level?'

'Very far from it, I believe. It's the British offshoot of one of those phoney American churches. Homes for the hopeless and homeless. Charismatic ministry, signs and portents, that kind of nonsense. They hang about universities and try to get their hooks into youngsters with more money than sense.'

'Nicky?'

'Precisely. Poor Archie is not going to be pleased when he hears that his only son has given up reading for the Bar in order to devote his energies to charity work.'

Everard considered this information, wondering how he could turn it to advantage. He said explosively, 'That little bitch! I'd like to break her neck.'

'So I gather. Well, you may find that Joss Page beats you to it.'

'Joss?' He was pleased to find a fellow-guest in the same boat. 'What has that old whited sepulchre been up to, then?'

'All I know is that when we were walking along the river path this afternoon, she started asking him questions about some share support operation, and Joss looked absolutely pea-green and said he'd come to Scotland to forget all about the Square Mile. Then he walked away so fast that he left *me* with the pleasure of Beverley's company for the last mile back to the lodge. That was when I found out that she and Eliza McNeil had worked together.'

'Good old Priss. You're not such a fool as you look,' he said grudgingly.

'Thank you. Now for God's sake leave my make-up alone. That stuff costs the earth.'

'*Captive Loveliness. Reveal your true imprisoned beauty,*' he said mockingly. 'My God, Prissy, why do you bother? I mean, it doesn't make much difference, does it?'

'We're not all blessed with your devastating allure,' she snapped, and he grinned.

'Trust you to have the last word.' His hands slid over her shoulders, sensuous and caressing. 'Come on, old girl. How about it? All cats are grey in the dark.'

'Leave me alone.'

She shook off his hands and stood up, gaunt and sallow in her peach silk nightdress. 'If you're that way inclined, you'd better try the maids' bedrooms. Straight up the stairs and on the right. I expect you'll find what you want there – at a price.'

Everard clenched his fists. After all these years, despite his wealth and success, she was still capable of making him feel inadequate. Hairy-heeled, as her father used to say. The private jet, the racehorses, membership of The Squadron still counted for nothing because plain, dowdy, old Prissy, with her horse-teeth and bony figure, possessed what money could not buy him.

Silently he turned and went into the dressing-room.

Chapter Four

AT NINE NEXT morning, the dining-room was deserted. Untidily stacked plates still smeared with egg, porridge, and marmalade, coffee-dregs in abandoned cups, chairs pushed back and scrumpled napkins showed that those bound for a day in the open had eaten heartily, but in haste.

Their promptitude surprised Beverley. She had imagined Sir Archie's guests idling about the house in dressing-gowns on this far from alluring morning, with grey rain sluicing down the tall sash windows, and gusts of wind bending the trees around the whipped-cream loch. She had glanced through the window after Ishy brought her tea and pulled back the curtains, and guessed that last night's plans would be cancelled, or at least postponed until the weather improved. Guessed wrong, apparently.

She checked the covered dishes on the sideboard's heater, grimacing to find that the choice lay between kippers, sausages, black pudding, bacon, and three kinds of eggs. Replacing the lids, she poured a glass of fruit juice. There was barely half a cup of coffee left in the percolator. She unplugged it, and went in search of more.

In the cave-like kitchen, Mary was rolling thin strips of pastry on the flour-strewn table, while the girls peeled potatoes, nudging and giggling at private jokes.

'Good morning, Miss Beverley. Och, ye didna have tae bring that here,' said Mary, hurrying forward to take the coffee pot. 'The bell's beneath the table. Just ring for Elspeth if ye're needing anything.' She refilled the pot. 'Now, is there toast enough for ye? Everyone's breakfasted except her leddyship.'

'Where's Nicholas?' She had expected to find him in his room at the end of the corridor, covers still pulled up to his chin.

Mary glanced out of the window. She knew very well where Nicky was, having watched him squeeze into the Land Rover behind Miss Ashy, bound for the Black Corrie.

'Would he be on the river? He was out in the rod-room after dinner last night.'

'Fishing? In this?'

Mary smiled. 'It's the first rain we've had for a week, and needed sair. I've never known it so dry at the time of year. The salmon will be running, the morn, and there's a good chance of a fish.'

Beverley sighed impatiently. 'Whereabouts on the river?'

'That I couldna say. It could be anywhere on the Lower Beat – the Upper will be running too brown just now. If ye go tae the road bridge and walk on up the path, ye're like tae find him.'

'Thanks.' Beverley took the coffee pot and went out.

As the door swung shut, Elspeth looked round from the sink. 'Mr Nicky's away to the hill.'

'Aye, so he is.'

'Then why – ?'

'Save your breath tae cool your porridge, lassie,' advised Mary, cutting delicate pastry leaves. 'If he didna tell that one, why would I?'

Sipping coffee and orange juice, Beverley decided to walk up the river as soon as the rain stopped. She was worried about Nicky. There had been a subtle change in him since they arrived here: he was less willing to agree with her, less interested in her plans for the place. The influence of his family was stronger than she had realised. In particular, she resented Ashy Macleod's casually proprietorial manner towards him. Ashy the insider, with the right voice, the right connections. Nicky would probably have married her, reflected Beverley, if his father had not made his approval of such a match so obvious.

Nicky could be led but not driven, as she had discovered in the course of her own exploitation of his feelings of guilt towards the under-privileged.

'You have no conception of what it is like to be poor,' she often told him, and he usually agreed humbly.

'I know, but I do what I can to help.'

Then she would laugh, and rebuild his self-esteem. 'If other poor little rich boys were like you, the world would be a better place.'

But Nicky trying to right the world's wrongs at her direction in the anonymity of London was a different being from this new persona as the laird's son on forty thousand acres of the Western Highlands, which he would, in all probability, eventually inherit. Unless John Forbes got there first, or it was sold to that fat-cat Everard Cooper. There was many a slip...

She frowned, drained her coffee, and left the dining-room.

A packet of neatly-wrapped sandwiches lay ready in the boot-room, clear indication that she was not expected back for lunch. Breathing shallowly in the stifling atmosphere of the drying-room, she saw that the pegs and racks which last night had been festooned with wet jackets and sodden socks were now bare. Only her own boots, freshly dubbined, and her green padded jacket hung in their corner. She stuffed the sandwiches in her pocket, and set off resolutely into the drizzle.

A screen of ramping ponticum separated the river Buie from the pot-holed, rock-ribbed track that led over the shoulder of Ben Culichan, and then continued through high, sedgy uplands, to the spawning-pools beyond the Glen Buie march. The map showed it as a dotted line thereafter, a thread of path fit only for walkers and mountain bikers where it crossed the steep, shaley slopes of Meall na Shallachan and eventually descended, through forestry plantations clothing the hills around Little Kintulloch, finally joining the main road at Westerbrae.

Half an hour's brisk walking along the river path brought her to the junction of tracks, where the left-hand branch veered away towards Strathtorran House. The stone bridge spanning the water marked the separation between Upper and Lower Beats of the Buie, but there was no sign of Nicky – no movement except that of a heron, which rose heavily and flapped upstream.

Beverley perched on the parapet of the bridge, and studied the outline map with which every guest was provided. This must be the Greeting Pool, where the Auld Laird's teenage daughter, Lady Helen McNeil, had drowned a quarter of a century ago. Against it on the map was written: *Not Fished.* Above the bridge was the pool labelled *Falls,* and beyond that were *Alt na Chorain, Mill Race, and Miss Hazelrigg's Catch.*

The rain had stopped, and looking back down the glen she took in the wide panorama of hills clad in russet and episcopal purple, sapphire water and emerald sward on the sheep-nibbled flats down by the estuary. The small cluster of whitewashed buildings – pub, post-office and general store combined – with the harbour and toy-size ferryboat, was as self-consciously scenic as a postcard.

Here was her brochure cover, no doubt about that. The PR people would go mad for it: the view that said it all. Bonnie Prince Charlie, the Road to the Isles, Will Ye No' Come Back Again? Every corny Highland fantasy the tourist heart desired.

She half closed her eyes, visualising a Visitor Centre down by the ferry, craftshops and an audio-visual introduction to the Highlands; a colour-coded Nature Trail to suit every degree of mobility from superfit to zimmer-bound; railed-off viewpoints where tourists could pose with their arms round a stuffed stag; a piper in full regalia outside the Snack Bar...

Daydreams for the future. There would be opposition, of course, and she would be foolish to under-estimate its strength. Backward people clung to the past, and feudal habits died hard. Park-Plans Inc. would have its work cut out to win hearts and minds here, even when legal possession of the peninsula was assured. Her own first task must be to sow seeds of discontent with the old regime, and prepare the ground for the new.

Where to begin? A group of nearer buildings caught her attention, and abandoning the search for Nicky, she walked away from the river, heading for the squat, low-browed cottage standing isolated amid the remnants of ancient Caledonian forest, half a mile up the glen.

A sagging wire fence enclosed an acre or so of coarse grass and rushes, where a shaggy white pony, its sweeping tail blown forward to wrap round its knees, was backed into the scanty shelter of a corrugated iron shed. As she approached, a pack of kennelled terriers set up a shrill yapping.

What a dump! she thought, arranging her face in a smile of greeting. 'Anyone at home?' she called, pushing open the half-glassed door of the porch.

On the hillside across the river, sunlight flashed against glass. Someone was watching her.

★★★★★

I was a fool to come, thought Maya. She kept her eyes focused on the basket-weave tops of Sir Archie's thick heather-mix stockings, and tried to match their steady advance. Follow my leader. Mark my footsteps, good my page.

She felt light-headed, as if she had been walking for ever in this muffled, dripping, midge-infested purgatory. Her boots were full of water and beginning to press on her toes, ski-pants dragged at waist and knees, quilted jacket was sodden inside and out.

Left, right, left. Slip, stumble, squelch over boggy ground, stony ground, coarse wet rushes and mossy rocks. Slowly they were gaining height, working across the broad bowl of Corrie na Shallachan, tormented by insects, longing for a breath of wind, with the shale slopes of the mist-shrouded Ben rising steeply above them.

From time to time the men stopped, scanning through binoculars the high ground at the very edge of the mist. They muttered together, ignoring her. She caught garbled, meaningless phrases: 'The carry, no' the true wind...draw back to the Sanctuary.' Maya swept her own binoculars across the slope, but they showed her nothing but rocks and bracken, grey and brown, a barren landscape.

Shouldn't have come, shouldn't have come, repeated maddeningly in her mind. She didn't belong here, among these chilly, disdainful people. *The Romans, masters of the fairest places on earth,* Gibbon had written, *looked with wonder and horror at the wilderness of Caledonia and its savage inhabitants.* The Romans had had more sense than to try to live here. They recognised the end of the civilised world, and built a wall to keep the barbarians outside it.

She should have followed their example, but because she had loved Alec, she had clung to the hope of finding some lingering echo of him among his own beloved hills. Glen Buie had been his Land of Lost Content.

'I want to take you to the cairn on top of Ben Shallachan, and show you my kingdom,' he had said. 'Highlands and islands spread out as far as the eye can see. That's where we'll ask them to scatter our ashes, my love, fifty years hence.' And he had quoted softly,

West of these, out to seas
Colder than the Hebrides
I must go,
Where the fleet of stars is anchored,
And the young star-captains glow.

Tears stung her eyes. There had been no fifty years, no ashes even, when those seas colder than the Hebrides stole his life and her happiness. She would find no trace of him here.

On the ferryboat from Tounie, she had had a premonition of what it might be like, and when she drove the hired car on to the jetty, instinct forced her to turn left, away from the sign to Glen Buie. She had gone ten miles in the wrong direction before conquering her nerves and deciding to go through with the visit.

Now she knew that instinct had been right. America and Britain were indeed two countries divided by a common tongue. Understanding the words fooled you into believing you knew what they meant, but half the time you got it wrong. The British would tell you to look them up, but to take the words at face value was a big mistake.

Gwennie's invitation had been no more than a social gesture. On impulse, Maya had rung her when she reached London, but even over the phone, her mother-in-law's surprise had been obvious. 'Come up here? Of course. My dear, we'd be delighted. By car? Well, take the ferry from Tounie, and after you dock turn right and follow the coast road until you see the sign. About four miles from the harbour. We'll look forward to seeing you, my dear.'

But all the 'my dears' in the world could not hide the tiny giveaway signs that she was an embarrassment. At dinner last night she had felt like Banquo's ghost, and today was the same.

Only the young second stalker's greeting as she followed Sir Archie into the gun-room gave an impression of genuine warmth. 'Good morning, Mrs Alec. Ready for the hill?'

Unlike the ginger-browed, ruddy-faced head stalker, Fergus was slim and olive-skinned, dark-eyed as any Spaniard. Even in his heavy hill boots and thick tweeds he moved with a dancer's step.

Mrs Alec. The form of address had surprised her initially, but now she felt pleased by the implication that she belonged here. She had smiled tentatively. 'Ready as I'll ever be, I guess.'

Sir Archie had handed his rifle to Fergus, who slid it out of the sleeve and checked the bolt.

'Ammo?'

Fergus patted his pocket. 'Aye, sir.'

Sir Archie gave Maya a quick up-and-down glance in which she sensed disapproval of her clothes, but he said only, 'Got a stick? Take one of these. You'll need a third leg on the rough stuff. Sandwiches? Good. Come on, then.'

The men had turned away, leaving her to follow, and so it had continued for the next three hours. She wondered if they had forgotten she was with them. This was what it must feel like to be a dog, she thought, unsure of what its master wanted or where he was going, following obediently, ready to sit or go forward at the word of command.

'Antlers!' whispered Sir Archie urgently, reaching forward to tap Fergus with his stick. Both men flung themselves flat.

'*Get down!*' they hissed at Maya as she hesitated, looking for a dry patch to lie, and dog-like she dropped into the wet peat, feeling water ooze through knees and elbows. She began to wriggle backwards, as the men were doing, although she could see no reason.

In the shelter of a rock, they re-grouped, and the men began a low-voiced discussion. She grasped that there were some small stags in front of them, and they believed there might be more lying in the hollow below. The problem was first to find out if there was a shootable beast among them, and then to get past the staggies without disturbing them.

'Up to the top and come down behind,' murmured Sir Archie.

Fergus plucked a tuft of cotton-grass and tossed it in the air, testing the wind. 'I'm thinking we can get past below them if we keep in the burn.'

Maya looked up at the misty heights and hoped they would adopt Fergus's plan. Already she was more tired than she cared to admit, and feared she might not be able to keep up if they tackled the climb.

'How many are there?' she whispered.

They looked at her in surprise. 'Did ye no' see them? Three wee staggies lying in the rocks,' said Fergus softly.

Useless to complain that she couldn't see past them both. They resumed their whispering, heads close, and being unable to influence their plans she turned away, staring down the hill at the dark pattern of peat hags through which they had threaded their way to this vantage point. Moisture dripped from her hat and her body temperature dropped. Bored and uncomfortable, she began to shiver, but she knew there was no going back now. Sir Archie had made that clear. The stalking-party had to stick together.

'People wandering about during the cull are a menace,' he had said. 'They shift the deer about, whether they mean to or not, and there's always a degree of danger when using high-powered rifles. A bullet could go astray, hit a rock, ricochet. We ask walkers to stick to the paths – most of them are pretty sensible.'

'And if they don't?'

'Our chaps have a friendly word with them. No question of intimidation, just pointing out the danger.' He had smiled. 'On some forests it's not unknown for a stalker to put a shot over their heads, but I don't approve of that, do I, Fergus?'

'No, Sir Archibald,' agreed Fergus, butter-wouldn't-melt.

'Don't you forget it.'

Fergus said nothing, but his grin suggested that he would put a shot over any interloper's head if he thought he could get away with it.

She had to stick it out. Maya wriggled her toes inside the sodden boots and tried to take an interest in the bleak, dripping landscape. To see it through Alec's eyes. 'Animal or vegetable, anything that survives in the Highlands is a miracle of adaptation,' she remembered him saying once. Obviously this applied to the little white-winged ptarmigan she had glimpsed among the rocks, and the blue hare which would turn white in the snow.

It was probably true of the scrubby sapling a few yards below them now, with its branches apparently growing directly out of the peat. Curiosity stirred: it sure was a strange place for a tree. As she put up her binoculars for a closer look, the branches moved and she drew a sharp breath. Not daring to speak, she tugged Sir Archie's sleeve.

'What?' His gaze followed her pointing finger.

Huge and black-bodied from rolling in peat, the stag came up the bank, and the three humans shrank back in the shelter of their rock, easing up collars and pulling down brims to hide the flash of skin. Unalarmed, the stag came on.

Maya pressed herself into the rock, peering sideways, noting all she could. His shaggy throat and brisket dripped moisture, his head was carried high, and she saw that on one side his antler was not branched, but formed a long single point, like a scimitar. His thin, delicate legs trod lightly over the rough ground. She could smell the hot, throat-catching stink of the rut on him, and feel his power and passion as he passed within yards of them: angry, alert, looking for trouble.

Would he wind them? See them?

The stag paused, snuffing the air, then laid his antlers flat against his neck and uttered an ugly, challenging roar, almost a bellow, that held his mouth wide open seconds after the sound had gone bouncing round the corrie. At once a whole forest of heads appeared. The small stags were on their feet, plus a dozen others, all staring at the newcomer. They turned, without haste, and trotted away, the big beast following.

Maya let out the breath she had been holding. They were gone.

'Yon's the muckle switch from Beinn a Heurig!' Fergus said excitedly.

'He's a long way from home, then.'

'It's him, right enough.'

'Good girl! Well spotted.' Sir Archie patted Maya's shoulder, and she experienced the baffled pleasure of a dog who has unwittingly done the right thing. 'We've been trying to get that beggar for years.'

'Why's that?'

'Didn't you see his left antler? No tines on it. Just a single point. Makes him a dangerous fighter. Better off the hill.'

'It sure looked kinda mean.' She was puzzled that the men showed no inclination to pursue the stags, which were now mere dots in the distance, brown against grey-green. 'Won't you go after him?'

'All in good time.' He sat down and took out his sandwiches. 'We'll give them a while to settle.'

'They may go for miles!'

Both men laughed at her anxiety. 'Och, they'll no' go far,'

said Fergus. 'Ye're doing well, Mrs Alec. Not too tired?'

She shook her head, for both boredom and weariness had vanished as soon as she saw the big stag. *The switch.* She was in a fever to catch up with them before they vanished in this vast wilderness. How could the men sit munching quietly while their quarry moved ever farther out of range?

Faintly across the wide bowl of corrie came the muffled groaning bellow.

Fergus nodded towards the sound. 'There he goes. Dinna fash, Mrs Alec, we'll come up with him soon enough.'

She tried to contain her impatience while they finished their food, and Fergus accepted a Turkish cigarette from his employer's battered silver case. When he had smoked it to an inch, he pinched it out and rose, easing the haversack off his shoulders.

'Best give Callum a call. We'll be needing the pony.'

'D.V, ' said Sir Archie, touching wood.

Fergus withdrew to a small knoll, and the walkie-talkie crackled. 'Wake up, mon. Wake up!' he muttered, pressing buttons.

At the third call, Callum answered. Far below them, a white blob with a black blob preceding it emerged from the stone building beside the jetty, where the launch bobbed at anchor, and began to move slowly up the path beside the burn.

'All set, then?' Fergus rejoined them. 'We'll have one up the spout now, sir, to be on the safe side.' He slid the rifle from its sleeve, and loaded it with quick, sure movements. For all his respectful bearing, he was in charge, and Sir Archie content to let him take decisions.

A gleam shone through the clouds, transforming the dull landscape into subtly glowing shades of bronze and gold, purple and pink.

'Ready, sir? Mrs Alec?'

They nodded, and Maya lowered the binoculars through which she had been scanning the far slope of the corrie. The stags were grazing, spread out over a grassy ledge about halfway up the hillside. They looked very small and far away, and she could not pick out the big switch, who might be anywhere in the broken ground between. Lying cudding, rolling in the hags, grazing some hidden gulley. It would be so easy to pass without seeing him.

Sir Archie guessed her thought and smiled. 'Don't worry. If we go cannily we'll spot him before he sees us. It's steep, though, so tell me if you need a breather. No need to kill yourself! All right, Fergus, let's go.'

Forty minutes later, they lay on a rocky ledge near the summit of Ben Shallachan, an icy wind stinging their eyes as they looked down on the stags a couple of hundred feet beneath them. They were still grazing quietly, undisturbed, scattered along a grassy runner above the bracken line, with the big switch conspicuous among them, blacker and heavier, the one lethal antler contrasting with the other stags' branched heads.

This was the view that Alec had wanted her to see: hills and islands rising like emeralds from a sapphire sea, stretching in a blue-and-silver haze towards the Outer Isles; but by now she was too caught up in the drama of the chase to give the great panorama more than a cursory glance.

She had lost all sense of direction as they zigzagged back and forth, but after the sweating, scrambling climb, cold air acted as a tonic, banishing the lethargy of the lower slopes. As they moved stealthily over rocky outcrops sparkling with chips of mica, she felt full of running still; her only worry was that the slow, careful approach had taken too long, and that the stags would suddenly gallop away.

Fergus crept along warily, his tweed fore-and-aft cap moving continually as he scanned the ground ahead. Suddenly he dropped to all fours, gesturing to freeze the others. Alone he crawled to peer over a rock, then turned a jubilant face.

'They're there,' he mouthed.

They inched down to join him. Fergus slid the rifle out silently, and checked it again. 'Safe. Right, sir?'

'Give me a minute.'

Maya glanced at Sir Archie and felt a stab of anxiety. His broad face was running with sweat and blotched red and white. He breathed fast and heavily, with a little grunt at the end of each exhalation, and she remembered her mother-in-law's worried look last night when he opted to take Everard's place.

'Take your time, sir. They'll no' move yet awhile.'

In tense silence they waited, while below them the stags chose sheltered places to lie, their backs to the slope, gazing out across the sea-loch. A flurry of rain swept in, blotting out the view, stinging their cheeks with icy needles. When it passed, Fergus planted his stick in the ground at an angle, and slid out of his knapsack, retaining only his telescope.

Maya ferreted in her pockets and found a long-forgotten stub of Polos, which she offered to Sir Archie. For a moment he hesitated and she thought he was going to refuse; then his hand reached out to take one. Rapidly he crunched it up.

'Thanks.'

Like Fergus, he divested himself of extra equipment.

'Stay here, ' he whispered to Maya. 'You'll be able to see most of what happens, but don't on any account move until you see one of us waving you forward. Understand?'

'Sure.' She swallowed her disappointment. A moment ago, she had been one of the team. Now she was again reduced to the status of faithful dog.

'Even after the shot, don't move.'

'OK.'

'We may have a bit of a wait. Keep out of the wind.'

She nodded. 'Good luck.'

He grinned and raised a thumb, and she thought with relief that he looked himself again. She watched them slither downhill on their stomachs, the soles of their boots the last things to disappear. Then the mist swirled in, and when it lifted again, they were gone.

Chapter Five

UNDER A LOW heather bank near the summit of Carn Mhor, Nicky and Ashy huddled companionably shoulder to shoulder, eating sandwiches.

'Swap you bacon for cheese-and-chutney?'

'Done.'

They munched in silence, the wind tearing at their clothes and teasing blonde wisps of hair from under Ashy's cap.

The relief of the confessional warmed Nicky to his core. An hour earlier, when Sandy left them and crawled away to reconnoitre the ground ahead, she had said, 'Tell me, Nicky. Now!' and almost without thinking he had unburdened his soul. She had put a hand on his shoulder and squeezed hard enough to make him wince.

'I thought it must be something like that.'

'What can I do?'

'Stop worrying,' said Ashy calmly. 'Don't do anything. Just leave it to me: I'll fix it.'

'But how?'

Her blue-green eyes crinkled. 'Don't ask.'

Uneasily he had studied her profile. Ashy had a reckless streak and sometimes went too far. 'You won't do anything – well – dangerous?'

'*Nicks!* What do you think I am? *Sticks and stones can break my bones, but words can never hurt me.*'

'They can, though.'

'Balls! I'll talk to her – that's all. It'll work, you'll see.'

Now he lay back out of the wind, gnawing an apple, glad to leave his problem with someone else. Ashy propped elbows on knees and studied the hill opposite, sweeping her binoculars in a slow arc to scan it section by section.

A thin plume of smoke rose from the chimney of the cottage far below, set back from the silver thread of river. The old white pony was a cottonwool blob against the woodshed. Her binoculars swept across it, paused, came back.

'Hullo! Kirsty's got a visitor,' she said quietly. 'No car, though.'

'M or F?'

'Can't tell. Sandy!' she called to where the head stalker sat eating his own piece at the distance required by convention. 'Can I borrow your glass a moment?'

No answer. Sandy didn't like lending his telescope, and he often found it convenient to foster the myth that he was hard of hearing.

'Deaf as a post!' Ashy rolled her eyes, pushed herself upright, and strolled the few paces to where Sandy was sitting, his baggy tweeds a perfect match for the sedgy grass around him.

'Lend me your telescope a minute?'

Ashy was a favourite. Reluctantly he handed it over. 'Dinna go dropping it, now.'

'As if I would.' She returned to her place under the bank and pulled out the heavy brass sections, frowning with concentration until the image leapt into brilliant focus. 'Guess who?' she murmured after a moment.

Nicky shrugged and shook his head, the sun glinting on his golden eyelashes. 'Tell me.'

'No. Take a butcher's.'

Nicky opened his eyes, took the telescope, and stared. Before he could comment or hand it back, Sandy's guttural rasp behind him said, 'Now if ye've done wi' ma glass, Miss Ashy?'

'Thanks.' Hurriedly she gave it to him, and he snapped it shut with three decisive clicks, his face stony. Without another word, he picked up the rifle and pulled down the peak of his cap. In single file, they followed him over the shoulder of the hill.

★★★★★

For twenty minutes after the men crawled away, Maya watched the stags through binoculars, but when her wrists began to ache and her fingers to turn a sinister grey, she withdrew behind the rocks that kept off the worst of the wind, and tucked her hands into her armpits to retain all the body-heat she could.

She eyed the heap of jackets and sweaters. After a brief hesitation she stripped off her sodden nylon blouson, and put first Sir Archie's and then Fergus's wool sweaters on top of her brushed cotton shirt. The blouson would not zip over such a bulk, so she substituted Fergus's rolled waterproof cape, pulling down its hood and curling up her legs until it covered her from head to toe.

Half an hour passed, but the stags still lay peacefully, unmoving. Maya hunched more tightly, knees to chin, resigned to an indefinite vigil.

A bit of a wait, he had said. How long was a bit?

Forty minutes crawled by. An hour. The wind blew shredded wisps of cloud past her eyrie, and she hugged her knees ever more closely. Nothing to read, nothing to look at, nothing to do but worry. What had gone wrong? That awful streaky look on Archie's face: should she have tried to stop him? Would he have listened if she had?

'You'll love my stepfather.' She remembered Alec's voice. 'What's more, he'll love you. He's always had an eye for the girls. He and my father were best buddies at school, and shared digs at uni. They used to rent this forest between them, and when old Lord Strathtorran went on the rocks in the early '80s, they scraped up the money to buy Glen Buie from him, fifty-fifty. The only pity is that they couldn't raise the cash to buy Strathtorran as well. There are two McNeil boys, the Auld Laird's sons, and they've inherited what's left, but they're having uphill work trying to make it pay its way. If they do decide to sell up, they've promised me first refusal. I'd like to own the whole peninsula: it should never have been split up in the first place.'

Even in the first flush of love, Maya had found this a daunting prospect.

'Then, when Dad died, my mother married Archie,' Alec had explained. 'He and I have always got on like a house on fire, and so will you.'

Not quite like a house on fire, she thought. The fact remained that sooner or later Archie would want to know what she meant to do with her half-share of Glen Buie.

'There aren't many places like it left in Scotland,' Alec had said seriously. 'I see it as my duty to protect it.'

From Nicky and his flaky girlfriend? 'Poor Nicky! He does hang out with the most disastrous people!' Alec had said, then checked himself, half-laughing. 'There I go – just like the rest of the family. We all say *Poor Nicky*, but he's not poor at all. In the financial sense, quite the opposite. He's had millions in trust ever since he was a schoolboy. That's why these frightful people latch on to him, I suppose.'

Maya shivered. Nothing Alec had told her about deerstalking had prepared her for being abandoned on a freezing mountain. But then, she thought wryly, he would never have been abandoned. He would be up there with the others, discussing, advising, planning the next move. No one would dream of parking Alec behind a rock and forgetting all about him.

Rebellion stirred in her. If ever she did this again, she meant to be at the sharp end, but for the moment she was effectively trapped. Stuck where the men had left her. If she broke ranks and made for home, could she be sure of walking in the right direction? In a couple of hours it would be dark, and she was not equipped for a night on the hill.

Think of something else. Consider her fellow-guests, that bunch of oddballs who made up a North British stalking-party. Take Gwennie, with her large calm blue eyes and dewy complexion, her seated tweed skirts and triple strand of pearls that made her almost a caricature of an English lady. Yet there were aspects of Gwennie which undermined that image.

On her first evening at the lodge, Maya had opened a door by chance and found her mother-in-law and Mary, the cook, standing ankle-deep in feathers, plucking small birds that smelt as if their Best Before date was long past.

'That bloody pompous fart! Too mean to bring whisky, so he gives me these and expects me to thank him,' Gwennie had been saying. 'God damn all guests who bring high grouse with them!'

Mary, dragging out a handful of blackened entrails, had clapped her on the shoulder and screeched with laughter. Gone was the deference that made Maya's toes curl. For the moment they were simply two women sharing a distasteful chore which they scorned to foist on the maids.

'Dinna fash, my leddy, dinna fash! What eye doesna see, hairt won't grieve ower,' Mary declared. 'By the time I'm done wi' them, none will ken when the wee birds were shot.'

Silently Maya had withdrawn, and in due course the grouse had appeared at table, sauced and unrecognisable, accompanied by fulsome compliments from Gwennie to Everard Cooper, who had brought them; but Maya, remembering that gory scene, had felt her appetite vanish.

In Lady Priscilla, too, there was a hint of hidden steel. 'Not such a fuddy-duddy as she looks,' had been Alec's view. 'She can be damned sharp at times. Everard's her second husband – a bit of a bully, and a bit of a shark. Archie doesn't like him, but puts up with him for Lady P's sake. When they were younger, Everard used to knock her about, but he's too scared of Lucas to try that nowadays.'

'Lucas?'

'Their son. A human pit bull terrier. No one in his senses gets the wrong side of Lucas.' Alec had smiled. 'When Glen Buie is ours, we'll invite our own friends, but until then, we'll have to put up with Archie's old gang...'

Boom! Boom-boom-boom!

At last! Shaking with cold and excitement, she knelt up and focused the binoculars. The stags were all on their feet, the big switch among them, apparently undamaged. Their heads faced the wind. They moved restlessly, trying to locate the danger.

He must have missed, thought Maya, waiting tensely for the rifle to crash again. Had there been two shots close together, or one and the echoes? She imagined the men creeping forward, finding another firing point.

Then she saw the switch was weaving and staggering as he tried to follow the other beasts. He took a few uncertain paces, then sank down gently, legs folding under him, as the rest of the herd streamed away across the slope. For a moment the wide antlers were visible against the pewter dazzle of the sea-loch, then they bowed slowly until just a single tip could be seen. She watched it through binoculars for a full minute. It did not move.

She found she had been holding her breath, and let it out on a long sigh. Stiffly she rose and looked for the men, then remembered she had been told to stay where she was until she saw them signal. Whereabouts would they be? She had no more idea than the switch where the shot had come from.

Sinking back on her heels, she scanned the ground impatiently. Why didn't they show themselves? The switch was dead. Surely they could now release her from this freezing vigil?

Ten minutes passed, and still nothing moved. The light was beginning to fail, but she could just make out the tip of antler sticking up from among the stones. What on earth were they doing? Had they lost her? Forgotten about her?

Better stand up and show herself. She collected the kit they had jettisoned – sticks, ropes, thermos flask, satchels, jackets – shuddering convulsively as she draped the straps about herself. Just as she was about to emerge from her lair, a movement caught her eye. In the nick of time she crouched and froze, as five more stags trotted into view.

They halted, heads up, and she barely had time to register

that the one at the rear was holding a hind leg off the ground, when it suddenly bounded forward. A split second later, the rifle's heavy explosion sent shockwaves across the hill.

The lame stag gave two stiff-legged bounds, then pitched down the steep slope, the body rolling over and over until it came to rest some fifty yards below the dead switch.

This time Maya remained motionless, horrified by how close she had been to spoiling the shot, or being shot herself. There, at last, was the white flash of a handkerchief, and two small figures far below, gazing upward, trying to spot her.

She rose and waved back. Her feet were numb, and the sticks and binocular-cases made an awkward bundle, constantly threatening to trip her as she began to stumble downhill.

By the time she reached the ledge where the dead switch lay, Sir Archie was barefoot, sitting on a lichen-covered rock and wringing black, peaty water from his stockings. Fergus had taken off his coat and rolled up his sleeves. He bent over the carcase, heaving out steaming coils of intestines. Both men were streaked with peat and sweat, but at least they looked warm, thought Maya, her teeth still chattering.

'Nice shooting!' she said.

'My dear girl, you're frozen. Sorry we were so long. Here, take a dram.' Sir Archie offered a dented flask. 'We spotted the little lame staggie when we began to crawl in on the switch, and decided to try for them both.'

'How did he get that way?'

He shook his head. 'Looks as if he's been in some wire. We'll see when we get down to him. He's only a knobber – a two-year-old. Callum can come back for him tomorrow.'

They sat relaxed, sipping single malt, watching Fergus about his work. A glint of late sun slanted under the grey bank of cloud, waking pink tints across the sweep of hill and water. A good place to live and die, thought Maya. Beverley was mistaken: there was nothing cruel about this.

She felt neither pity nor triumph, only satisfaction for a

difficult job well done. A blue film spread across the stag's large liquid eye, and his long slender legs looked impossibly delicate for their task of carrying the big body over rough ground. In the coarse, gingery hair about his neck, black insects crawled into the light.

'How much would he weigh?' she asked.

'What d'you think, Fergus? Fourteen stone? Fourteen and a half?'

'Aye, sir. He'll be all of that.' He was serious and professional, intent on his task, but now that the adrenalin had stopped running, Sir Archie looked terrible. His skin was grey, with a purplish tinge about the upper lip.

'I'm all right,' he said firmly, reading her expression. 'Don't go worrying Gwennie, now – promise?'

'OK.'

'I know how to pace myself.'

She didn't contradict, but nor did she believe him.

Fergus twisted a rope round the switch's nose and antlers, and attached another to the slender hind legs. Finally he slit open the pale, bulging bag of stomach that he had removed, revealing a mass of coarse greenery.

'Can ye see the eagle, Mrs Alec? When there's a stag shot, he's never far away.'

Two soaring specks rode the winds, flight-feathers spread fan-wise, fierce eyes on the ground, waiting for the humans to depart.

'Sure, they're there, looking for their dinner.'

He smiled at her, and she thought those dark, aquiline features and glowing eyes must cut a swathe through the Tounie lassies. 'They're bonny birds, ' he said quietly. 'Mr Alec was aye glad to see the eagles. He called them the stalker's friends.'

Tears stung her eyes again, and she turned away to hide them. Already Fergus was back at work, hoisting the dragging-rope over his shoulder, and settling against it like a draught-horse testing the traces.

'If ye'll take the brake-rope, sir, and Mrs Alec can manage the rifle, we'll be getting on.'

'Right you are.' Sir Archie bent stiffly to gather the rope attached to the hind legs, and the two set off downhill, with the stag's limp body slithering between them, undulating over the stones and heather, slipping and twisting and sliding, the sharp switch point dangerously close to Fergus's thighs, while Sir Archie leaned his weight back against the second rope, steadying the awkward burden by digging his heels into the slope.

Home is the hunter, home from the hill, thought Maya, watching the ungainly, spasmodic descent. According to Alec, the death of the stag was just the beginning of the stalker's work. Now the carcase must be hoisted on to the pony's saddle, carried to the boat, and thence to the game-larder. There the head and lower legs would be cut off after the body had been weighed, and the anonymous truncated carcase, still in its skin, locked into the chiller with the week's other stags for collection by the game merchant's refrigerated van, for eventual export to Germany.

Chapter Six

SANDY'S NOSTRILS TWITCHED as he opened the claw-marked porch door of his cottage and shut it firmly in the faces of the three dogs pressing to follow him in. He bent stiffly to unlace his boots.

'Kirsty?'

No answer. A single unshaded bulb lit the dingy ground floor, divided by a formica-topped counter, that served both as kitchen and sitting-room. Packets of cornflakes and biscuits, encrusted dog-bowls and tattered copies of *Hello!* took up most of the counter space. On the scored oilcloth which covered the table were the remains of a meal: an empty jam-jar with a sticky knife-handle protruding, a hunk of cheddar, tea-cups and a few pallid slices of white bread, curling at the edges.

More cups and dishes crammed the sink, half-submerged in cold greasy water, and the acrid smell of the Rayburn brought a bleak message. He touched the top and frowned. Out for hours, by the feel of it.

In stockinged feet he padded towards the stairs. 'Kirsty!'

As he passed, a long-haired tortoiseshell cat leapt off the sagging sofa that took up most of the back wall, and fled with arched tail for the cat-flap. Sandy pressed the TV power-button and sank down on the sofa, grimacing as his stiff knee was forced to flex.

'I'm home,' he called above the chatter of talking heads on the screen. 'Where's ma tea?'

No answer, and the familiar chill of fear that she would

vanish from his life as suddenly as she had drifted into it forced him to his feet again. It was two years since he had taken her into his home, but deep down he knew that this was only a temporary refuge for her, and he was but her temporary protector against the violent husband from whom she had fled early one Sunday morning, taking her six-month-old baby with her.

Her greatest fear was that Kevin would discover her whereabouts and try to claim the toddler whom Sandy now regarded as his own. It took a year for her to stop trembling when the telephone rang, and slipping out to the woodshed whenever a strange car drove up the track.

Sandy had found her perched on the parapet above the Greeting Pool one wet November morning, shivering in her denim jacket, with the baby in her arms and less than the price of a meal in her handbag. Their coming had transformed his solitary existence, unleashing long-stifled emotions: tenderness, pride, the joy of posession.

She was twenty-five years his junior, slender and delicate, with a pale, heart-shaped face and big brown eyes that reflected her changing moods. She was untidy, unthrifty, and her slapdash housekeeping left him more than his share of domestic chores. He knew that his mother thought him a fool, yet he could not regret what he had done. Kirsty could neither sew nor bake, and could hardly be trusted to sit in front of a fire without letting it die.

'I'm learning,' she would say, with a lift of the chin that went to his heart, and he would stroke her long brown hair and pull her close.

'Ye're doing fine, never fret.'

I'm ower old for her, he thought, and steeled himself not to glower when Fergus's bold eyes smiled at her. He knew Fergus was too canny to risk his job by letting things get out of hand.

The silence upstairs sent a chill through him. Had she gone without warning, unable to face his reproaches? Had Kevin tracked her down at last? Then the floorboards creaked and he relaxed, lowering himself to the sofa again. Kirsty appeared feet first down the steep stairs, moving carefully, carrying wee Dougie draped over one thin shoulder.

Sandy went to take him. 'Give him here,' he scolded. 'He's ower big for ye tae go carrying him.'

'He won't settle. Feel his head – it's burning.' She laid the child on the sofa, where he stared at them vacantly, whimpering a little, playing up. Sandy placed his calloused hand with the missing forefinger on the flushed brow, but he couldn't tell what he ought to feel.

'It's cold down here for him. Did ye forget the stove?' he asked, carefully unaccusing.

'That damned thing! I've no patience with it,' she exclaimed. 'If I take my eye off it one minute it goes out, and it's not for want of fuel. It got a full scuttle at dinner time, and look at it now!'

Sandy lifted the hot-lid, and hooked out the central plate to peer into the murky interior. There was coke to the rim, right enough, but as usual Kirsty had failed to riddle the ash out before she stoked. Unless a spark could be nursed back to life, he faced the grim and grimy prospect of emptying by hand, a lump at a time.

Kneeling, he moved the riddling lever back and forth, and a cloud of fine ash rose to settle on the table.

Kirsty said bitterly, 'Sir Archibald should put us in a modern stove in place of that old heap of scrap.'

'It's served well enough these thirty years,' said Sandy, to whom stoking and riddling came as naturally as breathing.

'There was a lady here from the big house, the morn. She said Sir Archibald should be ashamed to let his folk live in such conditions.'

'Did she so?' Sandy's tone was dry. 'Which leddy would that be?'

'Beverley was her name. Beverley Tanner. She said it was a disgrace that a rich man's servants should live in a hovel.'

'She called this a hovel?'

When Kirsty had been down-and-out, she had thought the

Stalker's Cottage little short of paradise, but now she nodded. 'She said the laird would do better to spend his money on improving his cottages instead of murdering defenceless beasts. She said things would be different when Mr Nicky was master here.'

'Och, aye, I don't doubt that, lassie. I don't doubt it at all.'

Within Sandy a slow anger began to smoulder. 'Well, we hope that won't be yet awhile, whatever Miss Beverley may say. It's bad enough tae have Strathtorran crawling with towerists and hikers, without letting them loose on Glen Buie ground too. Hark ye, Kirsty, and hark ye well. If yon lassie comes back with more talk of the kind, you can tell her from me that it's none of her damned business how I live, or what the laird does with his money. Tell her that, Kirsty, and if you want to please me, you'll show her the door.'

★★★★★

'How long do you think she'll stick it?' murmured Lady Priscilla to Gwennie as Beverley left the drawing-room towards the end of the week.

Gwennie sighed and shook her head. 'Can't tell. The last thing I want is to say something that might drive Nicky away, but honestly! I can hardly bear the way she bosses him around and then looks to make sure that I've noticed.'

'You're a saint.'

'You wouldn't say that if you could read my thoughts! But if we can't have Nicky without her, we'll simply have to bite the bullet and put up with her.'

'I'm surprised she allowed him to come. I'd have thought she'd be afraid he'd slip back into his old ways as, indeed, he is doing – up to a point.'

Marjorie Forbes raised her head from her tapestry. 'As far as Beverley's concerned, bringing him here is part of the programme. As a magistrate, I've seen quite a lot of the ways these cults operate: they all brainwash their recruits in the same way.

First they destroy a boy – or, indeed, girl's – self-confidence, and rubbish their preconceived ideas. Then they fill the recruit with their own propaganda. When they've got him where they want him, they put him back in his own environment and see if they can control him there, as well. Not much different from training a horse or a dog, when you think of it.'

'So arrogant – how dare she!' exclaimed Gwennie, flushing. 'Poor Nicky!'

'Rich Nicky,' said her sister-in-law dryly. 'You don't suppose it's his *beaux yeux* she's after? Pretty soon, now, I'd expect her to go off and leave him, then whistle him to heel a few days later.'

Gwennie said vigorously, 'I hope you're right about the going off. It's such a strain having her here. Archie can hardly open his mouth without her jumping down his throat.'

'I bet you a tenner she quits before the week's out,' said Marjorie, stabbing her needle into the canvas and folding it into her work-bag.

Nobody actually cheered aloud when this prediction was fulfilled, and Beverley announced one tea-time that she wanted to spend a few days exploring the islands alone, but the sense of relief was palpable.

Hidden by the tea-trolley, Gwennie groped secretly in her handbag, and passed Marjorie a crisp note. 'Never were ten pounds more happily lost!' she murmured.

'I've looked up the timetables,' Beverley went on, 'and there's a ferry from Tounie to Stornoway at 8.45 on Sunday. If I catch that, I'll get there with plenty of time to find a B&B.' She turned to Gwennie. 'I'll be back for dinner on Friday. May I leave most of my luggage in my room?'

'Of course.'

'I do hope you're a good sailor,' remarked Ashy, munching chocolate cake. 'Apparently there's a big blow coming this way.'

The other women frowned at her: *For God's sake don't try to put her off!* and Gwennie said briskly, 'I'll ask Mary to put you up sandwiches and a thermos. Don't forget to pick them up when you sign the Visitors' Book.' Before Beverley could protest, she touched the bell. 'Oh, Ishbel,' she said when the maid answered. 'Miss Tanner is leaving before breakfast tomorrow, so would you ask Mary to put her up a picnic?'

'Very good, my lady.'

'Tell her I'm sorry to put her to so much trouble,' put in Beverley, and cutting off Gwennie's protest that it would be no trouble at all, she rose abruptly and left the room.

'Lovely manners!' said Gwennie, with a wealth of feeling.

Lady Priscilla looked up from the window-table, where she was playing Patience and a smile which on less equine features might have been called impish spread across her face.

'Dearest Gwen,' she said softly, 'why look a gift horse in the mouth?'

★★★★★

Straggling down to breakfast on Sunday morning, everyone passed the table in the hall, on which lay the Visitors' Book. Across a fresh page of thick, creamy vellum sprawled a new signature.

Sir Archie bent to examine it. *Beverley Tanner, September 15-20th* was followed by the address of Nicky's flat in Walton Street. So that's where she parks herself, he thought angrily; but as he entered the dining-room and saw his son's strained expression, Sir Archie knew his hands were tied. He could not risk alienating him again. Now Alec was dead, Nicky was the heir to half Glen Buie, even if he had to wait a few years yet to take control.

In the meantime, he could encourage Johnny Forbes to take over more of the day-to-day management: Marjorie would be delighted.

Spooning down salted porridge as he paced back and forth across the big sash window, Sir Archie reflected on his elder nephew. He had turned out pretty well, all things considered. There had been that trouble at school, but it was surprising how short people's memories were. Johnny had lived down that blunder: it might even have been the making of him. If anything, he had become a touch self-righteous, a bit too much of an eager beaver, in contrast to his brother Benjamin, who showed every sign of developing into a proper little layabout, interested in nothing but loud music and the uncouth specimens who belted it out.

If Marjorie hadn't kept a sharp eye on him, young Ben would have slipped off to Tounie to watch videos instead of sweating up the hill with a rifle. The only time his uncle had seen him looking happy this week was when he found him sitting on the scullery draining-board chatting to Elspeth while she loaded the dishwasher. Apparently she shared his taste in music.

Freed from the strain of Beverley's presence, Sir Archie's guests drew together, just as Alec had told Maya they would, and to her relief they made it plain that she was included in their circle, as of right.

'It's strange,' she remembered Alec saying, 'but I've often arrived at Glen Buie and thought, Oh, lord! Same old faces. How can I bear two weeks of their company? But when you spend day after day with them, crawling up hills or wallowing in burns, sharing highs and lows, you develop a curious attachment...'

'Camaraderie?' she had suggested.

'Something of the kind. Tribulations and triumphs shared. By the time the party breaks up, you can hardly bear to see them go.'

As the week progressed, she saw what he meant, and noticed, too, how her own interest in the outside world dwindled. Newspapers were sent from Tounie with the groceries, but only the weather reports were read with attention. Everard still listened to the Stock Market report; the rest of the party knew and cared little about world affairs.

Each morning, Sir Archie stood at his bedroom window, scanning the distant tops, and when he saw them clear, came downstairs with a spring in his step. Steadily the tally of stags mounted.

'Halfway there,' he said with satisfaction on Tuesday evening, looking back through the Game Book before making the day's entry. Sandy's card, recording in neat, square script the weight, points, and location of the stags shot that day, had been slipped between the pages during dinner, and these details Sir Archie now copied into the book, adding his own comments on wind and weather.

Handing round liqueur chocolates, Ashy paused beside him. 'How many's that?'

'Thirty. Average weight – let's see – around twelve stone. Pretty good going, though we've been lucky with the weather. Do you remember 2003? Nine solid days of mist! We ended up a dozen stags short, and Sandy and old Jock had to pull out all the stops to get them before they started shooting the hinds. By then, of course, they had been rutting for weeks, and the weights were right down.'

'It always puzzles me why Nature gives stags such a hard time just before the winter.' Everard leaned back in his chair by the fire, velvet slippers embroidered with his initials stretched to the blaze. 'Just when they should be taking things easy, storing up fat for the hungry months ahead, they run themselves to skin and bone chasing hinds. Cock-eyed, when you think of it.'

'Still, it weeds out the weaklings,' said Johnny, glancing across the room to the windowseat where Nicky was leafing through a magazine, bony knees showing sharply through his jeans.

Yes, thought Sir Archie with a pang. If humans obeyed the same imperatives, Nicky would certainly go to the wall. 'How did you and Priscilla get on at the trout, my love?' he called as his wife entered the room.

'Pretty well, considering the loch was clear as glass, never a ripple. Rowing was hot work.'

'Numbers?'

'Eight to my rod, eleven for Priss. All much of a muchness – about three to a pound. The midges were terrible, though, so we

left after Marjorie joined us. Things might have got busier during
the evening rise.'

'Well done, plenty for breakfast, anyway.' He noted the
number and said, 'Now, Ben: you were on the river today, weren't
you? Catch anything?'

'N ... no,' mumbled Benjamin, flushing and glancing at his
mother, but she was deep in talk. He said rapidly, 'It got too bright
to fish, and there was a – a concert over at the Clachan, so Nicky
and I went across to it.'

'Culture in Tounie? You astonish me.'

'Well, a rock concert. A gig.'

'I see. ' Understanding the anxious glance, his uncle lowered
his voice. Ben would certainly catch it if his mother found out.
'No salmon, then?'

'Nicky caught one.'

'Excellent. Where was that, Nicky?'

'Tail of the *Turn Pool*. Seven pounds four.'

'Fly?'

'Small Stoat's Tail,' said Nicky, without looking up.

Again Sir Archie filled in the details and passed the book to
Ashy. She read:

TUESDAY, 22 SEPTEMBER
Wind: SW Weather: clear, warm
Stags:
*12.4 Eight points; Carn Mhor; John Forbes; A. McNichol
11.8 Eight points; Sir A. Hanbury
17.8 Royal; Carn Beag; Everard Cooper; F.Grant*
Salmon:
7lbs 4 oz Turn Pool; Nicholas Hanbury; Stoat's Tail
Trout:
19 Loch a Bealach; Lady P. Cooper; Lady Hanbury

'Hmm...' Ashy placed a finger on the seventeen-stone
Royal, and raised questioning eyebrows.

Sir Archie shrugged and grimaced. 'At least he's broken his duck,' he murmured.

'Telephone, my lady,' announced Ishbel from the doorway, and Gwennie followed her into the hall.

'I'm so sorry, I'll have to cry off tomorrow,' she told Sir Archie on her return. 'The Kingswoods asked if they could come over, and I couldn't very well say No.'

'You could have.' Sir Archie disliked having his plans altered. 'Blast them! That means I'll need another first rifle. Nicky?'

'Sorry, Pa. I'm going up to the trout loch.'

For the space of several seconds, Sir Archie wrestled with the impulse to tell his son to do as he was damned well told, and as if to assist him, Ashy said, 'Oh, but that's what I want to do. Maya and I have asked Donny to bring the pony here tomorrow morning, so I can take up my painting things. You go stalking, Nicks, and we'll take care of the trout. Two's company, three's a crowd.'

Nicky seemed unoffended by so clear a hint that he wasn't wanted. 'I tell you what we'll do,' he said diffidently. 'You can paint and fish while I walk round the loch. How about that? I gave my knee a bit of a twist scrambling about in the plantation after that roebuck,' he explained to his father, 'and I don't think it's quite up to a full day's stalking.'

Since 'scrambling about in the plantation' had provided the party with at least two meals, Gwennie took her stepson's part.

'Much better get it right first,' she said, nodding. 'Knees can be the devil. Why doesn't Johnny take the rifle?'

No reason, except that some inner monitor was telling Sir Archie that Johnny was getting not only more than his share of shooting, but also rather too big for his boots. However, needs must when the devil drives, he told himself, and nodded with the best grace he could summon. 'All right, Johnny?'

'Very much all right, Uncle Archie,' replied his nephew with a grin.

Chapter Seven

LOCH A BEALACH, the lake at the pass, was shaped like a great tadpole, with three miniature islands grouped at the head and a long curling tail ending in a reedy bog. On this brilliant autumn morning, the water's glassy surface reflected hill and cloud with perfect clarity, and the occasional spreading ring showed where trout were feeding.

Ten yards behind Ashy's chosen viewpoint, firmly tethered to an angle-iron fence-post, the solid white pony stood with underlip hanging and eyes half closed. Carrying stags home from the hill was his job, his attitude implied, not toting easels and paintboxes. In the stable-yard he had objected quite strongly to these unfamiliar objects being loaded on to his saddle, and had only been persuaded to move by a smart thwack from Donny's thumbstick.

'Keep him moving, Miss Ashy,' he had grinned. 'Dinna gie him the chance tae stop or he won't budge again. Grrr! Get on wi' ye, Rory, ye daft bugger.'

Nicky trailed behind as they climbed the winding track towards the pass, but when the two girls had unloaded the painting gear and set up the easel, he joined them at the water's edge, and shyly produced a bottle of white wine to enliven their sandwiches.

'You're not as useless as you look, Nicks,' Ashy told him by way of a compliment, and his cheeks flushed with pleasure.

When she had finished eating, and posted the apple cores into Rory's cavernous mouth, Ashy lay back in the heather, face raised to the sun.

'Just a tiny kip,' she murmured. 'Away with you both, and let me court my muse in peace.'

Nicky rose reluctantly, and the look of naked longing on his face as he gazed down at Ashy gave Maya a curious pang, reinforcing the need she felt to be on her own for a while.

'I guess I'll go catch some fish.' She picked up her borrowed trout-rod and walked quickly away.

The three small dots of islands shimmered in the haze, the best part of a mile away. Moving round the foreshore, making detours past inlets and squashy bogs, Maya at last found herself level with the little archipelago, where Gwennie had told her the fishing was best. Interlocking circles on the smooth surface showed trout feeding among the reeds, but the air was so still she found it impossible to put a fly over them. I need a boat, she thought. I wonder where they left it yesterday?

Continuing along the water's edge, stopping now and again to flick a fly into some promising bay, she reached a point where a feeder burn had created a delta of marshy tussocks, and there, some yards beyond the waterline in a sandy cove flanked by low cliffs, her eye fell on the unmistakable shape of an upturned rowing-boat.

And there in the middle distance was Nicky, a small, spidery figure climbing the side of a heather-covered spur with long strides. On impulse, she ducked down behind the boat to wait until he was completely out of sight. She didn't want him turning back and offering to row while she fished. For the first time in a week she had the chance to be alone, with no one to tell her where to go or what she should be doing.

The sun-warmed wood was friendly against her back as she laid down rod and net, stretched out her legs, and allowed the peace of this remote place to sink into her soul. Her breathing quietened, and by degrees, she became absorbed into what seemed like silence until her hearing adjusted to take in the soft *plop!* of a rising fish, insects buzzing in the heather, the muted, far-off cry of birds. Sounds and landscapes that had changed little since Bonnie Prince Charlie's call raised the clans over two hundred and fifty years ago.

Lifting her face to the sun, she closed her eyes, revelling in solitude. No need to please anyone or talk. No need to worry about what she said or did, or wonder what Alec's family thought of her. For this golden afternoon, at least, she could remember why she had come here.

'Alec,' she said softly. 'Are you here, my love?'

Silence; yet her sense of a presence was very strong.

'Stay with me,' she murmured. 'Don't leave me alone.'

The heather was springy, and smelled of honey. Overtaken by lethargy, Maya yawned and took off her sweater, wedging it between her head and the boat. Comforted by the feeling that Alec was near, she drifted off to sleep.

★★★★★

She awoke with a start, chilly and disorientated, unsure whether minutes or hours had passed. As she lay blinking the sleep from her eyes, light dazzled against them like the first blinding stab of a migraine. A breeze had sprung up, ruffling the loch into choppy waves, and the smiling hills now looked shadowed and forbidding.

Shuddering, she got up and pulled on her sweater, then considered the boat. Was it worth hauling it down to the water and rowing back to the islands? That depended largely on finding the rowlocks and oars, and the most likely place for them was under the boat.

She bent and raised the hull a few inches, and caught a glimpse of a polythene covered bundle. Oars! she thought, and with a strong heave rolled the boat the right way up.

The breeze plucked at the polythene as, suddenly uneasy, Maya squatted on her heels and laid a tentative hand on the bundle. Soft. Lumpy. More like a kit-bag than a pair of oars. Without allowing herself to speculate further, she grasped the nearest edge of plastic and twitched it aside.

Flat on her back, eyes turned sightlessly to the sky, Beverley's pale, shocked face and scarlet gash of mouth gaped at her. Maya gasped and stepped back quickly. A dark veil clouded her vision, and she swayed, wondering if she was about to faint. I'm not *seeing* this, she thought wildly.

Yet as her head cleared and the first shock passed, she knew it was real enough. Her mind took in details: a contusion above the right eye and scrapes down the right cheek; scraps of dry bracken in her hair; the astonished, outraged expression, as if her next words would be, '*This can't happen to me!*'

What had killed her? *Who* had killed her? How long ago? Maya stretched out a hand to touch the dead cheek, then drew back before making contact, fearful of destroying evidence.

I must get help, she thought confusedly. Nicky. Ashy. They're the nearest. I must find them, quickly.

She stared round at the empty hills. High in the rocks directly above the burn, something flashed as it caught the light. A deadly chill spread through her and her heart began to race, for who would be hiding in the rocks, spying on her, but the murderer?

Adrenalin surged, and she heaved the boat back over the body as easily as if it had been balsa wood. With no thought beyond escape, she fled away from the loch, making for the dark shelter of the forestry that clothed the lower slopes of Ben Shallachan. That twinkling light came from binoculars, or possibly a telescopic sight. How far away was it? 'A bullet can travel two miles,' Sir Archie had said, 'unless it hits something on the way.' Any moment she expected to hear the crack of a rifle, or feel the jolting thud that would end her life.

With bolting eyes and breath rasping in her throat, she reached the trees and plunged into the scratchy gloom of interlaced conifer branches. Pine needles carpeted the slope, and at first she made good progress, thankful to be out of sight of that long-distance eye. But as the trees thickened and the slope became ever steeper, she began to regret leaving the open hill where she could see ahead.

Here was no path, not even a game-trail, and soon she lost all sense of direction as she veered this way and that, unable to see the sky through the thick canopy of firs. All she could do was keep moving downhill, praying that sooner or later she would strike a track.

Chapter Eight

IT WAS AFTER two in the morning when the tramp of boots over boards warned of the search-party's return. Sir Archie pushed open the drawing-room door, and his wife and Lady Priscilla, seated either side of the embers, rose quickly.

'Nothing,' he said wearily, in reply to their unspoken question, and headed for the drinks table. 'Sweet bloody eff all. That girl's a fantasist.'

'Where are the men?'

'Just coming. I told them not to worry about their boots. Ah!'

The men clumped in, tired and pale. Sir Archie sloshed malt whisky into glasses. 'Sandy, Fergus, take a dram. By God, you've earned it. Johnny? Nicky? The same?'

'Thanks.'

'Sit down, all of you,' Gwennie urged. 'Tell us what happened. Did you find the boat?'

'Aye, my lady,' said Sandy. 'Abune the jetty, just where it should be.'

Gwennie shook her head in puzzlement. The men drank, slumped in their chairs, the tension draining out of them. Sir Archie took a long pull at his whisky, set it down, and rubbed his eyes.

'We found nothing,' he said heavily. 'The boat was in its proper place, as Sandy says. Hauled up, with the oars under it. No polythene sheet. No body. We walked the whole way round Loch a Bealach, and disturbed a lot of deer and a couple of hill foxes.

We fell into holes and stumbled over rocks, but in the matter of dead women, we drew a complete and utter blank.'

'She must have seen *something*,' said Gwennie. 'She was in a real state – well, you saw her yourself. I mean, why would she – ?'

'God knows. Where is she now?'

'I made her go to bed. She was tired out, but I think she was having second thoughts as well, especially when we heard about the message from Beverley.'

'What message?'

'Apparently she rang about five o'clock. One of the maids took the call. It was Beverley, saying she'd caught a cold and wouldn't be back for a day or two.'

'Thank God for that.'

'She wanted to speak to Nicky, but of course he wasn't back by then.'

'One for the road, Sandy?' Sir Archie heaved himself out of his chair, but Sandy rose, too, shaking his head.

'No, thank you, sir. I maun' be awa' or Kirsty will wonder what's keeping me.'

'Of course. Well, thank you all, and I'm sorry we had such a wild goose chase. If you'd like to call off tomorrow's stalking, that's all right by me.'

'Nae need for that, sir. Fergus and I ha' done without sleep afore now, and none the worse,' said Sandy with his slow smile. 'Good night to you now, my lady.'

When the boots had retreated, Gwennie said sombrely, 'I'm afraid that's not the last we'll hear of it.'

'Oh, I think we can trust our chaps to keep their mouths shut.'

'You're forgetting the lad from the fish-farm.'

A pub-bound pick-up had found Maya shivering, scratched, and almost incoherent beside the sea-loch road, and brought her back to Glen Buie. In a place where every tiny incident provided food for gossip, her rescuer was bound to talk.

'And he works for young Ian McNeil,' said Sir Archie slowly.

'Damn and blast!'

They thought it over in silence, then Gwennie nodded to Lady Priscilla and rose. 'Nothing we can do about it now. Let's get some sleep. So long as Beverley is alive and kicking in Stornoway, there's really no great harm done.'

Next morning, Maya found it hard to face the breakfast table. Curious faces turned when she came in, but they greeted her without comment and the usual chatter quickly resumed.

So British, she thought. Pretend something doesn't exist, and with luck it will go away. Close ranks. Freeze out the alien. It worked with Bev, after all. Perhaps I, too, should go explore the islands, or remember an urgent appointment in London.

She sought out Gwennie to apologise, and waylaid her in the passage, going to discuss menus with Mary Grant.

'Silly child!' Gwennie smiled and patted her arm. 'There's no need to cut short your visit. Archie's an old bear, I know, but surely Alec told you that his bark is much worse than his bite?'

'I really did see her, you know,' said Maya unhappily.

'Oh, my dear, I don't doubt that for a moment.' Her mother-in-law's tranquil eyes showed neither impatience nor surprise. 'People see the oddest things up here. I expect what you saw yesterday was what we call a Fetch. Have you heard of them? Sort of a ghost in advance.'

'A Hant?' Maya shook her head. 'Sure, I've heard of them, but this was *real*. Look, I broke my nail when I turned over that boat. I wasn't dreaming.'

'I'm not suggesting you were. What you experienced was real enough, only it hasn't happened yet.'

'You mean it will happen again?' Maya wondered which of them was mad.

'Maybe not for years. Maybe not in the form it appeared to you. Strange things happen here on the rim of the world. There seems to be a particularly fine line between reality and fantasy. Past, present, and future tend to blur.' She looked attentively at Maya's troubled face. 'I remember a friend of my parents' – the stuffiest, most blimpish old brigadier you could imagine – who was sitting on the river bank one day when he saw – or claimed he saw – a little man in a green hooded cloak, about the size of a six-year-old child, hurrying about on the opposite bank, picking up sticks and tying them in bundles. Every time he put up his binoculars for a better look, the little chap vanished, but he could see him clearly with the naked eye. What do you make of that? We all teased him terribly, of course, and said he must have had a dram too many, but he swore that he was wide awake and stone cold sober. To his dying day he was convinced that he had seen one of the Wee Folk.'

'But what *I* saw was …'

'I know, I know. Your apparition belonged to the future, and his to the past, but when you think, they're not so different. Just a blurring of time-zones.'

Gwennie gave her a moment to consider this, then said, 'What do you plan to do today? I'm afraid both stalking-parties have gone, but will you come with me to the river?'

Maya hesitated, then said quietly, 'It sounds weird, I know, but I'd like to take a look at that boat again. Or the place where I thought I saw it. I guess I won't get it out of my mind until I've done that.'

'Excellent idea,' said Gwennie briskly. 'May I come with you?'

How could she refuse? 'If you're not too busy, I'd appreciate it,' said Maya, bowing to the inevitable.

'I must have a word with Mary, and after that my day's my own. Shall we say halfpast ten?'

★★★★★

It was all very different from the gold-and-purple landscape through which she had climbed with Ashy and Nicky. Now a sharp wind buffeted them head-on, and when they got their first glimpse of the loch, white horses were cresting the surface that had yesterday lain smooth and shiny as treacle.

Gwennie pointed. 'There's the boat.'

The green, clinker-built rowing-boat lay hull-up above the stone jetty where they had picnicked in the sun.

'It wasn't there yesterday,' said Maya. 'Leastways, I don't believe it was.'

'Are you sure? One can easily walk past something without noticing if you're talking and not actually looking for it.'

Uncertain now, Maya stared about her. The green and russet hill. The loch with its humpy shore-line and many little inlets and bays, were at once familiar and alien. Yesterday's small clear burns had been turned into jets of white water by overnight rain, and low cloud obscured the skyline.

'I can't be sure,' she admitted. 'Shall we go on?'

Hurrying as if to grasp at memory before it faded away, she led Gwennie along the thread of path worn by fishermen round the loch's eastern shore.

'Steady!' panted Gwennie. 'Was it really this far? We never bring a boat past the islands, because of the reeds.'

'I can see the place from here.'

Silent now, conserving breath, they climbed to the ridge from which Maya had first seen the boat, and paused to look out across the narrow bay into which the feeder burn was now discharging a lazy trail of foam. In the dull light, it was hard to tell where water ended and land began, but it had been there – just above the crescent of shingle –

'Who's that?' Maya exclaimed. A few hundred yards below them in the bay, a kammo-clad figure moved to and fro, head bent, scanning the ground.

'Not one of our chaps.' Gwennie was perched on a rock, binoculars to her eyes. 'Could be a hiker.'

'That's just where the boat was.'

They stared at one another. 'Whoever he is, he has no business there,' said Gwennie firmly. 'Let's see what he's up to.'

When they got near the stooping figure, Gwennie said

with a hint of steel in her tone, 'Good day to you. Have you lost something?'

The man straightened and swung round. Tall, square-shouldered: a Viking, thought Maya, taking in the long-featured, Nordic face, straight nose, straight mouth, the dusty-fair hair tied back in a queue.

'Ian!' exclaimed Gwennie, in a voice that left no doubt of her irritation. 'What are you doing here?'

'I was told you'd had a spot of bother hereabouts,' said Ian McNeil easily, smiling at Maya. 'I came up to see if I could help at all.'

'Bringing your rod on the off-chance of doing some fishing at the same time?' Gwennie picked up the slender split-cane from where it lay against a gorse-bush, and swished it to and fro.

'Not mine – wish it was,' said McNeil. 'Actually, Gwennie, it belongs to your husband. See?' He pointed to the name engraved on the butt. 'Odd sort of place to leave it...'

Maya said quickly, 'I left it there. I'm sorry. I forgot all about it.'

'Finding a body under a boat does tend to drive other things out of one's head.'

'What rubbish!' snapped Gwennie, but without conviction. Obviously the story was all over the peninsula.

'Is this where you found the boat?'

'I – I guess so,' said Maya. 'But there's nothing to show I didn't dream it all.'

'Why should you dream something like that?'

She raised her hands, then let them fall. 'I just don't know. It was hot. I went to sleep...' her voice trailed away.

As abruptly as if she had thrown a switch, Gwennie's hostility became sociability. 'So good of you to come and check, Ian, but I think we've seen all we need to. As Maya says, the oddest things appear normal in this part of the world.' And while Maya struggled with her inclination to point out that this was Gwennie's theory, not her own, she added in the same bright, brittle manner, 'How's your brother? And Janie? We were hoping to see more of them this year, but they're always so busy.'

'True enough.'

'Have they had a successful tourist season?'

'Busy, anyway.' His quick grimace hinted at his own view of the summer invasion. 'Plenty of punters, mostly foreign, and they tend to come in waves. It's pretty difficult for Janie, never knowing how many she's got to cook for.'

'I can't think how she manages.' Gwennie didn't quite hide her disapproval that the laird's wife should be running a hostel.

'Needs must when the devil drives,' said McNeil cheerfully. 'Anyway, we're all looking forward to seeing you and your party at the Ceilidh after the Sports on Saturday. Oh, and at the Sports too, of course. We'll catch up with your news then.'

'I do wish you'd persuade Janie to let us feed the hordes at Glen Buie for once.'

'Not a hope. She wouldn't hear of it – and nor would my brother. You know how they love opening up the old house once in a while, and it makes a change to entertain their own friends and neighbours, after all those backpackers.' He picked up the net which Maya had left beside the rod. 'Don't forget this! You'll all be coming, then?'

'Yes – if you're sure it won't be the final straw for Janie?'

'The more the merrier.' McNeil fished in a pocket and drew out a scrap of paper. 'I suppose you dropped that yesterday?' he said, turning to Maya.

Crumpled, unbleached tissue, sodden from last night's rain, but its waffle pattern overprinted with tiny formalised trees was still clearly recognisable.

'Recycled paper,' he pointed out. 'Can't have been here long or it would have disintegrated.'

Maya shook her head. 'Not mine.'

Her eyes met Gwennie's, and she knew the same scene was in their minds. Pre-dinner drinks round the drawing-room fire. Beverley sniffing, fishing in her sleeve, blowing her nose. Moving away, leaving on the carpet a crumpled whitish scrap overprinted with tiny green trees.

Lady Priscilla stooping to retrieve it, tossing it on the fire, rubbing her fingers on her skirt, saying with distaste, 'I can never understand why girls like that won't carry a proper handkerchief.'

★★★★★

'The one person I'd prefer not to find poking his nose into our affairs,' exclaimed Gwennie, striding downhill. 'It's lucky you were with me, though, or I might have been rude to him, and that would have made Archie cross. He tries to keep on good terms with our neighbours, no matter how tiresome they are.'

'You don't get along?'

'Oh, the Strathtorrans are all right, poor things. They work like – like slaves to keep the place together, and live on a shoestring. Ian is a different kettle of fish altogether. He's poached too many of our stags and salmon for one to feel easy about seeing him on this side of the ground.'

'Poached?'

'Stolen. He was hauled up before the local Bench last year, but of course they're far too soft. All they gave him was a miserable fine, because he's Torquil Strathtorran's brother. What sort of deterrent is that? One of these days he'll go too far and land up in jug.'

Gwennie brooded, hurrying downhill so fast that Maya had to jog. 'Of course it's hard luck on Torquil, and worse for Janie. Torquil takes his paying guests out sailing and climbing, but Janie has to do all the cooking and admin with only a half-witted old woman to help. That's why I tell her we should host the Ceilidh at Glen Buie Lodge. At least we've got enough staff. But Janie battles on and won't hear of it. I'm afraid she's heading for a nervous breakdown.'

'What is this Cayley?' asked Maya.

'Oh, just a general jollification. Sports in the afternoon

on the football field, and then the Strathtorrans open up the old house for the evening. Music. Dancing. All that sort of thing. Some people recite ballads that go on for ever. Archie presents the prizes, and the ferryman plays the pipes. It's a lot of work for Janie, and I don't suppose either Torquil or Ian is much use when it comes to setting up trestles and peeling spuds.'

'Does Ian live with them, then?'

Gwennie nodded. 'Archie says if Torquil and Janie can put up with that lazy layabout, why should he annoy me? I'm sorry, but he does. I can't bear deliberate idleness, especially in someone who was brought up to know better. He battens off his brother, spends half his time in the pub, and does a bit of poaching on the side. He's a rotten example to the local riffraff. If the laird's brother can get away with it, they think, why shouldn't they?'

They walked for a time in silence, then Gwennie said abruptly, 'Odd about that paper hankie, though.'

'I know.'

'You couldn't have dropped it? You're sure?'

'I never use that stuff. It makes my nose sore.'

'Still, lots of other people do.' She sounded as if she was trying to persuade herself. In thoughtful silence they made their way back to the lodge.

Chapter Nine

ON SATURDAY AFTERNOON, Everard Cooper cried off
the Strathtorran Sports. 'I'll join you for the Ceilidh this evening,'
he said. 'That's more my style nowadays.'

'Oh, but I was counting on you to partner me in the Three-
Legged Race!' wailed Ashy in mock anguish, and he gave a snort
of disgust.

'You can count on someone else, you horrible child. I've
better things to do than break an ankle for your amusement.'

As soon as all the cars had driven away, and he was sure the
Lodge was deserted, he installed himself in his host's study, locked
the door, drew the curtains across, and settled down to peruse the
contents of the files stacked in an untidy heap on the corner of
the desk. He would have liked a cigar, but that would have given
him away. Archie might be deaf, but he had a nose like a labrador,
and even a man of his absurdly trusting nature might wonder at
Havana fumes in his private sanctum.

It was always instructive to see where Archie Hanbury
was putting his money. Last year, Everard had gleaned advance
warning of a bid for a brewery, and managed to buy shares before
the price rocketed. One couldn't expect that sort of luck every
time, but there was no harm in sniffing the wind.

He spread open half a dozen files and copied what information
he needed, then re-stacked them with artistic attention to how
it had looked before. Next he looked about for some indication
of his host's intentions regarding the future of Glen Buie itself.
Gwennie had admitted to Priscilla that the doctor insisted this

should be Archie's last stalking season, so would he hand the place over to Nicky, and what would Nicky do with it if he did? Sell, or follow in Torquil Strathtorran's footsteps? Plainly that bossy bitch Beverley Tanner had spotted the tourist potential of this unspoilt wilderness. If she should get her hands on Glen Buie, bang would go his own plan of buying it for the entertainment of corporate sportsmen.

Everard poked in drawers and riffled through correspondence, but found nothing to show what Archie planned. No luck today, then. He sat back in his chair, hands planted on his broad thighs, and considered his next move.

Already it was four-fifteen, and the races on the football field would be in full swing. Every man, woman and child on the peninsula would be watching or taking part, and the coast was as clear as it would ever be for him to put a spinner through the Greeting Pool.

He had been careful to keep his spinning-rod concealed in the boot of his Jaguar. Sir Archie allowed only fly-rods on his river, even though most of the pools had lies which could not be reached by casting. The Greeting Pool was potentially the best fishing on the river, and it had always annoyed Everard to know that it was out of bounds.

He sauntered into the gun room to pick up his fishing-bag and the spiked stick he used for wading, then drove down to the river.

Although there wasn't much chance of anyone seeing him, he parked the car behind some bushes which concealed it from the track. The evening sun slanted low through the trees, and the Greeting Pool lay still and dark on either side of the strong, sinuous current that swept from the Strathtorran bank at the head of the pool to the Glen Buie bank at its tail.

Under the bridge's central pier, a marker showed the water's height: four feet – just about perfect. Everard heaved himself on to the parapet and stared towards Strathtorran House, whose roof was visible in the distance, and the glittering sea beyond. Between them lay the football field, where glints of sun on serried ranks of windscreens showed that the Sports were, as usual, attracting a capacity crowd.

Satisfied, he pulled on his waders and took the spinning-rod from the boot. He eased himself waist-deep into the water, and began deftly flicking the silver-winged, triple-hooked 'spoon' into a dark backwater just below the bridge, systematically covering every foot of water, and moving a couple of paces on alternate casts.

At first he was tensely expectant, placing the spoon meticulously, his nerves fine-tuned to the movement of the twinkling wing as it rotated through the water. At any minute, he expected to feel the thrilling bump on the line that tells a fisherman he is in business: that in the unseen depths his lure has been noticed, inspected, and is about to be swallowed. But as time passed and no swirl of interest disturbed the dark water, he grew blasé and began to spin carelessly, mind easing into neutral.

When he reached the unfishable shallows at the tail of the pool, he climbed out, disillusioned, and sat on a log to smoke a cigar. What the hell was the matter? This pool must be stuffed with fish – fat, lazy, undisturbed. Why wouldn't they look at his spoon? The water was the right height and temperature. He had been careful not to show himself against the sky, yet nothing had stirred since he arrived.

Quarter of an hour later, after some desultory conscience-searching, he threw away the stub of his cigar and crossed the bridge. After another careful look round to be sure he was unobserved, he lowered himself into the stream on the Strathtorran side of the river. Now he was compounding his felony, breaking the law as well as Archie's fuddy-duddy rules. If caught, he would have difficulty explaining his conduct. A guest of such long standing could hardly plead ignorance of who owned which bank.

The pool was easier to fish from this side. The swirling current carried his spoon in a long arc, right under the opposite side as he reeled it back towards his own waders. Now he could be sure he was covering every inch rather than every foot of water.

No action.

Everard reeled in, cut off the spoon, and substituted a sand-eel lure, its hooks attached to a hank of yellow tow. Was he fishing deep enough? After some thought, he chose two small lumps of split shot from his weight-box, and bit them on to the line a couple of feet from the lure.

Then he waded up to the top of the pool again, just below the bridge. He thumbed the bail across the top of his reel, slung the weighted lure into the current, and began to wind in.

Immediately he felt a quick, snatching tug of resistance, and his heart jumped. At last! Trembling with excitement, he counted to five then struck, but to his intense disappointment the hook floated free.

Never mind, things were looking up. He tried to cast again at the same spot, but the weighted line overshot and caught the bushes on the opposite bank. Too impatient to go across and free the hook, he heaved brutally until it snapped, sacrificing both the weights and the sand-eel lure. These he replaced with a golden articulated minnow and slightly smaller split shot, returned to the bridge-pillar, and tried again.

This time the minnow dropped exactly where he wanted, and once more he was rewarded by a tug – not a quick snatch, but steady, heavy resistance.

By God, this is more like it! he thought. And then, more doubtfully, Am I on the bottom?

Gentle exploratory pulls proved to his satisfaction that the fish was definitely moving, though lying so deep in the pool that his line disappeared almost vertically.

A big one. A really big one! he thought, heart hammering. Thirty pounder? Even bigger? His mind raced ahead. How could he bring such a monster to the bank? Would it fit in his net, or must he use the gaff? It seemed little disposed to fight, but he had often heard that real leviathans were sluggish. They towed you down to the bottom, and might simply sulk there for an hour.

You had to be patient.

He glanced at his watch – ten past seven – and took long, calming breaths. He imagined carrying his huge fish back to the house, and the excitement it would cause. Very lucky that he had brought a fly-rod in the car: he could pretend he had caught it on that.

The relentless pressure was making his arm ache, and bending the stiff, short spinning-rod, but as soon as he relaxed a fraction, the line pulled away from him. Slowly, with many pauses, Everard began to reel in, using the brake on maximum, and moving downstream so that the fish had the current against it as well as the line. The light was fading behind the trees, and in the black water it was difficult to tell just where the long silver shape would break the surface.

Net and gaff to hand, he peered into the murky depths, waiting tensely for the flurry of foam, the desperate plunge for freedom which the fish would make when it caught sight of him.

A paleness showed under the surface, and his heart raced again. God! It was enormous. No chance of getting *that* in a net. He would have to beach it where the shingle curved steeply at the tail of the pool. Carefully he waded backwards, feeling for submerged rocks that might snag the line. His arm was tiring, the muscles lumped in one solid ache from shoulder to hand, and he was blowing hard.

Three steps to the beach...two...

Reaching the shallows, the fish grounded on underwater shingle and lay still. No struggle. No frantic thrashing. Just a long, inert...shape beneath the glimmering surface.

His elation drained away. What have I caught? he thought, bending forward to peer into the water. A dead deer? A sheep?

The current plucked at the obstruction, trying to float it away. Everard gripped his line and heaved, and a human arm rose out of the water in macabre salutation. Horrified, he stumbled backwards. His foot skidded on a weed-covered rock, and he toppled into the pool.

An icy wave flowed into the bib of his chest-waders, weighing him down, while the air trapped round his feet forced his legs upward. He dropped his rod and clawed at the clip on the shoulder straps of those deadly waders, but the more he thrashed about, the faster they filled.

With his feet in the air and his head under water, Everard realised he was about to drown.

Chapter Ten

'TWENTY-EIGHT, TWENTY-NINE, thirty... That's the lot, then, Morag,' said Janie Strathtorran. 'Go and tell his lordship we're ready to eat. Morag!' she said more loudly as the old woman stared blearily into space.

'Verra guid, my lady.' Eyes glazed and snowy hair already escaping from its pins, Morag teetered away more unsteadily than could be explained by her best shoes.

She's been at the sherry, thought Janie, and hoped she wouldn't drop anything that mattered.

Critically she surveyed the rows of heaped plates which had taken her most of the day to prepare. Boring food for boring people, she thought heretically, and wished – not for the first time – that tradition played a smaller part in local eating habits. She was a first-class cook, and this standard of fare was anathema to her.

She imagined the shocked faces of the stalkers and ghillies, the ferrymen and crofters and shepherds and fish-farm lads, if she followed her own inclination and served Indonesian curry or garlicky goulash as refreshments after the Sports, instead of plastic sliced ham and heavily-Heinzed potato salad. Or sushi. Or a bubbling, wine-laden fondue.

The women were more adventurous, gastronomically speaking, and might welcome a change, but their men would not; and here on the Western rim of the world, feminism was a lost cause.

She shrugged and turned to the ornate gilded mirror which, together with half a dozen portraits of long-dead Strathtorrans in heroic kilted poses, was all that remained of the original dining-room furniture. She was slender, tense, mousy: the deep groove between her eyebrows and perennially anxious expression testifying to the strain of keeping up appearances on too little money, and running a business with too little help.

Smile, she told herself. Look serene. This is meant to be fun. It *is* fun. Tonight's guests are friends and neighbours, not PGs. She could see that Torquil was enjoying himself, and so would she be if only they could afford to do things properly for once, with shining mahogany instead of trestles from the village hall, and waiters to serve the food instead of herself and Morag – and Ian when he remembered.

She tried to look on the bright side. As from this evening, the hostel was closed for the season. Just to be free of greasy breakfast fry-ups and the finicky, time-consuming chore of wrapping packed lunches should be enough to raise her spirits. From now until Easter, she would have no ashtrays to empty, no lavatories to unblock. For six glorious months, she need not brace herself to enter a bedroom which she had left fresh and pretty, its bathroom sparkling clean, knowing she would find it soiled and despoiled, the crumpled sheets stained, wet towels littering the bathroom, waste-basket overflowing with nameless horrors, mirror daubed, taps dripping, lavatory unflushed. Why did tourists have such filthy habits?

The flip side was that there would be no money coming in. Never mind: once tonight's meal was out of the way, and their guests began to recite, or dance, or sing for their supper, she would stop feeling hard done by and enjoy the party, she knew. She loved these people – really. It was just that from time to time the domestic drudgery and constant demands on her energy and goodwill made her want to scream.

Mercifully, Torquil never felt as she did. He accepted the burden of his inheritance as easily and naturally as he did its privileges. He should be called Tranquil, not Torquil, she thought affectionately, watching him move round the long, high-ceilinged hall, courteously making his guests welcome, from angular Lady

Priscilla to the cocky, chippy Macdougall twins from the fish-
farm, with their slicked-down hair and aggression in every swing
of their kilts, looking for a chance to show their mettle to their
girlfriends, all eye-black and over-exposed thigh.

Torquil stooped over old Mairi Kilbride's wheelchair, his
dark head attentively bent to catch her toothless mumbling. He
looked the flower of Scottish chivalry in the old style, needing
only a periwig atop his sleepy-eyed, long-featured face to pass as
a Stuart pretender.

Moving on, he exchanged a word with Sir Archie Hanbury,
red-cheeked and jovial in the tight circle of the Glen Buie party;
then smiled his sympathy at Colleen Taggart, the publican's
daughter, pipped on the post in the Ladies' Sprint. 'Can't win them
all, Colleen,' she imagined Torquil saying. 'Got to give someone
else a chance now and then!' and she saw Colleen's chagrined face
break into a reluctant smile.

Fergus had covered himself with glory, winning most of
the men's races, though Johnny Forbes had hung doggedly on his
heels and finally passed him to win the Men's Mile. That was one
in the eye for the cocky devil, thought Janie, who often crossed
swords with Fergus over the harassment of hikers.

'It's Sir Archibald's orders, my lady,' Fergus had told her
with barely veiled insolence when she had complained of the way
he had frightened a middle-aged Dutch couple.

'What harm were they doing?'

'They were ower the march.'

'You can't expect foreigners to know that a broken wire
fence is a boundary,' she had said, trying to sound reasonable, but
Fergus wouldn't give an inch.

'I'm only doing my job, my lady. Sir Archibald doesna like
his deer disturbed.'

His deer! As if they didn't move freely from Strathtorran to
Glen Buie and back several times a day!

'I've a good mind to have it out with Archie,' Janie had said
later to her husband. 'I bet he doesn't know the half of what his

stalkers get up to when he's not there. Poor Kaatje was scared stiff, and Hans said that Fergus actually threatened him with a gun.'

'Leave it, old girl. Leave it,' Torquil had said, as if she had been a spaniel about to roll in a fox-dropping. 'It'd only make bad blood.'

'All the same –'

'I said, leave it.'

'If Fergus is going to scare our guests away, we might as well shut up shop,' she'd replied angrily.

'Oh, come on, darling, it's not as bad as that. And even if you get Archie to read him the Riot Act, it won't do a blind bit of good in the long run. The Hanburys are only *somerlid*, after all. We mustn't let them get under our skins.'

'Somerlid?'

'Summer raiders, like the Vikings who used to harry this coast. Scots called them *Somerlid buie* – yellow-haired summer raiders. They'd come here for six weeks or so when the weather was good, and grab all they could lay hands on, but as soon as the winter gales began, they'd be off. Since we live here all year round, we might as well make up our minds to get on as well as we can with the Glen Buie people. No sense in starting feuds.'

In her heart, she knew he was right. The Hanburys would always be outsiders, even though Sir Archie now owned the bulk of the peninsula. Any orders he gave to his stalkers and ghillies would be observed while he was there to see they were enforced. Once he went back down South, Sandy would again reign supreme, with Fergus as his second-in-command. There was no point in making enemies of them.

Even now the Glen Buie party looked isolated, she thought. They were standing together, facing inward – all except Ashy, who was chatting up the fish-farm boys with the ease of long acquaintance, while Nicky stood with his shoulders propped against the wall, following her with his eyes. He looked strained and unhappy. Janie had heard the gossip about his girlfriend, and wondered if it was true that he obeyed her orders like a dog.

It was strange how inherited riches could make a person miserable. If someone left *me* a few million, I'd know what to do with it, she thought.

'Oil and water,' murmured Ian, appearing at her side. He nodded at the Glen Buie party.

'Just what I was thinking. They hardly even try to mix – except Ashy, of course.'

'Have a drink.' He gave her a glass and touched her forehead lightly, smoothing out the frown-line. 'Relax! Everything's going beautifully. Torquil's about to herd them through into the dining-room.' He scanned the room. 'Where's little Kirsty?'

'Where would she be but minding the bairn?' Janie pitched her voice into a prim Edinburgh lilt.

'Couldn't she bring him?'

'He's not well. Got a bit of a temp.'

'Poor kid,' said Ian, and she knew his sympathy wasn't for wee Dougie. 'Perhaps I'll pop up there after supper. Take her a few goodies. All right, you needn't look at me like that.'

'Just watch it,' she warned. 'The last thing we need is a row with Sandy.'

Ian smiled and moved away. She watched him cross the room and sit beside Maya Forrester. The Black Widow, the locals were calling her. Janie observed her curiously. Who would have expected Alec to marry a coloured girl? No wonder his mother had been a bit tight-lipped, and wedding photographs were not on display.

A heavy crash in the kitchen, closely followed by a keening wail, put an end to her musing, and she hurried out to assess the damage. Morag's luck – and that of the crockery – had finally run out.

★★★★★

Dougie had at last fallen asleep, though his face was flushed and he whimpered from time to time. Kirsty held him until he settled into deeper slumber, then laid him in his cot and crept to the door.

All day she had been up and down stairs, trying everything she could think of to soothe his fretfulness. She felt stiff and stale, her nostrils full of the sickness smells of Vapex and Friar's Balsam.

I'll run to the bridge and back, just for a blow, she thought. It won't take more than ten minutes.

She was sorry to miss the Ceilidh, which would have given her a chance to wear the ruffled and pin-tucked emerald silk blouse which Sandy had given her on the anniversary of their meeting. She had admired it in a magazine, and he had sent secretly for it, getting the size right, and waylaying the postman to preserve the surprise. It suited her, just as she had guessed it would, making her skin very white and her eyes big and dark. She had looked forward to seeing Colleen Taggart's envious glance, and perhaps admiration from Ian McNeil.

Half past seven, and the long gloaming was easing into dark. They would be eating their supper now at Strathtorran House, with the laird filling their glasses, and the company mulling over the events of the day. Then the prizes would be given out, and the pipes would squeal and drone...

Just down to the bridge and back: wee Dougie wouldn't wake for a while. She opened the door and sped lightly down the twisting path to the river, leaping the planks laid over culverts, flitting through the twilight with her long hair streaming. When she reached the bridge, she leaned panting against the parapet, her chest heaving and the taste of blood in her mouth. After the stuffy cottage, the sharp nip of autumn air was intoxicating, making her almost light-headed in her exhilaration.

With her heart slowing to normal, she straightened and looked about. The confluence of two small rivers, the Torran and the Buie, had formed a broad triangular pool, with twin waterfalls above the bridge, and a long tail sweeping tightly under low cliffs on the Buie bank, while the Strathtorran side extended in a steeply shelved shingle beach overhung by a sheer wall of rock.

For the few moments she had been standing there, a

subconscious layer of her mind was registering the sound of splashing at the tail of the pool, and now her ears caught a hollow groan, not quite the grunting roar of a rutting stag: closer to a sheep's cough but curiously prolonged.

Suddenly alert, she strained her eyes into the dusk. Something was floundering against the water-smoothed rock, trying to hoist itself, then falling back. Superstitious fear gripped her. This was the pool where the laird's young sister, Lady Helen McNeil, had drowned...but ghosts did not flounder and splash .

Kirsty moved cautiously across the bridge, then scrambled over flat rocks interspersed with clumps of deep heather. On hands and knees, she ducked under lichened hazels fringing the cliff, and crawled to a spot where she could look straight down.

An injured stag? One of Sandy's ewes?

'Oh, God!' it groaned, and she caught her breath.

'Hold on! I'm coming.'

She looked in vain for something to use as rope, but the cliff was sheer and even the tough heather stalks would give a drowning man no support. Carefully she climbed to a ledge where she was close enough to see the big pale face and desperate eyes only inches above the water.

A gentleman from the Lodge, she thought. One of Sir Archibald's guests, and even at this anxious moment a corner of her mind found time to wonder how a fisherman in waders came to be in this forbidden pool.

Kneeling on her ledge, she stared down at him. His hands were stretched out, grasping a knob of rock, but the current plucked at his sodden clothes, threatening to sweep him away.

'Can't reach,' he gasped. 'Done for.'

'I'll get help.'

'Hurry!' he groaned, but she needed no urging. Heedless of scraped hands and knees, she scrambled up the gully and across the rock slabs to the bridge. There she paused, remembering that all the men were down at Strathtorran House, the best part of a mile away.

'Oh, God, what'll I do?' she murmured.

Back at the Stalker's Cottage were ropes, blankets, stretchers, all the kit required for rescue work in the hills, but without assistance she could do nothing. Yet by the time she got to Strathtorran to raise the alarm, the waterlogged fisherman would surely have drowned.

As she stood there, irresolute, with the light fading rapidly from the surrounding hilltops, an echo of that despairing groan goaded her into action. Dropping her sweater, she began to run as she had never run before.

★★★★★

The ham salads had been eaten, the plates stacked, and the company now faced the choice of chocolate mousse, treacle tart, or a selection of lurid trifles.

'I've been totting up points, and you've won the Ladies' Cup. Well done!' said Ashy, depositing a plate piled high with creamy goo on the trestle table, and clambering over the bench to plump herself next to Maya.

'Got to keep up my strength before the dancing,' she explained, intercepting Maya's amused glance. 'Oh, what a shame, what a waste,' she went on without a pause, following Ian McNeil with her eyes. 'Such a dish as never was seen in days gone by, and look at him now. Gone bush, but totally. *De mortuis* and all that, but I can't help blaming Eliza.'

'His wife?' prompted Maya, guessing there was more to come.

'Did Alec tell you about her?'

She thought back: had he? 'He talked about so many people. I'm confused.'

'You'd know if he'd talked about her,' said Ashy positively.

'Was she very beautiful?'

The corners of Ashy's expressive mouth turned down. 'Depends what you call beautiful. *I* thought she looked like

Cruella de Ville, all flashing eyes and floating hair, but *men*, well – you know.'

Maya had no difficulty in imagining Eliza's effect on men.

'She was a form above me at school,' Ashy went on. 'I had a pash on her, actually, when I was in the Lower Fourth, but I soon grew out of it. After she left school, she teamed up with Beverley Tanner, and they started *Gentlemen's Relish*. They did City lunches, Livery Company dinners, that kind of thing. Corporate entertaining. Did you hear about that?'

'Your mom told me.'

'A few years ago Gwennie had a kitchen crisis when Mary Grant was carted off to hospital for a hysterectomy, and Eliza came here at zero notice to take over the cooking. I must say, she was a marvellous cook. Then the next thing we heard was that she and Ian were engaged. Bingo.'

Ashy fortified herself with a swig of the pinkish Europlonk which Maya thought would do a good job stripping paint, and held out her glass to the Macdougall twin who had taken charge of the bottle. 'Yes, please, Hamish, while you're at it. More for you, Maya? Truly? Where was I?'

'Telling me about Eliza.'

Ashy cocked an eye at her mother, two places away, but Lady Priscilla was absorbed in conversation with John Forbes. 'You may think it strange that she didn't try to land Torquil while she was about it,' she went on in a slightly lower voice, 'but poor Torkie was extremely groggy just then, something wrong with his innards, so the smart money was on Ian to succeed to the title.'

'But – ?' prompted Maya, and as if reassured of her interest, Ashy plunged on.

'Torkie made a miraculous recovery and married his nurse' – she nodded towards Janie – 'the Auld Laird popped his clogs and left him all that remained of Strathtorran, and poor Ian was sent to Northern Ireland on an unaccompanied tour of duty. So after the wedding, Eliza found herself stuck here at the back of beyond, in the wettest winter in living memory, living with in-laws with whom – tell it not in Gath – she didn't exactly hit it off. Not with Janie, anyway. Two women in one kitchen...' She shuddered, and lowered more of the pink paint-stripper.

'Couldn't she go back to work in London?'

'She and Bev had sold out to one of those celebrity chefs – Julian something, can't remember the name – and Eliza tried to start a restaurant up here with her share of the money.' She pulled a face. 'Didn't work. The locals don't go for what they call *messed-up food*, and Janie wasn't keen on losing the tourist trade. So what d'you think happened?'

'They had a bust-up?'

'In a manner of speaking. When Ian showed up round about Christmas, Eliza told him she had had enough. According to old Morag, who was in the next room doing what she called 'dusting,' and Janie calls 'stroking the furniture,' when the fur began to fly, Eliza told him she couldn't stand it here any longer. She said she was in love with someone else, and was going to have his –'

'Astrid!' Lady Priscilla's voice was sharp. 'Everyone's waiting for you.'

Ashy flushed, plunged a spoon into her trifle and finished the plateful, but not before Maya's mind had completed her sentence: *baby*. Whose baby? Surely to God she didn't mean Alec's? He had often come up here at Christmas to shoot hinds, and since the house at Glen Buie was closed for the winter, he had told her he used to stay at Strathtorran.

'Sorry. Rabbiting on as usual,' mumbled Ashy with a sidelong glance.

'No, really. It's interesting.' Maya's lips felt stiff as she tried to smile. 'You must tell me more.'

To her relief, a ripple of applause heralded the after-supper speeches, and Ashy swung her legs over the bench and stood up. 'I'm off. I've heard Archie do this umpteen times. I'll go and give Morag a hand with the glasses.'

She slid through the door that led to the kitchen, and Maya wished she could go with her. The voices around her seemed suddenly too loud, the heat oppressive, the bonhomie forced. What was she doing here? Why didn't she catch that flight home, and leave these people to their outlandish traditions and recreations? No one would be sorry if she quit, herself least of all.

Torquil was on his feet, flushed and jovial, splendid in his jabot and silver-buttoned velvet coat. After a few words of welcome, he called on Sir Archibald Hanbury to present the prizes.

'My lord, ladies and gentlemen,' boomed Sir Archie. The Macdougall twins sniggered and offered round cigarettes. Nicky tipped back his chair against the wall. Easing away from table and covertly loosenng waistbands, the company relaxed and waited for the evening's familiar pattern to unfold.

'I'm not going to make a speech.' The easy confident voice washed over them like warm treacle. ' I know everyone wants to get on with singing and dancing, so I'll just say how honoured we are to be with you again, and I'm sure I speak for everyone here when I thank our charming hostess, Lady Strathtorran, for the wonderful feast she has put before us tonight...'

He chuntered on agreeably, but by degrees Maya became aware that down at the far end of the room the audience's attention was not with him. Heads were turning towards the door to the hall, through which came a piercing outdoor draught. A rising tide of whispers brought disapproving shushes from the top table.

As the commotion increased, Torquil left his seat and squeezed round behind the benches to reach the hall door. A moment later he clapped his hands, and the room fell silent.

'Sorry to interrupt you, Archie,' he called, 'but there has been an accident. One of your guests is in the Greeting Pool. Can I have some volunteers?'

*****

Even with manpower a-plenty, it was a struggle to raise Everard's sodden and helpless bulk from the pool. By the glare of roof-mounted spotlights trained down from the line of 4x4 vehicles on the bridge, he was slowly hoisted to the ledge, and carried to the flat ground at the top of the cliff.

'Damned dangerous, these chest-waders,' growled crusty Doctor Ferguson, slitting them and releasing a stream of water. 'Stand back, all of ye. Give the man a chance.'

The cliff and bridge were thick with spectators. 'He's coming to himself now,' they told one another as Everard stirred and groaned, blinking in the white light.

His gaze wandered vaguely over the assembled faces. 'Where's Archie?' he said hoarsely.

'Here I am.' Sir Archie shouldered through the throng and knelt beside him. 'So sorry. Terrible thing to happen.'

'Listen,' said Everard painfully. 'Got to tell you.'

'Take it easy, old chap. Don't try to talk. We'll soon have you home and dry.'

'*Listen!*'

'All right. All right, I'm listening.'

'Got to tell you.' He paused to gather his breath, then said faintly, 'There's a body in the pool. Tried to get it out.'

'What?' The word was repeated in widening ripples through the crowd. 'What's that he said? A body?'

'Tried to pull it ashore. Slipped. It's – it's that girl.'

'What are you talking about? What girl?'

'Awful creature. Nicky's girl,' said Everard and closed his eyes. 'In the river. Dead.'

PART TWO

Chapter Eleven

'CAGEY LOT,' said Detective Sergeant James Winter of the Highlands and Islands Constabulary, as he entered the book-lined study which Sir Archie had allotted to the police team. 'Don't suppose they've ever heard of the Classless Society. Not exactly falling over themselves to assist the police.'

He was a lean, light-framed thirty-year-old, whose cropped dark head and El Greco looks would have been attractive but for his habitual aggrieved expression.

Detective Inspector Martin Robb waved him to a chair. 'What can you expect? Nobs don't like finding bodies in their salmon pools, and nor do their staff. Upsets everyone. Have some coffee. It's good.'

As Winter poured and sipped, Robb added, 'Tell me how you got on in the kitchen.'

Winter grimaced and said with sudden intensity, 'If *I* worked my guts out to let a lot of rich layabouts indulge their passion for slaughter, I'd be glad enough to spill any beans I had. With this lot, it's blood from a stone.'

Robb said soberly, 'You can't blame them. Jobs are scarce around here. Anyone who gets on Sir Archibald Hanbury's payroll is going to do his damnedest to stay there, and if that means being cagey with coppers, too bad. You'll have to work at it, Jim. Buddy up to the cook. Offer to peel spuds.'

Winter made an impatient noise. 'What gets me is the way they *grovel* to these people.'

'I doubt if they see it that way.'

'No? You ought to hear them. Yes, sir; no sir. Miss Ashy did this; Mr Nicky did that. Lady Priscilla said the other. Why *Lady* Priscilla, anyway, if her husband is just Mr Cooper?'

'Duke's daughter. Courtesy title,' Robb said absently and then, catching the full force of Winter's glare, 'Don't blame me, Jim. I didn't invent the system.'

'Rotten system, if you ask me. Do you know what the cook's paid, after twenty years in the job? Have a guess.'

'Basic agricultural?'

'Sheer exploitation! Just think what Hanbury himself must be raking in. Chairman of TABC, isn't he, and non-exec of God knows how many other companies. Three houses, wife breeds racehorses...'

'My word, you have been doing some digging.' Robb tried not to smile. Winter was new to his team, a Londoner with a red-brick degree and plenty of environmental idealism. What Robb privately dubbed a City Green – crusader for whales and rain-forests, champion of the ozone layer and enemy of agri-business – who could spout all the fashionable dogma without having any personal experience of country work. Finding himself among people to whom field sports were a way of life was bound to cause culture shock.

Robb himself was country born and bred, and forays after rabbits and pigeons with his trusty .410 were among his early memories. He said briskly, 'Well, Jim, how Sir Archibald spends his money is nothing to do with us. We're here to find out how Beverley Tanner came to be in that river, right? We'll concentrate on the matter in hand. There won't be anything from the lab for a bit, but meantime we can get on with taking statements. Where's that list?'

As Robb studied it, Winter sipped his coffee and watched him, hoping they'd be able to work together. A big man, Robb. Forty-five years old, six-two and solidly built, with strong square hands and a permanently stiff knee, legacy of county standard rugger. Dark curly hair had retreated from his forehead, leaving a thick island above each ear. The baggy tweed jacket and brown cords in which he had travelled from the mainland looked as well suited to this background as Winter's own jeans and bomber jacket were out of place.

Easygoing, dependable Robb. Everyone's favourite uncle until you had occasion to look closely into those light blue eyes and see the frost behind the twinkle.

It was eleven on Sunday morning, and sun streamed through the long sash windows of the library, which overlooked the broad sea-loch and the faraway blue hills of Carse Morrish. In the middle distance, the twin funnels of a toy-size steamer puffed black smoke into a sky of duck-egg blue. The *Lady of Spain* was making her thrice-weekly round trip from Tounie.

For the police team, the day had begun early with a rough voyage over heaving black water which Robb, no seaman, preferred to forget. Still fighting queasiness, he had watched as Beverley Tanner's battered and pulpy body, with a triple-barbed hook embedded in the left arm, and a climbing-rope lashed round a boulder attached to her waist, had been removed from the lower end of the Greeting Pool. In the rocky funnel where it had lodged, the water had given it a pounding.

'The wonder is that she's still in one piece,' said Rhys, the police surgeon, squatting on the bank to examine the remains. 'When you look at that weight of water, you'd think flesh and blood would disintegrate in twenty-four hours. Amazingly resilient, the human body.'

'Roughly how long do you reckon she's been there?' Robb had asked, and Rhys had pursed his lips and paused long enough to make it clear that guesswork wasn't his style.

'Best part of a week,' he said at last. 'Four to five days, maybe. From the general state of breakdown, I'd put it in the four to six-day bracket. Can't be more exact until we run some tests. All right, Dave,' he called to his assistant. 'That's all I want. Bag her up and we'll get back to the lab.'

He had risen with a gymnast's neatness, and said, 'Over to

you, then, boyo. I'll be in touch.' He had nodded to Sir Archie, hollow-eyed in the chilly dawn, with Sandy a dour, protective shadow at his shoulder. Then he had snapped shut his flat black case and looked round carefully, fixing the scene in his memory.

'Be seeing you,' he murmured, and walked away.

'We'll go to the house, sir,' Robb had said then. 'Constable McTavish can take charge here and see no one comes collecting souvenirs.'

'I'll drive,' said Sir Archie, opening the Land Rover door. 'Would you two mind sitting in the back, Inspector, so that Sandy can deal with the gates?'

With an effort, Robb hoisted his bulk over the tailgate, pushing aside the labradors squirming in greeting. 'It's all right, Jim,' he said as Winter hesitated. 'Plenty of room.'

'All aboard?' Sir Archie let in the clutch with a jolt and drove a few hundred yards before stopping again at the high gate in the deer-fence. 'Bloody nuisance,' he muttered.

Robb thought he was cursing the gate, but a moment later Hanbury added, 'Why did the stupid little bitch change her mind? Why make all that song-and-dance about visiting the Isles if she meant to sneak back here? What the hell did she think she was doing?'

In the driving mirror he caught Robb's eye. 'All right, Inspector, I can tell what you're thinking, but it's no use pretending I liked her. She was a pain in the neck alive, and now it looks as if she's going to be just as much trouble dead.'

An hour later, when Robb had been installed in the study and a green baize-topped card table set up for Wpc Margaret Kenny's tape-deck and laptop, he invited Sir Archie to sit in his own leather armchair and tell him about Beverley Tanner. The anger Hanbury had expressed in the Land Rover still simmered below the surface.

'Nothing annoys me more,' he began, 'than people who come here and get into difficulty through their own stupid fault. I warned that girl it was no place to wander about on her own, but would she listen? Well, she's paid for her pigheadedness now, and damned nearly drowned that ass Cooper into the bargain, not to mention putting the rest of us to no end of bother and fuss. Wherever she is, I hope she's satisfied.'

Well, that's one way of putting it, thought Robb. Aloud he said, 'I understand Miss Tanner was invited here by your son Nicholas?'

'Correct.'

'She was not someone you yourself would have chosen as a guest?'

'Also correct. A thorough-going proselytising Anti. Disapproved of stalking, hunting, shooting and fishing, although she didn't know the first thing about any of them and didn't want to learn. Why she wanted to come here is, frankly, beyond me, but my son brought her, and since this is the first time in three years that he has shown the slightest interest in Glen Buie or his family, my wife and I didn't feel inclined to criticise his choice of companion.'

'Is Nicholas your only son?'

'My only child, yes. His mother – my first wife – died when he was eight. Tell me, Inspector,' he said with a half-smile, 'have you firsthand experience of teenage revolt?'

'I've three daughters, sir. Nineteen, fifteen, twelve. They have their difficult moments, believe me. Now, let me get this straight. Miss Tanner – Beverley – was here at your son's invitation, and although you found her uncongenial, you put up with her rather than risk antagonising him?'

'That's about the size of it.'

'May I ask if the rest of your guests shared your opinion of her?'

'They'll tell you themselves, of course, but my guess is that they felt much the same as I did. We're all old friends. Most of the party have been coming here for years. They know the form. Beverley didn't fit in, and she made no effort to. No one was sorry when she left to explore the islands.'

'Not even your son?'

Sir Archie shook his head and took his time about replying. Finally he said, 'The fact is, Inspector, I've had precious little contact with Nicky for three years, and relations are still – shall we say – delicate.'

'Why is that, sir?'

'He took up with some frightful pseudo-religious sect while he was at university,' said Sir Archie bitterly. 'My wife and I have been at our wits' end trying to wean him away from them.'

'What sect is that, sir?'

'It's an unregistered charity that calls itself *Home from Home*. Ostensibly their aim is raising money to help house the homeless, but as I see it, their real business is latching on to rich young idiots like my son, and bleeding them white.'

'Is your son rich?'

Sir Archie drew a deep breath and exhaled heavily. 'Nicholas's maternal grandfather died when Nicky was fifteen, and left the bulk of his fortune in trust for him. The papers went to town over it at the time: *Schoolboy Inherits Mines Millions*, that kind of stuff.'

A poisoned chalice, thought Robb. His girls would have to work for their living, and he preferred it that way. He said, 'Did Beverley belong to this organisation?'

'I imagine she was one of the top brass.'

'What was her personal relationship with your son? Were they lovers?'

The question seemed to surprise – even startle – Sir Archie. 'Good lord, I didn't go into that. Separate bedrooms here, in any case. My wife's – well – old-fashioned about that. But quite honestly, I wouldn't have said he was up to her weight. She looked the sort to eat Nicky for breakfast. Domineering. Bossed him about. Liked to show us her power over him. If I asked him to do something, she'd tell him not to. I thought the less notice we took the better.'

Robb recognised the problem. Kick up a fuss and provoke

a row, or let sleeping dogs lie? He'd tried both with Sally, his rebellious middle daughter, and neither had worked particularly well.

'How did your other guests react?'

'Oh, they tried to pretend everything was normal. Ashy Macleod was the only person to tackle him head-on. She more or less told him not to let himself be trampled.'

Robb consulted his list. 'Lady Priscilla Cooper's daughter?'

'That's right. My god-daughter: lovely girl. She and Nicky were great pals as children. She led, he followed.'

'Did Nicholas take her advice?'

Sir Archie nodded slowly. 'Up to a point, I suppose he did. He started going stalking again, and fishing, which seemed a hopeful sign from our point of view, although I thought Beverley would give him stick for it later. Then she tried a different tack by going off on her own. My sister Marjorie – that's Mrs Forbes – said she'd probably ring up from the islands and make him join her there.'

'But instead she came back herself,' said Robb thoughtfully. 'I wonder why?'

'She came back,' echoed Sir Archie, 'and I wish to God she hadn't.'

★★★★★

'Inspector Robb? I'm Nicholas Hanbury. How do you do?' The young man's manner was polite but nervous. 'My father said you want to talk to me,' he added, hovering in the doorway as if poised for flight.

Robb had expected sandals and a beard, but Nicky was conventionally dressed in a tweed jacket and polo-neck, upmarket jeans and well-polished shoes. He was a slim, goodlooking boy with his father's fresh complexion, but his features were narrower, more finely drawn, and his mouth was set in a defensive line.

Robb shook his hand and made introductions, adding that

Wpc Kenny's grandparents used to live in one of the Strathtorran crofts.

'Overlooking the Sound of Gash,' said Peggy. 'My grandfather was shepherd to the Auld Laird.'

'Fas Buie – I know the house. A birdwatcher's got it now.' Nicky was disinclined for small talk. He said jerkily, 'Have you found... I mean, do you know...?

'Just a minute, sir. I understand that Beverley Tanner was your guest?'

'That's right.'

'But she wasn't interested in deerstalking or fishing, I gather?'

Nicky raised his head defiantly. 'There are other things to do here besides killing wildlife.'

'Of course. So she enjoyed her visit, did she? Got on well with your father's friends?'

Nicky said shortly, 'No. They didn't even try to be friendly.'

'Was that why she decided to leave early?'

'Partly. Yes.'

'Had you quarrelled?'

Nicky's colour rose, but he said composedly enough, 'We didn't live in one another's pockets, you know. Bev liked her space. She wanted to explore a bit, see the islands, but she promised she'd keep in touch.'

'Did she?'

'Keep in touch? Well, yes. A bit.'

'What do you mean?'

'Well, she knew I couldn't use my mobile because there are only a couple of places on the peninsula where I can get a signal, but she rang the house a few times. She was going to come back –'

'That's the question, isn't it?' Robb broke in. 'When *did* she come back? Did she, in fact, ever leave?'

'Of course she did. I took her to the ferry on Sunday morning before breakfast. Then a few days later she rang from Stornoway and said she'd had a very rough crossing and had caught a cold.'

'Did you actually see her onto the boat?'

'Well, no.' Nicky fidgeted with his watchstrap; then, seeing Robb watching, put both hands in his pockets. 'We were early, and she told me not to wait. I left her in the queue at the ticket-office.'

'So she could, in theory, have walked out again without buying a ticket?'

Nicky shrugged and said querulously, 'What would be the point?'

'Check with the ferry line, Jim,' said Robb, and Winter left the room.

'According to the police surgeon, Beverley's body has been in the river at least four days. There's no way she could have crossed to Stornoway and back *and* spent that long in the water.'

Nicky was silent, and Robb continued, 'Why did she want you to think she had gone away?'

'I don't know.'

'Another thing. We need to notify Beverley's next of kin, preferably before the newspapers get hold of the story. Can you help us there? Parents?'

'Dead, I think.' Nicky had gone very pale.

'Anyone else you can think of? Brothers and sisters? Husband?' He stared hard into the haunted eyes. 'That's you, isn't it?'

Nicky drew a long, uneven breath, and his shoulders sagged.

'How long have you been married?'

'Ten – no, eleven months. Nearly a year. Must you tell my father? Will I – will I have to – ?'

'Not if you don't want to.' Robb gave him a moment to compose himself, then said, 'Why did you keep your marriage secret?'

'You've met my father. Do you think he would have been pleased?'

'Is pleasing him important to you?'

Nicky slanted a glance from under his brows and said, '*I*

don't care what he thinks. Keeping it quiet was Bev's idea. She didn't want to muck up my chance of being given Glen Buie when my father gives up stalking.'

'Is he likely to?'

'His heart's been playing up and the doctor wants him to stop. My stepmother has been piling on the pressure, too. The plan used to be that he would hand over to me and my stepbrother, Alec Forrester, who was anyway co-owner here...but then Alec was drowned at sea.'

'So what will your father do now?'

Nicky shrugged. 'I don't know, but by the terms of the partnership he'll have to get Maya's agreement before he does anything.'

'Maya?'

'Alec's widow. The … the black girl. She inherited Alec's share.'

Again Robb consulted his list. 'Ah, yes. So now you think your father will pass over his share to you when he retires from stalking?'

Nicky's mouth twisted. 'Bev thought he would, if I don't blot my copybook.'

'And being married to her would constitute a blot?'

Ask a silly question, said Nicky's expression. Aloud he said, 'Dad's blinkered. He didn't even try to understand Bev's point of view.'

'What was that, sir?'

'Well, obviously she was shocked at such a waste of resources. Land lying idle, cottages empty and so on, especially when so many people are homeless.'

'I doubt if they'd be willing to move to a Highland croft,' observed Robb dryly.

'No one was suggesting they should! Bev's idea was to develop Glen Buie as a tourist destination, which would generate income for *Home from Home*,' said Nicky earnestly, 'but I knew if my father got wind of it, he would make pretty damn sure that neither Bev nor I got the chance to do any such thing. Bev was so outspoken. She didn't realise how slow people here are to accept a new idea.'

'So in fact *you* initiated her trip to the islands?'

'I thought she'd be safer there.'

'Safer?'

Nicky leaned forward, biting his lip, his bony, boyish hands pressed between his knees. 'It worried me, the way she used to wander by herself, but when I told her to be careful, she laughed at me. She thought the hills were just a big theme park and she could go where she pleased because there's no law of trespass here. She didn't understand how dangerous it can be – how quickly things can go wrong.' He paused and then added sombrely, 'Especially if there's no one around to help you.'

Robb said, 'You were afraid she would be harmed by some*one*, not some*thing* – is that right? Someone who didn't like what she meant to do here? Who was that?'

For a moment there was silence, then Nicky said jerkily, 'She couldn't see how much – how much they hated her.'

'They?'

'My family. Pa's friends. Ashy, Sandy, Fergus – everyone who works here. Even Everard Cooper. Because they were polite to her face, she thought they were harmless, dinosaurs: a bit of a joke. But I know what they're like really, and I knew what they were thinking. Any one of them would have shoved her in the river if they thought they could get away with it.'

'If you were that worried, why didn't you leave with her?'

'I wish I had,' said Nicky wretchedly, 'but she wouldn't let me. She said if I didn't take an interest in Glen Buie, I'd find my father handing it over to my cousin, John Forbes. Ever since Alec was drowned, Aunt Marjorie has been pushing blasted Johnny under my father's nose, trying to persuade him I'd ruin the place.'

Robb said, 'When did you last speak to Beverley?'

'I told you she rang on Sunday night, just to say she'd arrived and found a place to stay; then again on Wednesday evening.'

'Wednesday? You actually spoke to her on Wednesday?'

'I wasn't there. One of the maids took the call. Bev gave her a message for me, saying she'd got a cold and was staying a few more days.' His mouth worked suddenly, uncontrollably. He said in a voice shaken by sobs,'And now she's dead. I – I still can't believe it.'

'Did anyone else know you were married?' Robb asked imperturbably.

'Ashy guessed. I made her promise not to tell.'

'Thank you, sir. I'll have another word with you when we've got the lab report. Please will you ask Astrid Macleod to come in?'

★★★★★

'Is this the Incident Room?' Ashy's eyes glinted with curiosity as her blonde head appeared round the door.

'I suppose you could call it that,' said Robb equably.

'Not exactly *Crimewatch UK,* but never mind.' She chose a chair and looked at him expectantly. 'What do you want to know?'

Five-ten, size 16-18, and as braw as she's bonny, thought Robb, who approved of big women, though no doubt any dietician would tell her she had a stone to lose. Like Nicky, she was clearly on edge, but where his answers had been terse, words poured from Ashy in a torrent. The difficulty with her was going to be sifting fact from hearsay, speculation, and outright fiction.

Even before he had framed his first question, she had plunged into the story of how she had missed the river rescue.

'Just my rotten luck. I went out to the kitchen while Archie was making his speech – I've heard it about a million times – to give Morag a hand with the washing-up so that she could come and dance her Highland Fling. It's an absolute hoot. She always says she's too old, but I can jolly her into it after a few drams.

'Anyway, there we were, gassing away, deep in the soapsuds, and we heard the cars roaring off up the drive, and when I went back into the hall there was hardly a soul left. Just Mrs McNichol, Sandy's mum, and a couple of other ancient biddies. They told me everyone had gone to the Greeting Pool because someone was drowning, so I simply flew up there – oh, my legs, I can hardly move today – but by the time I got there it was all over. They were just putting my stepfather into the doctor's car. I gather there's not a lot wrong with him, though I doubt if he'll show his face here for a while. Amazing luck that Kirsty happened to be passing the pool and heard him. If she hadn't gone out for a breather, dear Everard would have been done for,' she finished with a marked lack of sympathy. 'He had no business fishing in that pool, as he very well knew, and certainly not with a spinning-rod.'

'Why not?'

'Because it's out of bounds.'

'I thought Sir Archibald owned the whole river.'

'Not so. When old Lord Strathtorran sold up, he kept that one pool. It's where his only daughter drowned at the age of sixteen, poor kid. I suppose he didn't like to think of people wading about in her grave. Grue!' She gave him a sidelong glance and added, 'Sandy has a Thing about that pool.'

'Sandy McNichol? The head stalker?'

'That's right. My theory is that he and Lady Helen were secretly in love. He must have been quite goodlooking when he was young. I guess that her father found out, and sacked Sandy, and that was why Lady Helen drowned herself. It all fits, you see, only Sandy is such an old oyster you'll never get him to admit it. But he hates people messing about anywhere near the Greeting Pool. Once I dared Alec Forrester to take a peek in Sandy's hideyhole under the bridge, but when Sandy found out he was furious.'

'What's this hideyhole?'

'It's where Sandy puts sweets for the Wee Folk whenever he takes a stalking party across the bridge. For luck, you know.' She saw Robb's smile and said seriously, 'He doesn't like people to laugh about it, either. I've noticed that if anyone teases him, he makes pretty damned sure that they don't shoot a stag that day.'

'How can he do that?'

'Very easily. After all, the Rifle is entirely in the stalker's hands. He only shoots when he's told to.'

Robb sensed that he was being decoyed away from the matter in hand. 'Let's talk about Beverley Tanner, Miss Macleod.'

'Do call me Ashy. Everyone does.'

'If you prefer. I understand you were the only person who knew that the deceased was Nicholas Hanbury's wife.'

'The deceased – how horrible.' Ashy grimaced, sighed, then said with her usual energy, 'I may have been the only person Nicks actually *told,* but the others very likely guessed. I mean, it was obvious from the way she bossed him around. Poor Nicky! He's too clever to be sensible, if you know what I mean. You or I could have seen at once that Beverley was after his money, but he thought she simply wanted to help the homeless. He wouldn't hear a word against her, not even when I told him she was trying to blackmail my stepfather.'

'Was she?'

'Well, trying to get money out of him. Same thing, isn't it?'

'How do you know about this?'

Ashy picked up a pipe-cleaner from a box on the table and began to twist it into a rabbit. Her face had gone attractively pink.

'I heard them. It was pretty embarrassing, actually. I was in the smoking-room, looking for a book after dinner. I was kneeling on the floor behind the sofa, to see what was on the bottom shelf, when they came in. No, don't tell me, I know I should have leapt up and shouted, but I didn't do it quickly enough, and after I'd been listening for a minute or two, I just couldn't.'

'Awkward,' Robb agreed.

'At first I thought he'd lured her in there for a spot of – you know,' said Ashy, flicking back her ponytail. 'He's a terrible groper. Mary – that's the cook – has to tell the maids not to turn their backs on him. But she – Bev – was talking about his business.

Some company called Mona Peat. She asked if Archie knew about their report on the West Coast peat extraction project, and said she wouldn't mention Everard's involvement if he made a donation to *Home from Home.*'

'How much did she want?'

'Ten grand. He practically exploded. He called her a lot of revolting names,' said Ashy sedately, though a smile twitched the corner of her mouth, 'and he said he'd break her bloody neck if she said a word about Mona Peat to Archie.'

'What did she say?'

'Oh, she was pretty cool. I think she liked seeing him in a stew. She said, "Take it or leave it. Makes no difference to me," and went out of the room.'

★★★★★

John Forbes was next, anxious to make a good impression and, specifically, to emphasise that he was as unlike his cousin Nicholas as a man could possibly be.

This, he told Robb, was his second visit to Glen Buie. 'I've still got a lot to learn about it, but in a strange way I do feel I belong here. Must be in my blood.'

Robb refrained from pointing out that the deer forest had been in his family's hands for less than thirty years. By his own account, John Forbes's life to date had been singularly lacking in roots.

'Father was a missionary, you see. We never spent long in one place, and were always on the move because some of his parishes were huge, especially in Africa. My brother and I had no chance to come here when we were boys, and anyway, Father wouldn't have liked it.'

On leaving university, he had been taken on by Shaw and Selkirk, the estate agents. 'I was lucky to get a job, with so many bright chaps out of work,' he said, managing to imply that S&S would have been fools to turn him down.

'Auctioneers, aren't you?' Robb had seen their signs at many a cattle mart.

'Among other things. We also do estate management, sporting lets, forestry. It's the sporting side that interests me most. Take a place like this. It's crying out for someone with professional training to take matters in hand. Of course Uncle Archie is a gem – I won't hear a word against him – but he hasn't the foggiest about management. Why should he? He's never had to count the pennies. But even with my level of experience I could save him a packet.'

'How do you mean, sir?'

Johnny said, 'Anyone with half an eye can see that he's being ripped off right, left, and centre. Oh, nothing criminal...' – for a moment he recalled to whom he was speaking – 'just general slackness and bending of the rules.'

'Can you give me an example?'

'Well, no names, no packdrill, but it's an open secret that Sandy's pals from the pub are allowed to fish where and when they damn well please, and I've no doubt that a fair few of the hinds shot here in the winter don't figure in the estate accounts. That's the first thing I'd crack down on.'

'Have you told your uncle this?'

'Only in a general way. The odd hint. I don't want him to think I'm criticising.'

'Of course not. Did Sir Archibald appreciate these – er – hints?'

'I think so,' said Johnny complacently. 'He said that as far as Sandy's concerned, you can't teach an old dog new tricks, and he's due to retire soon, anyway; but it did no harm to let Fergus know you're not blind. He had trouble in his last place, you know. Selling venison on his own account – the old story.'

'It's not an easy life.'

'Oh, I wouldn't throw the rule book at them, heaven forbid! Uncle Archie wouldn't stand for that. I'd just tighten things up a bit. Cut out the worst abuses.'

Smoothly Robb guided him away from these ambitions and on to the subject of Beverley Tanner. Needless to say, Johnny hadn't liked her.

'Beats me why Nicky brought her here, unless he wanted to wind up Uncle Archie,' he said, shrugging. 'Of course it was one in the eye for Ashy, too. You should have seen her face when Nicky arrived with that creature in tow! Bang went her hopes of marrying millions.'

'You think she hoped to marry him?'

Johnny laughed. 'Ashy's got no money of her own, and she's a girl with expensive tastes. Oh, she looks very sweet and charming, but don't be fooled. She's as tough as they come. Grallochs her own stags — not a job for the squeamish — and she collects the bullet from every stag she shoots. Cuts them out and keeps them. How weird is that? If Ashy wanted to marry Nicky, she wouldn't let anyone stand in her way.'

The dislike Robb had been feeling for this self-satisfied young man crystallised into controlled anger. 'Be careful what you say, sir. There is such a thing as defamation.'

Johnny flushed. 'I thought you'd need background information,' he said defensively.

'Information, yes. Malicious gossip and speculation, definitely not. All right, sir, let's recap. You thought Nicholas had brought Beverley here in order to irritate his father. When did you realise they were, in fact, married?'

Johnny said sulkily, 'I heard them talking. My bathroom is next to the room Beverley was in, and it's only a thin partition.'

Robb imagined him lying in the bath, ears straining, careful not to splash to avoid alerting the couple next door. 'Did you tell anyone else?'

'No,' said Johnny, so quickly that Robb immediately wondered to whom he had relayed this tasty morsel of gossip. 'Can't say I envied him,' he added, meeting Robb's eyes defiantly. 'Quite honestly, I thought he'd made a big mistake.'

'Were you pleased?'

'Why should I be?'

'Didn't you think that when your uncle discovered the truth he would jib at putting his deer-forest into Beverley's hands? Word had already got about that she wanted to make it a tourist destination. A Highland honeypot.'

'Pie in the sky,' said Johnny scornfully. 'It could never have broken even.'

'Didn't it occur to you that even talking about such a possibility improved the chance that Sir Archibald would ask *you* to take over the management of Glen Buie? He might retain ownership and pay the bills, but you would be in charge. Didn't that look to you like the best of all possible outcomes?'

'You've no right to say that!' Johnny's cheeks flamed. 'You're putting words into my mouth.'

'Let's see. Am I putting words into Mr Forbes's mouth? Play that back, Peg, will you?'

Wpc Kenny pressed buttons, and Johnny's voice, amplified and malicious, filled the room. *'Ashy looks very sweet and charming... but she's as tough as they come... Can't say I envied him... made a big mistake...'*

'All right, it may have crossed my mind that – that Nicky's marriage did my chances here no harm, ' he said sulkily. 'What's wrong with that?'

'Nothing, sir.' Robb's voice was coldly formal. 'So you had good reason to hope your uncle would find out about it. And it was in your interest that Nicholas's wife should enjoy the best of health?'

'Well, yes. Of course.'

'Thank you, sir. That's all for the present,' said Robb breezily.

With a puzzled look, John Forbes left the room.

Chapter Twelve

SERGEANT WINTER RETURNED at noon from his researches, and found Robb settling down to canned Guinness and game pie, courtesy of Mary, the cook.

'She never even booked on the Stornoway ferry,' he said, taking a can of fizzy orangeade off the tray and yanking the ring-pull. 'Went over to Tounie, spent the morning buying camping gear and drinking coffee, then slipped back here sometime before five o'clock. That's when she appeared at the Strathtorran Hostel and booked in for the week.' He looked with suspicion at the game pie. 'What's in this?'

'Hare and venison, at a guess, and you can't get much more organic than that. Try it. It's good.'

'I'll stick to cheese, thanks. As I said, she booked in at the hostel, calling herself Kimberley Skinner. Lady S wasn't too keen to take a whole week's booking, because they were due to close the hostel on Friday, but in the end she agreed, and Tanner – aka Skinner – spent the next two days like a good little backpacker, without saying a word about having been here at Glen Buie the previous week. Quiet, but knew her own mind, according to Lady Strathtorran. Gave no trouble, except that on Wednesday evening she didn't come back.'

'Leaving her bill unpaid?'

'No, Lady S gets them to pay upfront, so in fact she was quids-in.'

'Where and when was Beverley last seen?' Robb hacked off another wedge of pie. 'You don't know what you're missing, Jim.'

'Tuesday morning, she asks for a packed lunch and a map. Wants to walk to a local landmark known as the Prince's Rock, or Charlie's Stane, which happens to be just on the boundary between Strathtorran and Glen Buie ground. To get there, she walked up the path beside the Torran river, then followed a walkers' trail marked with whitewashed stones over the back of the hill, and round to the head of the glen. I'll show you on this.'

He moved to the big wall-mounted map of the peninsula, studied it a moment, then drew his finger in a big loop around the rim of hills.

'How long would that take her?'

'Between two and three hours. Then she planned to walk on to the next hostel at Glen Alderdale, spend Tuesday night there, and come back next day.'

'Wednesday.'

'Right.'

'Go on.'

'When she hadn't turned up by dusk on Wednesday, Lady S sent her brother-in-law, Ian McNeil, up the forestry track in a Land Rover, in case Beverley had been benighted. But when he got back at about half-eight, Lady S told him the Glen Alderdale warden had rung to say that Miss Skinner had decided to go straight back to London, and would they please cancel the rest of her reservation?'

'What about the luggage she'd left at Glen Buie?'

'No mention of that. She probably thought Nicholas would bring it back.'

'Right.' Robb thought for a moment, then swallowed the last morsel of pie and drained his glass. 'Go up and have a word with Kirsty McNichol, the stalker's wife. Find out why she went walking by the river last night. After that you'd better fix us up with rooms at the pub. I'll carry on here, and hope we get an interim report from Griff Rhys before we're much older. It looks as if his guess is right about how long she'd been in the river, but I can't see why she lied about going over to the islands.'

★★★★★

'She went to meet a man,' said Gwennie.

She sat with ankles neatly crossed and knees pressed together like a caricature of a Tory lady on a platform, with her well-tailored, well-worn tweeds and double row of pearls. Iron-grey hair curled in little horns at her temples, and her make-up was limited to a dusting of loose powder and lipstick of a shade that had to be called *English Rose*. Her manner was friendly, if a trifle remote. Only the cool grey eyes and firm mouth suggested that she could pull rank if she chose to.

'What makes you think that, Lady Hanbury?'

'I don't think. I know. I heard them on the telephone. There's an extension by my bed,' she went on without a trace of embarrassment, 'and Beverley can't have realised that I always breakfast in my bedroom, because I heard her say that everyone had left the house. I was just picking up the receiver to make a call, and checking the number I wanted, and I heard her talking to this man.'

'What impression did you get of him?'

'Not a gent,' said Gwennie definitely. 'Apart from that, difficult to tell. I'm afraid I'm hopeless with accents.'

'Could it have been a local accent?'

'Not – not exactly.' She shook her head. 'I can't really say what it was.'

'Can you remember what they said?'

'It was really more what they *didn't* say. I don't know if he guessed I was there, but he seemed to want to get off the line. Beverley was asking questions, and he laughed and said, Wait until Sunday, and he'd tell her then. So when she told us she was going across to Stornoway, of course I thought she was meeting this man. And when we got the message that she had a cold and wouldn't be back for a few days, I couldn't help hoping she had decided to ditch my stepson in favour of – '

The telephone rang on Wpc Kenny's table. 'Mr Rhys for you, sir.'

'Right, Peg, I'll take it over here. If you'll excuse me a moment, Lady Hanbury?'

'You carry on, Inspector,' said Gwennie graciously, but she made no move to leave the room.

'We've done the prelim on your lady of the lake,' said the rich Welsh baritone. 'Been in the water a minimum of four days. It's hard to be more precise, because in a spate river, as you know, the volume of water varies almost from hour to hour. So, since last Wednesday or Thursday.'

'Thanks, Griff. We'll base it on that.'

'Hang about,' said Rhys testily, 'I said the body went in the water then.'

'So?'

'She was already dead. Shot through the chest at least 24 hours earlier.'

'Shot!' he exclaimed, taken by surprise, and both women stared at him. No matter. Everyone would know soon enough.

'At close quarters?'

'No, from a fair distance. Over a hundred yards, I'd say. The bullet passed through the thorax, penetrated the left ventricle, and exited just over 2 mill to the right of the spine. High velocity bullet from a heavy calibre rifle, something of the kind you'd use to shoot deer.'

'Ah!'

'I expect there are a few of those not far from where you're sitting, eh?'

'Have you got the bullet?'

'No joy,' said Rhys, 'but don't give up hope. I may be able to fill you in when my samples come back from the lab. I'll keep you posted.'

'So it wasn't an accident,' said Gwennie flatly, as he replaced the receiver.

'Doesn't look like it.'

'But it's *inconceivable!*' Between the kiss-curls, her brow furrowed. 'It must have been some maniac – the man she spoke to – '

'Lady Hanbury, Beverley was shot dead with a rifle, not the sort of weapon that could easily be concealed. From what I've heard, I don't imagine your estate staff would allow any stranger to roam Glen Buie with a loaded rifle.'

'You're saying it was one of us. That's – that's horrible.'

'Murder is horrible.'

There was a moment's silence. Then Gwennie said carefully, 'Beverley may not have fitted in very well here. No, that's wrong: start again. Beverley may have made herself very much disliked in the short time she spent here, but I don't have to tell you, Inspector, there's a big difference between disliking a person and murdering him or her.'

'That's correct. You don't have to tell me.'

Gwennie flushed and said stiffly, 'I'm sorry. I'm not trying to teach you your business. It's just that I – I'm not used to being on the wrong side of the tracks.'

Robb shuffled his papers and said briskly, 'Well, since this is now a murder enquiry, I would like you to make sure that no one leaves the premises without my permission.'

'Not even Mary?'

'Not even Mary.'

'Oh, dear. That's going to be difficult.'

'What's the problem? Food?'

Gwennie nodded. 'Mary always goes to Tounie on Sunday evening so she can get to the market early on Monday. She has a shopping list as long as your arm.'

'Give it to Wpc Kenny. She'll deal with it, won't you, Peg?'

She gave him a darkling look. 'Yes, sir.'

'Any other problems? No? Then I'd be glad if you'd ask Sir Archibald to come in again. I want to know what everyone was doing last Tuesday afternoon.'

'I've brought you the Game Book,' said Sir Archie, placing the heavy volume in front of Robb with the air of a faithful retriever. He leafed through the pages. 'Here you are: *Tuesday, September 22nd.* As you see, we had a busy day. Lovely stalking weather, although the wind was in the south-west, so we were all up the same end of the ground. Two stalking-parties out on Carn Mhor and Carn Beag respectively, and we got three stags between us. My wife and Lady Priscilla were up at Loch a Bealach, and caught a lot of small trout; and Nicky and Benjamin were on the river.'

And somebody shot Beverley Tanner, thought Robb, studying the page. Where the devil were all these places? Carn Mhor. Carn Beag. Loch a Bealach. He'd have to get to know the layout of the forest.

He rose to take a look at the wall-map, but the faithful retriever had something else to present. He moved heaps of paper and old magazines from the lower deck of a trolley covered with a green baize cloth, and wheeled it up to the desk. 'Here you are, Inspector. You'll find this a help.'

Beneath the cloth was a contour model of the whole peninsula, beautifully modelled and painted, with tiny houses, huts, silver threads of river and burn, trees, fences, paths, bridges all marked and identified.

'Work of art,' said Sir Archie proudly. 'It took Sandy two years to complete, but it's all there, right down to the names of the fishing-pools.'

'Wonderful,' said Robb. 'Just what I need.'

He studied it carefully. The elongated triangle of the peninsula was more or less bisected by the River Torran, which was joined by its tributary the Buie at the Greeting Pool for the last two miles of its journey to the sea-loch. On either side of the Buie rose the long dragon's-back ridges of Carn Mhor and Carn Beag, the latter's lower slopes forested with conifer plantations, which in turn were intersected by a grid of forestry tracks.

Above the deer fence, the trees gave way to rock with only a patchy covering of turf, while the broken, boggy nature of the

Carn Mhor low ground was indicated by camouflage green-and-brown mottling.

At the head of the glen the two long ridges came together in a narrow defile, and between them nestled the turquoise tadpole shape of Loch a Bealach, with its three small islands.

'Can you show me where you went that day?' he asked.

'Me, personally? Yes, of course. I was with the Carn Mhor party. Sandy was in charge. I was first rifle, and John Forbes, my nephew, was to take over if we had time for a second stalk. Ashy came along for the walk.' He reflected a moment, putting his fingertips to his eyes, then said, 'Sorry, it was the other way round. I remember now. Johnny shot his stag first, and went down to fetch the pony. Ashy and I went on with Sandy, and I got a shot around four o'clock.'

His thick forefinger traced a path along the ridge of Carn Mhor, up and down, up and down, finally climbing once more to end near the pass at Corrie Dubh. 'We dragged my stag down to this track for the pony to pick up, then walked on home by the Devil's Staircase.' His fingers took little steps over the shoulder of the hill and down behind the lodge. 'Is that what you want?'

'Clear enough. Thank you, sir. So you and Sandy and Miss Macleod were together from – say – nine in the morning until five-thirty; and John Forbes was with you until – when?'

'One-ish, I suppose. His shot was 12.15, or thereabouts.' He hesitated, then said, 'I'm afraid I can't give you a detailed breakdown of what the other party did. You'll have to ask our second stalker, Fergus Grant.'

Robb glanced at his list. 'Son of your cook, Mary?'

Sir Archie nodded. 'His father works here, too. Gardener by day, butler by night. A man of many talents.'

'Right, sir. I needn't bother you for anything else just now.'

'One other thing,' said Sir Archie casually, 'I've been on the blower to the Chief Constable. Old friend: we were at school together. I wanted to check that it would be in order to keep on with the cull. Time is of the essence, you know.'

Thank you, God, for a lovely day! thought Robb, schooling his features to conceal his fury. Just what I need: suspects with a hotline to old Blood-and-Guts.'

'What did he say to that, sir?'

'Oh, he said fine: as far as he's concerned there's no problem. He's stalked here himself many a time, so he knows the form. If we're to get our quota of stags, we have to crack on while the going's good. He said you'd have no objection.'

One day not too far distant, thought Robb, when the girls can fend for themselves, I shall enjoy telling people like Sir Archibald Hanbury just how much I like being bypassed in the chain of command. Tell them what they can do with their Old School Ties. Not yet, though. Not quite yet.

He swallowed his anger, smiled his sleepy smile, and said, 'All right, sir. If that's the Chief Constable's view, I have no objection. Perhaps you'd allow my sergeant to go with tomorrow's stalking-party. I'm sure he'd find it instructive.'

'By all means. He'll be most welcome.'

Sir Archie withdrew, wagging his tail, and Robb took a few turns about the room. 'Damn, damn, and damn,' he said softly. Wpc Kenny propped her elbow on the table and regarded him with raised eyebrows.

'All right, Peg, you can wipe that grin off your face.' He dropped back into his chair. 'Send in Lady Priscilla Cooper, and for God's sake let's get on with the job.'

Building a driftwood fire on the shore of Loch a Bealach, Lady Priscilla had noticed a lone hiker climbing the path marked by whitewashed rocks.

'I remember thinking, Hullo, there's that girl Beverley; then realising it couldn't be, because she was away to Stornoway,' she told Robb. 'Of course it was some way off, the other side of the loch, and everyone wears those cagoules now: it's almost a uniform, but certainly my first thought was that it was her.'

She smiled at him: with her toothy, bony-nosed face and narrow, greyhoundy head she was – to Robb's way of thinking

– every inch a duke's daughter, so sure of her position that she felt no need to make herself fashionable or attractive. Yet she was elegant in a loose-limbed, very English way, even though her mannish Viyella shirt, ancient fawn cords and sludge-green quilted waistcoat had all seen better days.

'You don't mind if I get on with my tatting?' she had said as she took a seat, pulling a bundle of wool and canvas from a bag with wooden handles. 'Kneelers for our church. In a moment of madness I let myself in for a whole pew's-worth.'

Robb felt he could hardly object to so blameless an activity, but he found it distracting. 'Did Lady Hanbury see her too?' he asked.

'No. Nor did I point her out,' said Lady Priscilla wryly. 'I didn't want to spoil our day. There's a good deal of *feeling* about walkers using that path during the stalking season, and Gwennie's quite territorially-minded. I thought I would let sleeping dogs lie. As I said, I concluded I had made a mistake and it couldn't be Beverley. But next day, when Maya Forrester told us she'd actually found Beverley's body under an upturned boat at the far end of the loch, it did cross my mind to wonder if I'd been right in the first place.'

'She found *what?*' exclaimed Robb incredulously.

'Haven't you been told about that?' Her finely arched eyebrows rose. 'None of us believed her at the time, but now it looks as if she saw exactly what she said.'

'Which was?'

'You'll hear the whole story from her, but the long and short of it was that last Wednesday afternoon, Maya went off round the trout-loch to fish on her own, and she spotted a boat lying hull-up at the top end. By the Sanctuary burn – here.'

Laying aside her needlework, she bent over the contour model. Her bony forefinger moved round Loch a Bealach, and stopped at the southern end.

'Is that where the boat's usually kept? It seems a long way from the path,' said Robb, and she gave him a quick, keen glance.

'You're quite right – it's not. Normally it's tied up to the jetty at the northern end, and that, may I say, is where Gwennie and I had left it the previous afternoon.' She resumed her seat, the needle stabbing steadily in and out. 'Maya apparently thought she would row back to where my daughter was painting. She flipped the boat over, and got a nasty shock when she found Beverley underneath it, dead as mutton. Or so she said. The poor girl panicked, which was hardly surprising, tried to run back to the lodge, and got herself thoroughly lost in the forestry. She was brought home that evening, in a state of collapse, by one of Ian McNeil's truck-drivers.'

'Did anyone go and check her story?'

'You bet they did. Poor Archie, Nicholas, and Johnny were up there half the night, along with the two stalkers and Donny Lamont the ponyboy, but they found nothing. No boat. No body.'

'So they concluded that Mrs Forrester had imagined it?'

'I'm afraid we all did. But if you're right and Beverley was shot on Tuesday afternoon, I suppose it's possible that whoever killed her hid the body under the boat until he had time to dispose of it in the river. Horrible, but possible. All the same, it leaves a lot of questions unanswered.'

She's the one who'll be teaching me my job next, thought Robb wryly. She's no fool, though; I must watch my step. 'You said that Lady Hanbury would have been annoyed to see a hiker using that path,' he said, feeling his way. 'Haven't they a right to do so?'

'Yes, of course they have, but one can't deny that from the stalkers' point of view it's a nuisance, because the north wind, which is the best for this ground, carries the scent of anyone picnicking by the Prince's Rock straight back across Carn Beag, and puts any stags that are on that face into the Sanctuary.'

The word had an old-fashioned ring. 'Can't they be shot in there?'

'Only because it's impossible to drag out the carcase. You can imagine how frustrated Fergus feels when the stag he has been stalking suddenly vanishes into the Sanctuary because some hiker has decided to take some snaps of Charlie's Stane. In fact, that was the first thing I thought when I spotted Beverley going up that path. I hope to God the silly bitch doesn't ruin Everard's stalk.' She gave Robb an unexpectedly charmng smile. 'My husband isn't the greatest of shots — in fact, until last Tuesday he'd had a lot of misses — so he was hoping for a change of luck. Then I remembered that the wind was from the south-west that day, so it didn't matter if anyone was up at the Stane.'

'And the change of luck. Did Mr Cooper get it?'

'In the end, yes. But he had several misses first.' She shook her head. 'One way and another, my husband has not distinguished himself this year, and after last night's debacle, I very much doubt if he will be asked here again.'

'But you will?'

She gave him a cool look. 'I shouldn't wonder.'

'Do Lord and Lady Strathtorran encourage their guests to walk to the Prince's Rock?'

Lady Priscilla shrugged. 'Let's say they don't *dis*courage them. Can't blame them: they've got to give the punters what they want, and hikers are never happy unless they're hiking. But it does cause a certain amount of friction between Glen Buie and Strathtorran.'

'I see. But despite this friction, all the people concerned attended Lord Strathtorran's Ceilidh?'

She smiled. 'Only a fool picks a quarrel on a submarine. In a remote place like this, you've got to be civilised.'

'Tell me more about the brother. Ian McNeil. You say he works at the fish-farm?'

'I believe he puts in a few hours there when he feels like it.' The bony nose wrinkled. 'The rest of his time is spent on the hill or in the pub. It's Torquil Strathtorran who organises the hostel, with his wife: a bonny way for the umpteenth earl to earn his living. Personally, I think Janie is a saint to put up with her brother-in-law, but perhaps she likes to keep him under her eye.'

'He's not married.'

'Was.' She saw Robb's next question coming, and went on, 'I might as well fill you in and be done with it. He married one of the Graham girls from Abertulloch. The middle one – Eliza.'

Eliza McNeil? Robb's memory stirred. There had been a tragedy... 'She died?' he prompted.

'She was drowned – in that same bloody pool, would you believe it. The Greeting Pool or, as we Sassenachs would say, The Weeping Pool.' Lady Priscilla nodded sombrely. 'It has certainly caused more than its share of grief.'

'How did that affect Mr McNeil?'

'Just as badly as you'd expect. Worse. They had only been married a couple of years, and most of that time he'd been away, doing hush-hush stuff with the Army in Belfast. Eliza's death knocked all the stuffing out of him. He resigned his commission and simply dropped out. Friends and family tried to help, offered him jobs, but he didn't want to know. He came back here and grew that awful low-mow beard, and now it looks as if he means to stay here doing as little as he possibly can for the rest of his life.'

★★★★★

The library was on the western corner of the house, and its windows commanded a sweeping view across the broad shoulder of Ben Shallachan, ridged at the top with bare spines of rock, while the lower slopes wore the vibrant colours of autumn – yellow and russet, purple, silver and green – in the densely planted stands of broadleaf trees which gave the house and its many outbuildings shelter from the fierce nor'-westerlies, and were themselves protected from the depredations of deer by a seven-foot wire fence with high wooden gates.

As Robb stood at the window, a battered Land Rover drove up the track from the wood. Donny sprang down from the tailgate and swung open the barricade, then followed the slowly-moving vehicle across the courtyard to a square, buttressed stone outhouse with a steep slate roof, set apart from the other buildings. By the row of bleaching skulls with antlers attached that were propped against its wall, and the monotonous drumming of a refrigeration unit, Robb identified this as the game larder.

Fergus left the driver's seat and reached up to the lintel in a gesture that left no doubt that this was the customary hiding-place of the key.

Security! thought Robb. The two young men opened the door and vanished into the larder, and he returned to study the contour model. Work of art was a fair description. Hills and rivers, lochs and forests – a miniature kingdom was up for grabs as the reigning monarch prepared to abdicate. Who would succeed him? Who wanted Glen Buie enough to kill for it?

He abstracted a lump of Blu-tac from Peggy Kenny's supplies, and placed a small blob beside the Prince's Rock to represent Beverley Tanner. Glancing at his notes, he rolled more blobs to stick where members of the party had been on Tuesday afternoon. Two at the trout loch. Four on the slopes of Carn Beag. Another four on Carn Mhor. Two on the river.

Whereabouts on the river had Nicky and young Benjamin been? He must find out. Standing over the model, it was easy to suppose that each of his blobs knew where the others were. On the ground it would be very different. There would be obstacles and angles of sight that you couldn't guess at from here. Like it or not, he would have to heave his bulk up those hills and see for himself. He groaned softly, and his knee gave a sympathetic twinge. Long ago he had wrecked it playing rugger, and any unusual stress stropped up the cartilage and gave it merry hell.

How, he thought, could people like these, rich enough to indulge themselves in any exotic holiday they fancied, choose to spend their leisure sweating up hills and crawling through peat-hags? Give me the Costa any day, he reflected. He didn't share Jim Winter's outrage at the idea of killing deer. It had to be done, but how people could do it for pleasure was beyond him.

Chacun à son goût. Interrogate, don't speculate, as his

sagacious first sergeant used to advise in the far-off days when he was a young DC.

'Your tea, sir.' With a flourish, Wpc Kenny set a tray on the desk. Two kinds of scones, plain and currant; butter, strawberry jam, and several slices of dark, damp gingerbread.

'Peg, you're an angel!'

'Yes, sir, and don't you forget it when I ask for leave at Christmas.' Despite the pert tone, he thought she looked tired and wan. That husband of hers must be on the booze again.

He remembered that they would need a place to lay their heads tonight. He wasn't going back and forth on the ferryboat if he could help it. 'Did Jim book us in at the pub?'

'Sorry, sir. They don't do accommodation.'

'Damn.' He wolfed the gingerbread and washed it down with tea.

'Shall I ask Lady Strathtorran if she can put us up at the hostel?'

'Aren't they closed?'

'From what I hear in the kitchen, her ladyship is always keen to rake in the extra bob.'

'All right, then. No harm in asking. And before you go, send in young Benjamin, would you?'

★★★★★

Ben had none of his elder brother's eagerness to please. 'Cool' and 'laidback' were the adjectives he himself would have used to describe his baggy black clothes and slouching gait, but to Robb's eyes they merely appeared slovenly. The boy's round face was still childish, but his mumbled, adenoidal responses were those of the quintessential teenage rebel.

'Can you tell me exactly where you were fishing last Tuesday, Benjamin?' Robb decided he was damned if he'd call this bolshy little number 'sir.'

'Was I fishing last Tuesday?' Ben drawled.

'According to the Game Book you were.'

'Yeah, I remember. What a drag! Hours flogging the water, and I never got a bite.'

'You were with your cousin Nicholas, is that right?'

Ben considered the question from all angles, decided it wasn't a trap, and said warily, 'What if I was?'

'We are trying to establish where everyone was on the afternoon Beverley Tanner was killed. Take a look at the contour model, and show me whereabouts on the river you and your cousin were.'

Unable to think of a reason to protest, Ben waved a vague finger along the line of the Buie. 'Lower Beat,' he said. 'Below the Greeting Bridge.'

'How did you get there?'

'In Nicky's car.'

'Good. Perhaps you'd indicate your position at, say, one o'clock.'

Ben said petulantly, 'How can I remember? We started at the top and fished down. I wasn't looking at my watch all the time.'

'Did you stop for lunch?'

'Well, yes.'

'And ate it together?'

'Yeah. Actually we went back to the car, which was parked in the last layby before the bridge.'

'What about after lunch? Did you go further upstream?'

Ben flushed, and said reluctantly, 'Actually, we didn't go on fishing after lunch. There was a gig on at the Clachan, and one of the groups was Spurs & Sporrans. They're doing a tour.'

'How did you get to Tounie?'

'By the car-ferry, of course. We only just made it.' Ben shifted uncomfortably. 'Please don't tell my mum. She's fanatically anti-rock.'

'Did your cousin attend this gig?'

'Well, no,' said Ben after a fractional pause. 'It's not his scene. He's more into Classical.'

'What did he do, then?'

'He wanted some new boots, and went from shop to shop but couldn't find any he liked.'

'A wasted journey for him, then. What time did your gig end?'

'About five, I suppose. Yeah, round about five.'

'Rather a long wait for Nicholas?'

'He didn't mind. He'd brought his golf-clubs so he could play a round on the 9-hole course beyond the bus stop.'

'I see. Were you back in time for dinner?'

'Just about. Aunt Gwennie makes an awful fuss if anyone's late.'

'All right, Benjamin. That'll do for now,' said Robb, and wondered at the boy's look of profound relief. What pitfall did he think he had dodged? It would be worth looking closely at those timings. But despite the relief, the boy turned at the door to say again, 'Please don't tell Mum!' before his steps hurried away.

When Winter came in, Robb relayed the information extracted from Benjamin and said, 'Find out if anyone saw them at The Clachan. That car of young Hanbury's is quite distinctive.'

'Rich boy's toy,' said Winter, looking with disapproval at the low-slung red Caterham outside the front door.

'That's right. Someone's bound to have noticed it. And try the ferry. They probably know Nicholas by sight.'

'Right, sir. Who do you want next?'

Robb glanced at the ticks beside his list of names, rubbed his eyes and said, 'Seven down and three to go. It's time I had a word with Mrs Forrester.'

Chapter Thirteen

TO AN EYE by now attuned to muted tweeds, Maya's shiny jade and magenta shellsuit with its diamanté questionmark on the front and equally bold exclamation mark between the shoulderblades had a stunning visual impact: a hummingbird among terns.

I know that face, thought Robb, then realised that the features were familiar only because similar polished-bronze beanpoles with dramatic cheekbones and baby-giraffe legs stared provocatively from every celeb-mag his daughters left lying about the house. Wide-set eyes, sultry lips, flared nostrils and the untamed look admired by fashionistas the world over.

She prowled catlike across the room while Wpc Kenny, sweetest of uniformed dumplings, goggled in open envy. Robb wondered if such unadulterated allure would penetrate Sergeant Winter's frosty soul.

'Hi, I'm Maya Forrester. Glad to know you.' Beneath the warm drawl and professionally brilliant smile, Robb sensed tension. A police investigation was hardly what she could have expected on her first Highland visit.

He introduced himself and Peggy, and said directly, 'I've been told, Mrs Forrester, that you found Beverley Tanner's body under a rowing-boat up at Loch a Bealach last Wednesday, but when the search party went to look for it, it had gone. Is that correct?'

She nodded, and said in the unhurried voice that sounded as if it would run out of steam between phrases, 'Wednesday afternoon, huh? You heard that Ashy and Nicky and I went up there so she could do some painting? She asked me to go along to stop things getting heavy.'

'Between her and Nicholas?'

'That's what I thought, but I guess I got it wrong because when we got up there, she made it clear enough she wanted time alone. Oh, she didn't chase me off, not exactly, but she sure didn't want Nicky hanging around to watch her paint. I thought maybe they'd had a fight.'

'Would he have liked to stay?'

'I guess so, but she didn't give him the chance.'

'You don't think she was trying to take Beverley's place in his life?'

'It didn't look that way to me, officer. If Ashy's attracted to anyone, I'd say it was Fergus. Or doesn't that square with your British class system?'

Robb let that one go. 'So you all split up, and you went off alone and found the boat on the shore, right?'

'Correct. It was kinda warm, and we'd drunk a bottle of wine with our picnic, and although I could see Nicky way over on the track above the loch, I didn't feel like talking, so I sat by the boat to wait until he'd gotten out of sight. And...' she paused, shaking her head, 'then I guess I just dropped off to sleep.'

'For how long?'

'Maybe an hour, maybe just a few minutes. You know how it is when you go to sleep in the sun?'

'And wake up with a splitting headache?'

'Not a headache. Just kinda woozy. I couldn't think where I was. Then I saw by my watch it was half-four, and thought I'd row the boat back to where Ashy was and help her get her gear on the pony. I figured the oars would be under the boat, so I turned it over.'

She stopped abruptly and drew a shuddering breath.

'What was underneath?'

'There was this long bundle covered over in sheeting – the kind they use in construction yards.'

'Did you touch it?'

'Sure I touched it. Jesus! I didn't know there was a body in it. I took hold of the sheeting and pulled a little, and there was Bev...' Her voice trailed away and she put a hand to her mouth.

'A nasty shock,' said Robb sympathetically.

She swallowed hard. 'I guess I screamed. I thought my mind was playing tricks. I mean, she was meant to be in Stornoway, so how come she was dead under a boat? Her face – she looked really *amazed,* as if she couldn't believe it either.'

'Can you remember what she was wearing?'

Maya narrowed her eyes, but after a moment shook her head. 'I'm sorry. I can't be sure. Something dark...maybe a black turtle? I didn't spend time looking. You see, I had this weird feeling that someone was watching me. When I looked back at the hill, I could see the sun flashing on glass.'

'Binoculars? A telescope?'

'Something like that. I figured that whoever killed Bev was right there, watching me.'

'You ran away?'

'Just as fast as I could lay legs to the ground.' She gave Robb an apologetic smile. 'Not very heroic, I guess.'

'Very understandable.'

Maya shook her head. 'I should have taken a better look at her. I should have gotten my bearings so I could find the place again. You think of these things afterwards, but I guess just then I was on auto. I wanted to get the hell out, fast.'

'Did you run to where you'd left the others?'

'That's what I meant to do, but somewhere I went off course. These hills are real confusing, and out in the open I was so exposed. I wanted some cover, but when I reached the trees and stopped running, I couldn't recognise a darned thing.'

'Did you try to retrace your route?'

'No way. Whoever killed Bev could have been looking for me. I took the shortest route off of that hill, down through the trees.'

Robb moved to the contour model, his finger tracing a line from the loch to the river. 'Is this more or less where you came down? Through the plantation?'

'I guess so. I just kept heading downhill, praying I'd hit a track, and suddenly I came out on one.' She smiled faintly. 'It was like one of those nightmares where you're running and can't move your legs; then I woke up and found myself on the track with a truck coming towards me, so I thumbed a lift.'

No need to tell him of her terror that the truck-driver might be the killer, or how she had crouched in the culvert beside the track, hoping he would drive by without seeing her. But he had stopped, and she recognised the chatty, tousle-headed boy who had taken her ticket on the car-ferry and had felt instinctively that she could trust him.

'Had the others returned by the time you got back?'

'They were in their baths. Ashy didn't say much, but I knew she was mad at me for getting myself lost. And she'd had trouble loading up the pony with her gear. I never did get to see the painting she did up there.'

'So you all came back separately?'

She nodded, and he said, 'That all seems clear enough. Now, turning to something else, I'd like you to tell me about the previous day's stalking. You went along with Fergus to Carn Beag, didn't you?'

'With Fergus, yes; and Mr Cooper, and Mrs Forbes, and that black dog of hers. We had a long walk, and some of it was kinda tough, but Mr Cooper shot a stag in the end, so he won his bet and that night Archie broke out the champagne to celebrate.'

'What bet was that?'

'You didn't hear? Oh, Mr Cooper hadn't shot anything all week, so when he was talking to Ashy at dinner the night before, he said he hoped his rifle wouldn't let him down again. He's the kind of guy –' said Maya with a touch of scorn – 'who can't do anything unless he has all the best gear.'

'And this bet?'

'Oh, he was sitting next to Ashy and acting the good stepfather, you know, getting her opinion on which gun was best – she's quite an expert – and Lady Priscilla leaned across the table and said in this very cold, sneering voice that there was nothing wrong with the rifle; the trouble was the man with his finger on the trigger. Yes, she said that! I sure was surprised. She looks so – well, quiet, and he's always full of noise and bluster, but then she comes out with something like that. She said – wait, I remember her exact words – she said, "You're a rotten shot, and the best rifle in the world can't cure that, so why waste any more money? You haven't shot a beast all week, and I bet you won't tomorrow, either."'

'What did he say to that?'

'Who-ay! He was real mad.' Maya shook her head, smiling. 'He didn't like being told that in front of everyone. He bet her a hundred pounds that he would; and Ashy tried to smooth things over by saying if anyone could get him a stag, Fergus would. He didn't like that, either. I guess it sounded as if he needed special help.'

'And you say he won his bet?'

'In the end.' Maya rolled her eyes. 'Plenty of times that day I thought we'd go home empty-handed. He had four misses. Four! Easy shots, too, except for the time a hiker turned up out of nowhere and spooked the beasts. Fergus blew his top. He grabbed the rifle from Mr Cooper –' she stopped abruptly.

'Did he put a shot over the hiker's head?'

'Just in the general direction. Like a warning.' She gave Robb an anxious glance. 'I mean, there are these notices telling hikers to stay on the paths, yet this crazy dude was wandering right up the hill.'

'Are you sure it was a man?'

'Uh-uh. He was quite a way off, but the stags were all unsettled because they were downwind of him. The last we saw, he was running down to the path, so he'd gotten the message. That was when we all sat down to eat our sandwiches, because he'd cleared every stag off the back of Carn Beag. We gave them time to settle, then climbed to the ridge and started over.'

'Time?'

'Around half-one.'

'After which you were facing Carn Mhor across the loch?'

'I'll show you.' She came to stand beside him, bending down to read the tiny lettering, her breath warm on his cheek. 'See here: Corrie na Fearn. That's where we left the four-track. We walked up this path through the heather, see the dotted line? After we left it, we crawled up a stream-bed and out into this gully. That's where Mr Cooper had his third miss.'

Robb was impressed. His own brief experience of deer-stalking had been very much a case of follow-my-leader, and afterwards he hadn't a clue where they'd been. This hot-house bloom evidently had a good eye for country.

She went on outlining their route, her slim brown finger tracing the ridges and gullies. Between the scarp of Carn Beag and the Buie river lay a series of roughly parallel corries, as if the cooling rock had been scrunched into pleats. The topmost of these, close to the line marking the march between Strathtorran and Glen Buie ground, was identified as the Sanctuary, and across its mouth ran the path that led to the Prince's Rock.

'We didn't make it all the way to the Sanctuary,' said Maya, kneeling down for a closer look. She put her cheek against the edge of the trolley and squinted through the maze of bumps and hollows. 'He had another chance here, in Corrie Odhar – '

'Another miss?'

'Do you have to ask?'

'And then?'

'Let's see. It must have been getting on for half-three, and they don't shoot after four if they can help it, because it takes so long to bring the stag home, and it's difficult in the dark. So time was getting short , and it looked as if Mr Cooper would lose his bet. We slid down here –' she pointed – 'and crossed the burn at the bottom. That runs into Loch a Bealach, and we could see my mother-in-law and Lady Priscilla sitting by their little fire, with the boat tied up to the bank.'

'They spotted you, too,' said Robb, nodding as the jigsaw of movements began to fall into place.

The sight of the fishing party so peacefully employed had persuaded Marjorie that she had had enough of sweating and scrambling for no purpose.

'We'd better call it a day, Fergus,' she had said in her authoritative manner. 'No point in going on now.'

'I'm damned if I'm giving up yet,' Everard had countered aggressively. 'You girls go on home by all means, if you're tired. I quite understand. OK, Fergus? You game for one more try?'

'Verra guid, sir.' Had there been the faintest trace of mockery in his voice? The suspicion of a wink at Maya?

Marjorie had begun to argue, but Everard overrode her. 'How about you, my dear?' he'd asked Maya. 'Tired, eh?'

'I was bushed,' she admitted to Robb, 'but the way he said that made me mad enough to see it through, and I sure as hell wasn't anxious to walk all the way back with Marjorie complaining of the way Archie runs the place, and how much better her precious Johnny would do it. And...' – there was mischief in her smile – 'I was curious to see if Mr Cooper would win his bet, or if he'd find some sneaky way round it, so I said I'd go on. "That's the spirit," he said, but he didn't look too happy.'

'Did you go towards the Prince's Rock?'

'Not right off. We sat there spying the hill, until Marjorie and the dog got back to the pony path, and while we were still watching her, four young staggies came round the end of the corrie and stopped above us. Behind them were two big beasts, kind of pushing and shouldering each other. The one nearest had twelve points, which made him a Royal – but the other looked really strange, big and heavy in the neck, like a polled steer.

'Fergus said, "Yon's your stag, sir," and Mr Cooper turned down his mouth, just like a sulky kid. He said, "That won't look good in my boardroom." I asked what had happened to his antlers, and Fergus said he was a hummel – that's a genetic freak that had never had any. They had wanted a chance to shoot him for years because he was better off the hill.'

She paused, and asked doubtfully, 'Do you want to hear all this?'

'It all helps.'

'Right. It must have taken us another forty minutes to climb up above the stags, and I knew this had to be Mr Cooper's last chance for the day. We lay on the ridge looking into a corrie, but the small staggies were still between us and the one without horns. Mr Cooper tried to get Fergus to leave me there, but he wouldn't, and we crawled on our bellies right along a stream to get clear of the young stags. Real Marine stuff. When they did park their gear and leave me by some rocks, I was close enough to see everything.'

'They went forward without you?'

'Only about fifty yards. I could see them lying side by side, looking down below them. Mr Cooper wriggled about and took aim a couple of times, then he put down the rifle and lay with his face on the ground. I couldn't make out why he didn't shoot.'

'Could you see the hummel from where you were?'

'Sure. He was standing on a bank right opposite, and every now and then he'd lay his head back on his neck and give a roar. I thought he was as good as in the bag.'

She had cupped her hands over her ears, she remembered, anticipating the rifle-blast, but the minutes crept by and still Mr Cooper did not fire.

Fergus had leaned towards him, whispering urgently.

Then a movement had caught the corner of her eye. The young staggies were on their feet, alarmed, testing the wind, poised for flight. Any minute the hummel would catch their panic and vanish.

Go on! she had cried silently. Hurry! You'll lose him.

When the crash of Mr Cooper's rifle shattered the silence, the hummel had given a great bound, then galloped away undamaged, with the four youngsters at his heels. Another explosion rocked the ground, but the beasts' pace never faltered.

'You thought he'd missed again?'

'I was sure of it. I'd had my glasses right on that hummel, and I could swear he wasn't touched. The men were arguing, and then they crawled forward out of my sight. About ten minutes later, I heard another shot, much fainter – then I had to wait nearly half an hour before Mr Cooper came back to find me. He was like a dog with two tails, and guess why? While I was wondering why he took so long to shoot the hummel, he had been waiting for the Royal to show himself. When he got up, Mr Cooper dropped him dead.'

Robb frowned. 'You mean he shot the wrong stag – deliberately?'

'I told you he was sneaky. He wanted a nice set of antlers on his office wall, and he wouldn't settle for anything else.'

'What did Fergus say?'

'He was mad as fire, but what could he do? He said Sandy would have his hide, but Mr Cooper just laughed and said he'd make it all right with old Sandy.' She shook her head. 'I was amazed. It was a long shot, and he had to be quick or Fergus would have seen what he meant to do.'

Robb said slowly, 'You don't think it was actually Fergus who fired the shot?'

'Why, no. I was close behind them. I saw Mr Cooper with the rifle.'

'What about the third shot you heard? Isn't it possible that Mr Cooper missed yet again, and after the two of them crawled out of your sight, he persuaded Fergus to shoot the Royal to save his bet?'

Maya thought it over and shook her head. 'I don't believe it. Sure, Mr Cooper might try that, but I can't see Fergus killing a Royal just to oblige him.'

'Or for money?'

'Uh-uh.' The grunt was positively negative. 'Fergus wasn't

faking anything. He was mad at Mr Cooper, and concerned what Sandy would say. I guess he thought his job was on the line.'

'Then how do you account for the extra shot?'

She drew a deep breath that flared her nostrils, then blew it out with an apologetic shrug. 'I just don't know. It's been bugging me that since I've been here, I've begun to doubt my own senses – isn't that something? It's easy to imagine things when you're alone in these hills and wondering what's going on out of your sight.'

Robb said deliberately, 'It could have been the shot that killed Beverley Tanner.'

Maya nodded silently, and he added, 'What did Sir Archibald think of Mr Cooper's trophy?'

'He wasn't very happy.' After a pause, she said quietly, 'Fergus didn't tell him about the hummel, so I didn't mention it either. I don't want him to get into any trouble over it.'

'No, indeed,' said Robb, and let her go.

★★★★★

Fergus's account tallied substantially with Maya's.

'The damnedest fluke you ever saw,' he said disgustedly. 'Four good chances Mr Cooper had that day, and missed them all. I'd begun to believe his blether that the sight was agley, though I'd had his rifle at the target myself, and it was spot-on. A Rigby, too. None of your cheap rubbish. I'd my mind made up that the beasts on the hill had naught to fear from him, then what does yon bonny gentleman do but shoot the best head on the forest under my very nose! Man, I could have broken his bluidy neck!'

Indignation burned in his dark eyes. It crossed Robb's mind that this tough young man in a rage would be a very dangerous customer. Even the baggy tweed suit and clumsy boots could not conceal the power in his compact, athletic frame, and he was evidently not the type to suffer fools gladly. Arrogant, quick-tempered, reckless, thought Robb. Tailor-made to attract a girl like Ashy.

'Tell me what happened on the hill after you left Mrs Forrester. She said you and Mr Cooper seemed to be arguing.'

'I guessed he was up to something,' said Fergus savagely. 'He'd a fine firing-point, and the beast wasna disturbed, just standing broadside on to us and roaring his head off. Mr Cooper said he wasna just ready. He'd aye take off his glasses and give them a wipe, and I could see his hands shaking.

'"Take him now, sir," says I, but he put his head down in the grass and said nothing. Stag fever, I thought, and waited for him to steady. Every now and then he'd take a wee spy through the sight, then down would go his head again. Man, I was going mad, for yon's an unchancy place to stalk a beast. It's ower close to Charlie's Stane. One puff of wind from a hiker there, and a stag's awa' before the safety's off.'

'Was anyone at the Rock that day?' asked Robb, and Fergus hesitated.

'I couldna say, sir. But while the hostel's open, they're there most days.' His bold eyes challenged Robb to mention the warning shot. 'A damned curse they are to us, and on the best of my beat, forbye. Many's the beast I've lost when some damned tourist stuck his nose across the march. But Mr Cooper had no trouble that day. His beast didna move until the four wee staggies jumped up. "He's off, sir," I said. "Quick, now, or you'll lose him."

'With that, he loosed off, and awa' goes the hummel. "Missed," says I. "Give him another." He swung to the right, then, and before I could ask what the hell he was doing, he took another shot, but the hummel never broke his stride. "Missed again," says I. "Well, that's it for the day." "Wrong," says he. "Did ye no' see him drop? Come on, let's find him."

'Well, I thought he was fou, but we went forward on our knees. "That's where he'll be," said Mr Cooper. "By yon muckle rock." I had my suspicions, then, for there'd been no rock where the hummel stood. "Give me the rifle and bide here," I said. I thought he must have wounded one of the staggies.

'He smiled at that, and gave me the rifle, and there beside

the rock I found blood and knew something was hit. I followed the spoor cannily, and pretty soon I saw Mr Cooper down on the low ground among the hags, waving me up, to show me the Royal lying there, dead as a stone.'

'So he disobeyed your instruction to stay where he was?'

'You might as well talk to the wind,' said Fergus disgustedly. 'He saw the beast fall, and slid straight down to him. He wasna going to chance missing him among the hags.'

'Can you show me approximately where you found that stag?'

'Aye.' Fergus scrutinised the model with care and placed a black-rimmed nail on a spot directly above the top end of the trout loch.

'I see. Did you have to give him another shot?'

'No need, sir. When I came up to him, he was dead.'

'Mrs Forrester thought she heard another shot.'

Fergus frowned. 'If she did, it wasna from me. Mr Cooper had put his shot too far back, but what could you expect? At that range, it was a bluidy miracle he'd hit it at all.'

Robb said casually, 'You didn't kill that stag for him, by any chance?'

He expected an indignant denial, but Fergus smiled and answered equably, 'Och, he asked me, right enough! When the leddy was too far back to see what we were about, he said if I'd do it, he'd make it worth my while.'

'What did you say?'

'I told him I was a wee thing deaf in that ear. It's no unco' politic to punch the boss's guests on the nose, though I'd have liked to do it well enough. No, Mr Cooper won his bet fair and square, little as he deserved to, and little would he have cared had it cost me my job.'

★★★★★

Detective-Sergeant Winter wore an expression of satisfaction bordering on smugness when he returned from his afternoon's legwork tracing Beverley's movements on the Sunday morning that she had left Glen Buie Lodge. He had also checked out Ben's story of the gig.

'Most of the tourists have gone now, so non-locals tend to be noticed,' he reported to Robb. 'There's an annexe behind the Clachan where they hold these rave-ups every week during the summer, and one of the waitresses recognised Ben's photograph. She thought he was sitting with a bunch of girls, but that needn't mean they'd come together. By their standards, Spurs & Sporrans pulled a big crowd, seventy or eighty, she thought. They must have been jammed in cheek by jowl.'

'Odd time of day for a concert.' In Robb's experience, daughters disappeared until the small hours.

'They have to fit in with the ferry sailings. Half the fans come from the islands.'

'Any reaction to Nicholas's picture?'

Winter nodded. 'The barman cashed him a cheque. But none of the staff saw the red Caterham leave, because after most of the kids had gone, there was a hassle with one of the groups over someone's wallet that had walked. It looked as if it might turn ugly, but the barman managed to calm them down.'

He paused to command Robb's full attention. 'By the way, sir, I found out who Beverley went to meet. It was Ian McNeil. He's well known locally. Two separate witnesses.'

'*Not a gent,*' murmured Robb to himself.

'What's that?'

'In Lady Hanbury's opinion, the man she heard making a rendezvous with Beverley was not a gentleman.'

'Huh!' Winter snorted. 'Doesn't behave much like one, either, by all accounts. "If it wasna that he's the laird's ain brither, we'd no' let him within the hoose wi' his claes all smelling o' fush,"' he mimicked in hideous travesty. 'Apparently he takes his boat out after mackerel on Saturday nights, and turns up to collect the Sunday papers in Tounie before going home. He was reading them in the caff, waiting for the bar to open, when Beverley joined him. She'd come over on the early ferry, gone to the sports shop, and bought herself a rucksack before meeting him in the Clachan.'

'Too much to hope that anyone heard what they were talking about? Ah, well, never mind. You and I must have a word with McNeil before we're much older.' He rubbed his eyes. 'Sufficient unto the day... Let's go and see what kind of digs Lady Strathtorran has fixed for us.'

Chapter Fourteen

'IS EVERYTHING ALL right, Inspector?' Torquil Strathtorran paused by their table.

With its trussed rafters and rough, whitewashed walls, the hostel's refectory was plainly a converted milking byre, and the kitchen which could be glimpsed beyond the serving-hatch had started life as a dairy. The decor was severely plain. Trestle tables covered in butter-yellow oilcloth and backless wooden benches did not encourage post-prandial lingering; but in the soft gloaming light the view over the three stable-style half-doors was spectacular: a panorama of glittering silver sea and far-off humps of black islands between the cradling arms of hills that swept down in a natural harbour.

The food had been equally plain but good. Scotch broth followed by salmon steaks, with salad of a freshness rarely found in Scotland. After a day on the hoof, Winter ate like a starving wolf, and though it embarrassed Robb to have their host waiting on them, he was hungry enough to accept the arrangement.

Wpc Kenny had discovered cousins in common with Mary Grant, and had been invited to supper in the Glen Buie staff room.

'Fine, sir. My lord, I mean,' answered Robb, and sensed Winter's wince.

'No formality, please. Not when I'm doing my Willie-the-Waiter routine.' Torquil's easy voice was Eton-and-Oxford, with no attempt at protective camouflage. Robb wondered how much the current Earl of Strathtorran relished his threadbare inheritance.

'My wife wondered what you'd like now? Pudding? Coffee, then?'

Robb nodded at Winter, and said, 'Please. For both of us."

'Instant, I'm afraid.'

'That's fine. It's kind of you to put us up at short notice.'

'Glad to help,' said Torquil as if he meant it. 'All a bit rough and ready, but at least you'll have the annexe to yourselves. All our other rooms are being stripped for re-decoration.'

'Suits me,' said Robb heartily. 'The less room for the media circus the better.'

Torquil nodded. 'Lead story on tonight's news – local news, that is. The armed siege at the Greenock supermarket is hogging the national headlines.'

'Long may it last.'

'I doubt there'll be any great invasion of journalists anyway. There's a big blow on its way down from Iceland, and the *Spanish Lady* may not sail tomorrow.'

'Does that often happen?'

'Often enough. Sometimes we're cut off from the Tounie supermarket for a week at a time, and it's a long way round by the coast road.' He smiled and added, 'It's no big deal, really. We keep supplies of basics, and there's always venison and salmon. No one goes hungry these days.'

'Can you and Lady Strathtorran spare us a moment?' asked Robb. 'I'd like to hear your impressions of Beverley Tanner. I gather she didn't tell you she'd been staying at Glen Buie Lodge?'

After a moment's consideration, Torquil said, 'No, she didn't, but of course this is a small place. Word gets around. We thought she must have her own reasons for moving out, and it wasn't difficult to guess what they were. She was so obviously a square peg in a round hole among Archie's guests. So my wife and I thought if that was what she wanted, we'd play along. Janie saw more of her than I did. Darling!' he called, and she appeared in the serving-hatch. 'Leave all that and come and talk. Inspector

Robb wants to know what you made of La Skinner.'

Janie joined them, wiping her hands on her apron. They were reddened and wrinkled, as if they spent too much time in hot water.

'Quiet, competent, businesslike,' she said, perching on the bench beside her husband. 'Not shy-quiet, but deliberately keeping herself to herself. What we call a B-type. The As like lots of organised activities: climbing, sailing, barbecues, that kind of thing. They don't feel they're having a holiday unless they're constantly occupied. The Bs are just the opposite. They like to wander lonely as a cloud, and feel they're close to Nature.' Her tone betrayed more than a trace of contempt. 'They're the ones who tell me how lucky we are to live here all year round, away from the rat-race.'

'Well, we are, aren't we?' said her husband defensively.

'Sometimes I wouldn't mind a bit of rat-race if it meant less than 90 inches of rain a year.'

'I'll take you to the sun this winter, I promise,' said Torquil, and she gave him a look that said I've heard that one before.

'Did Beverley tell you how lucky you are?'

'Oh, yes. Ad infinitum,' said Janie rather wearily.

'How did she spend her time?'

'I gave her a packed lunch and a map, and she did various walks, checking out the local landmarks. She used to ring some friend or other in the evening and tell them what she'd seen, and what she planned to do next day. I warned her to stick to the paths, and to steer clear of the Glen Buie stalkers, who get stroppy about hikers, not that they've any right to drive them away.'

'That doesn't stop them,' Torquil muttered.

Janie shook her head vigorously. 'Oh, Kim would have told them where they got off if they'd tried it on her. She wasn't afraid to stand up for herself, not like some of the poor foreigners. That old brute Sandy McNichol scared one couple this summer, just because they sat down to eat their sandwiches beside Loch a Bealach. They were terrified, and it wasn't even during the deer-cull. I don't believe Archie Hanbury has any idea what his stalkers get up to when his back is turned.'

'Still, we've all got to rub along,' said Torquil uncomfortably.

'But if we don't say anything, they think they can get away with it,' she flashed at him. It was evidently a disagreement of long standing.

'There's no sense in antagonising our neighbours,' insisted Torquil. 'I don't want a repeat of that stupid business with Ian last year.'

Robb searched his memory. 'Was that when Sandy McNichol accused your brother of poaching deer?'

'As if we haven't more stags than we know what to do with!' exclaimed Janie. 'He just wanted an excuse to get at Ian.'

'Why should he want to do that, Lady Strathtorran?'

Janie made an exasperated noise, and her husband fielded the question. 'Let me explain: in my father's time, before Ian and I came here, Sir Archie had a lease on the Strathtorran stalking as well as owning Glen Buie, so Sandy could go more or less where he pleased. He can't get used to the fact that things are different now.'

'I see. I shall want to speak to Mr McNeil in any case. Do you expect him home soon?'

Janie glanced at her watch, and said, 'He'll be in the pub now until closing time. After that – God knows. Some nights he takes his boat out...'

'In a gale like this?'

'He's a grown man, Inspector, ' she snapped. 'We can't monitor his movements.'

Lady Priscilla had described her as a saint to put up with her brother-in-law's ways, but Robb thought that compassion-fatigue was setting in fast.

'We'll look into the pub before closing time,' he rumbled reassuringly. 'I daresay you could do with a pint, eh, Jim?'

'So long as it's Coke.'

'Filthy stuff.' Robb grinned. 'Right, let's see if I've got this straight. Beverley left here on Tuesday morning, to walk over to Glen Alderdale hostel via the Prince's Rock?'

The Strathtorrans looked at one another and nodded.

'We expected her back on Wednesday evening,' said Janie. 'When it was getting dark, my brother-in-law said he'd drive up through the Forestry, in case she'd been benighted. It's a long hike – about fourteen miles.'

'Was that your idea or his?'

'His, I think. Yes. I'm sure it was. He went out to look for her, and drove right up to the top fence, but no sign. By the time he got back here, we had heard from the Glen Alderdale warden, Jamie Lomax, that Kim – sorry, Beverley – had decided to cut short her holiday, and wanted to cancel the rest of her booking with us.'

'Were you surprised she'd changed her plans?'

'*Nothing* our guests do surprises us,' said Torquil ruefully. 'Not any longer.'

Robb turned to Janie. 'Did you speak to the warden yourself?'

'Morag McIntyre, who helps me in the kitchen – she took the call. Jamie is a nice fellow, and ringing up to stop us getting supper ready for someone who wouldn't show is just the kind of helpful thing he would do.' She paused, then added, 'Only he didn't.'

'What do you mean?'

Janie said deliberately, 'I saw him in the Tounie supermarket on Saturday, and thanked him for his message, and he asked what I was talking about. He'd never seen Kim at all. Whoever rang here that evening, it wasn't Jamie.'

She gave a little shiver and, rising abruptly, began to clear the plates.

'My job, darling,' protested Torquil, and she gave him a look that said, Why the hell don't you get on and do it, then? Robb had an uneasy sense of a quarrel simmering just below the surface, ready to burst out the moment they were alone.

He thanked them for supper and, followed rather reluctantly by Winter, went out into the dark, windy night.

★★★★★

The Strathtorran Arms hardly deserved the name of public house, being no more than a bar and snug attached to the peninsula's post office-cum-general store, but tonight, at least, the landlord Jock Taggart, gaunt and grey-faced as any lifer, was doing a roaring trade.

The car park was jammed. No hope of easing the borrowed Land Rover into that muddy morass of battered 4WDs, and both up and down the street vehicles cluttered the narrow pavement with cavalier disregard of parking regulations.

'When in Rome,' muttered Robb, bumping his offside wheels up to join the rest. Winter tried to lock his door, but every time he pushed it down, the button popped up again.

'Leave it,' said Robb. 'No one would want it except for scrap.'

They pushed through the narrow porch, and encountered an inner wall of backs packed as tight and symmetrical as a rugger scrum. The fug of turf smoke, tobacco, and damp oiled wool was choking. Robb saw Winter's nose wrinkle and suppressed the impulse to tell him he could get AIDS just by kissing the barman.

Why did he have this urge to tease the poor lad? Why couldn't he accept that the political correctness that seemed wimpish and affected was, in fact, a perfectly genuine part of Winter's personality?

He's the New Man, and I'm just an out of date, unreconstructed, Male Chauvinist Pig, he thought ruefully. Even so, he drew the line at ordering the New Man a coke.

'I'll have a Guinness, thanks,' he said, fishing a tenner from his wallet. 'Get yourself whatever muck you fancy. Here, it's on me. I'll be over there.'

Shoving the note in Winter's hand, he began to work his way towards the corner settle, where two whiskery old men were playing dominoes. Scraps of conversation as he squeezed past confirmed that Topics One, Two, and Three in the Strathtorran Arms that night were the police investigation into the death of Beverley Tanner. From the way people stared and dropped their voices, he knew that even in his old tweed jacket he was as conspicuous as if he had worn uniform. The classic response of a small community. He thought they had probably made the Vikings feel just as welcome.

Fishermen, crofters, ghillies, shepherds... As his eyes got used to the haze, he recognised other faces he had met that day. The big ponytailed ferryman, Ishy's husband. The tight-jeaned blonde who manned the petrol pump. Squint-eyed Donny, the Glen Buie pony-boy, and away in the far inglenook sat Sandy McNichol, head stalker, with the cares of the world on his shoulders, according to his expression, and his big hands crooked about his dram.

Fergus was there, too, deep in talk. As his companion turned her head, Robb recognised the blonde topknot of Ashy Macleod. He felt briefly sorry for Nicky, whose millions would never rival Fergus's effortless sex appeal.

Robb squeezed his bulk on to the unoccupied end of the settle, and Winter, following with the drinks, had no option but to prop his shoulders against the wall. He drained his coke quickly, said, 'Be with you in a mo,' and slid through the scrum towards the illuminated arrow.

Robb exchanged nods with the ancient men. 'Busy, tonight.'

'Aye, so it iss.' Their rheumy eyes surveyed him briefly and returned to their game.

'There's nae boats will sail the nicht,' observed a chatty voice in his left ear, and Robb turned.

'Because of the gale?'

'They're forecasting a big blow. The fisher-lads will have time enough tae drown their sorrows, if they've the inclination and the cash. That daft bugger Ian McNeil may run his boat across the Gash, but then it won't be fish he's seeking.' Small bright eyes twinkled at Robb from a ruddy, gnomic face topped with wiry white hair like an Old Testament prophet.

'*Be it wind, be it weet, be it hail, be it sleet,*
My ship must sail the faem.
The King's daughter of Norroway,
'*Tis we must bring her hame!*' he declaimed.

'Sir Patrick Spens,' said Robb with an effort of memory.

'You're in the right of it, sir; only it's no' the King's daughter he's seeking but a lassie whose man is awa' tae the oil-rigs. Frailty, thy name is Woman!' He put out a brown hand, ridged with muscle. 'Allow me tae name masel': Hector Logie of Fas Buie, above the Sound of Gash, from where I've the best view in all the West Coast, tae ma way o' thinking. And you, sir, will be Inspector Robb?'

'Pleased to meet you, Mr Logie. Are you a fisherman yourself?'

'Not in the way you're meaning – no, sir.' He chuckled and coughed. 'I was dominie in the School House for nigh on thirty years, and I promised masel' I'd retire here when the time came. It's a grand place for a birdwatcher and naturalist.'

'The deerstalking doesn't bother you at this time of year?'

'Och, no, no, not at all! There's naught like a sporting landlord for presairving wildlife and keeping down vermin, and the fewer young folks wi' rucksacks I see tramping the hills, the better I'm pleased,' said Hector Logie with emphasis. 'Torquil Strathtorran wi' his wee signs and nature trails is like tae ruin one o' our last remaining wildernesses. What good does it do tae draw in sich a rabble of towerists,' he demanded, thrusting his face close to Robb's. 'What do they ken of nature? Yon puir lassie, now, kilt as she walked where she'd nae business tae be. If she'd stayed on the path she'd be alive this minute, but no. She had tae go tramping the heather and disturbing the deer, for all she'd been warned o' the danger.'

Robb eyed him curiously, aware he had information to impart. 'How do you know she left the path, Mr Logie?'

'Man, I saw her do it. I was in ma wee hide, watching the osprey teach the young birds tae take fish.'

'You mean on Loch a Bealach, where Lady Hanbury and her friend had their picnic?'

Hector Logie nodded. 'The leddies frae the Lodge were down by the jetty, and they didn't disturb ma birds at all. It was yon lassie who turned off the path and walked clean past the cliff where ma birds were feeding.' His eyes sparked indignation.

'Didn't she go to the Prince's Rock, then?'

'I'm no' saying she didna go there,' said Logie cautiously, 'but she didna go by the proper route that's agreed between Sir Archibald and the laird. When she went out of ma sight, she was headed up Corrie Odhar towards Carn Beag.'

Robb turned this information over in his mind, visualising the topography. 'Where Fergus and his party were stalking?'

'Aye. She could have ruined their sport, but that wouldna worry her kind.'

Robb nodded. 'You had binoculars?'

'Leica 10 x 42,' said the old schoolmaster complacently. 'They're small but unco powerful. At two hundred yards I can count the flies on a stag's head.'

'So you got a good look at her?'

'Och, aye, good enough. I'd seen her about the place for the past week. A dark-haired lassie, bonny for all she'd a wheen paint on her face.'

'Who else did you see that day? The ladies fishing –'

Logie snorted. 'Is it fishing they call it? Swimming and frisking on the shore wi' never a stitch tae cover their nakedness? Ye'd think they'd have more shame.'

You didn't have to watch them through 10 x 42 lenses, thought Robb with an inward grin. Aloud he said, 'I don't suppose you could see the stalking party on Carn Beag, but could you tell where they were? Deer moving, and so on?'

He took Logie through the latter stages of Everard Cooper's stalk, and was not surprised when the former dominie confirmed

Maya's impression of two rifle shots ten minutes apart.

'I'm obliged to you, Mr Logie,' he said at last. Some gleam in the bright eyes, some hint of secrets yet untold, prompted him to ask, 'I don't imagine you were in the same place the next day: last Wednesday, that was?'

'Indeed I was,' replied Logie promptly, 'and I've pictures to prove it.'

He drew a number of talc strips from a bulging yellow wallet, and perched half-moon spectacles on his nose to peer at the date on each.

'There you are, sir.' He chose one set and slapped them on the table, stowing the rest away. 'Taken last Wednesday between sunrise and sunset, and I'd have had more if the leddies of the Lodge hadna taken the boat, for without it I canna bring up ma heavy gear tae the hide.'

'So *you* moved the boat,' said Robb, light dawning.

'I did, sir, just as soon as the leddies headed for home, for it's a weary way for an old man tae carry sixty pounds weight of photographic gear. When they'd gone, I took the boat up the loch, and had it all stowed safe in ma hide before the stalkers came off the hill.'

He beamed at Robb and lifted his glass, but the latter's brain was humming. Maya claimed to have found the body under the boat on Wednesday afternoon, but by Wednesday night, when the search party went up to the loch, the boat was back in its proper place at the jetty.

'When did you return the boat to its mooring?' he asked.

'Ah, there's the rub, sir. Someone else did that for me on Wednesday afternoon when I was busy wi' ma birds. When I was ready tae leave the hide, it had gone frae the bank by the islands, and me wi' ma tripod and three great cameras to carry! It was close on eight before I got them back tae where I had concealed ma vehicle, and while I was loading it in the moonlight I saw the Land Rovers go up the track frae Glen Buie Lodge, and guessed there was something amiss.'

'You didn't see who took the boat?'

'Have a look at the prints, sir, and ye'll have the answer tae that.'

Robb leaned forward and studied the photographs with care. The cameraman's focus of interest had been the untidy heap of branches that formed the osprey's nest, halfway up the cliff at the head of Loch a Bealach, and some three hundred yards from the water.

The first half-dozen pictures showed the almost-fledged nestlings perched on the lip of their eyrie, beaks agape, awaiting the approach of an adult. Subsequent shots showed the parent birds hovering, alighting, depositing fish in the greedy beaks, and soaring back over the loch for fresh supplies.

It was the background, though, that held Robb's attention, for there on the shore, fuzzy yet unmistakable, was the green boat, with a figure sprawled beside it.

'That must be Maya Forrester,' he said, and Logie nodded.

'She was there sunning hersel' for half an hour, but she was ower distant tae disturb ma birds, so I paid little heed.'

'Did you see her run away?'

'No, sir. The young birds were near flying, and ma mind was on them.' He brought out his yellow wallet and chose another set of pictures. 'There's the last I took that day – see what ye make of them. By then the light was going.'

Robb fanned them out on the table and obligingly the domino players shifted their game to give him room.

The same scene, from the same viewpoint, but now the shadows were longer and the colours muted, the loch no more than a glimmer of silver against the darkening sky. By the shoreline, the blurred shape of the boat was still visible, but now it was in the water, and amidships he could just make out a blob that might be an oarsman.

'Do you know who that was?' he said, pointing.

Logie shook a regretful head. 'If I did, he'd get a piece o' ma mind.'

'I'd like to borrow these,' said Robb. 'I'll give you a receipt. Maybe our boys in the lab can make something of them.'

Logie said with a touch of anxiety, 'Ye'll take good care o' them now, sir? I've a bird magazine buys every picture I can get.'

'I'll bring them back myself,' promised Rob. 'Your house is called Fas Buie, you said?'

'That's right, sir. Overlooking the Sound. Anyone will point you there.'

'Thanks.' Robb stowed them carefully in his own wallet. 'Is Ian McNeil here tonight?'

'On your right, sir. Talking to – would it be your sergeant?' With a touch of scorn Logie added, 'They say what's bred in the blood will come out in the bone, but in the case of Ian McNeil I take leave tae doubt it. Weel, as the Good Book tells us, Esau was a hairy man.'

'And Jacob was a smooth one,' responded Robb, who had served his time in Sunday School.

Logie's eyes twinkled. 'Verra true, sir. Verra true.'

Robb left him chuckling into his drink, and went to join Winter and the tall young man with the dusty ponytail, but when he tried to question him, the din of the juke-box made conversation impossible.

'Can we go somewhere quieter?

McNeil spoke briefly to the landlord, and nodded. 'Jock says we can use his parlour. This way.'

Scarcely were they settled in the bare little front room that had damp islands on the walls and smelled of must and lavender polish in roughly equal parts, than a tousled white head poked angrily round the door, like a hen surprised in the nesting-box.

'Yon's no' the Public! Get on oot o' it!'

'It's all right, Patsy. Jock said we could come in here. It's the Police.'

'I'll gie them Pollis!' squawked the head, withdrawing nevertheless, and McNeil grinned and gently closed the door.

'Now what can I do for you gentlemen?'

Both tone and address were in marked contrast to his earlier demeanour. Robb wondered whom the New Age scruffiness was designed to impress, but said merely, 'You'll have heard we're enquiring into the death of Beverley Tanner. Tell me, how well did you know her?'

'Hardly at all, Inspector. In fact I met her for the first time about a fortnight ago, but of course I've known *of* her for several years, because she and my late wife once ran a catering business together.'

'That would have been *Gentlemen's Relish*?'

'That's right. My wife sold her share when we married, but I believe Beverley carried on for some time. It was quite a successful operation.'

'Were you surprised when Beverley contacted you here?'

'Frankly, yes. I'd understood from my wife that by the time they parted company, there was precious little friendship left between them.'

'Why was that, sir?'

McNeil shrugged. 'Oh, you know how these things go. People get across one another at work.'

'Nevertheless, you agreed to meet Beverley?'

'I couldn't see any reason not to. *Gentlemen's Relish* was water under the bridge as far as I was concerned, and I knew that Eliza and Beverley used to swap letters from time to time, so it would have been unfriendly to try to avoid her. She said she wanted to get in touch with various people who had been their clients – mostly Eliza's friends – so I suggested we met for a coffee in Tounie on Sunday morning.'

'Did it surprise you to find she was staying with the Hanburys?'

'Well, yes and no. There's not a lot of contact between us and the Hanburys, but I had heard rumblings about Nicky's unsuitable girlfriend, so I wasn't entirely unprepared.'

'Can you give me the gist of your conversation, sir?'

'Yes, of course.' He thought for a moment, then said, ' She

turned up on the early boat, as promised, and I stood her a cup of what the Clachan calls coffee, and after beating about the bush for a bit, she told me what was bothering her – namely that she had a week of holiday still to run, and she didn't want to upset Nicky or offend the Hanburys, but she didn't think she could stand the atmosphere at the Lodge that long. She hadn't realised what she was letting herself in for, couldn't stand the killing, and so on. Did I think my sister-in-law would let her stay at the hostel for a week and get in some proper walking? That was what she enjoyed, and she'd been terribly disappointed to discover that most of the Glen Buie ground is off limits to ramblers at this time of year. Well, of course I said that would be fine.'

'Of course?'

McNeil said impatiently, 'Janie's always glad of an extra booking, and I could just imagine Archie's disgust when he found a rambler in his midst.' The corners of his mouth drew down. 'Would you believe it, I even felt sorry for her.'

'When did that change?'

'Not soon enough,' said McNeil grimly. 'All that rambler stuff was pure eyewash. What Beverley really wanted was to find out if our business was viable, and if not whether we could be persuaded to sell out. And since I wasn't there to stop the rot, poor Janie simply played into her hands.'

'Where were you?'

'Fishing. The mackerel were runnng, and I was away in the boat for the first part of the week. When I got back just after midday on Tuesday, the only person in the house was old Morag – you've met Morag?'

They nodded.

'She was keening away to the hoover, and saying what would become of Strathtorran if her ladyship quit? Well, I didn't like the sound of that, so I sat Morag down with a cup of tea, and out it all came. High words between Janie and my brother, who never *ever* quarrel – "all on account of yon thrawn lassie." Morag said Janie had pitched into Torquil, and told him she couldn't face another winter here, she wanted out, she wasn't prepared to go on slogging her guts out for nothing. The business was doomed, they were fools to think they could ever make it pay, they must sell up and get out before it destroyed them both. All the things my brother least wanted to hear. Morag said he was shaking like a leaf, and when Janie ran out of steam, he simply turned and went out without another word, while Janie jumped in the car and drove off "greeting sair," as Morag put it. And she's not a girl who cries easily, believe me.'

'So you immediately deduced that Beverley had been getting at her?' said Winter, hardly bothering to cover his scepticism.

McNeil gave him an angry glance. 'I did indeed.'

'So family feeling impelled you to go looking for her?'

'Wouldn't you have?'

Antagonism sparked between them.

Robb frowned at Winter and said peaceably, 'I thought Lady Strathtorran said it was nearly dark before you went up into the forestry?'

'She was talking about Wednesday,' said McNeil after a moment's hesitation.

'So you went looking for Beverley on Tuesday as well?'

'Yes.'

'Tell me about Tuesday.'

McNeil said reluctantly, 'Morag told me Beverley had taken a packed lunch and was walking to Glen Alderdale via the Prince's Rock. I thought if I took the steep path over the back of Ben Torran, I might catch up with her before she got to the Rock.'

'Then what would you have done?'

'Talked to her.'

'Is that all?'

'Yes.'

'I suppose you took your rifle?' put in Winter.

'I always do.'

'Habit?'

'That's right.'

'Go on,' said Robb, irritated by their sparring. 'Did you catch up with her?'

'No. Either she was a faster walker than I imagined, or she branched off the path. I got to the Rock well before two, but she wasn't there.' He glanced from Robb to Winter and back. 'Did she leave the path?'

'Mr Logie saw her turn off and cross the hill towards Loch a Bealach, passing right beneath the cliff where he was taking photographs.'

'Logie told you that? He's got a nerve! What he means is that she stuck to the proper path marked on the map and refused to be deflected by the fact that he had moved the stones that mark it.'

'Why should he do that, sir?'

'Because the Prince's Rock path passes too close to his damned nest, that's why. We've had no end of trouble over it. My brother takes the view that history is history, and you shouldn't alter the line of an authentic ancient path just because a rare raptor has decided to nest there.'

'Mr Logie disagrees?'

'Bloody old dog-in-the-manger. Of course he does. He is the self-appointed guardian and official photographer of the Strathtorran ospreys, and he would very much like to re-route the Prince's Path round the back of Ben Torran, which is steeper and shorter and altogether less attractive.'

'The way you walked up last Tuesday, in fact?'

'Precisely. As I said, I keep the proper path marked with whitewashed stones, but whenever the coast is clear, Friend Logie turns the sign round to point in the other direction, and kicks my marked stones into the heather. As a result, we get furious complaints from hikers who go astray and miss the monument altogether. We find the activities of Mr Logie a confounded nuisance.'

Robb nodded, reflected, and then said, 'All right, sir. We've got you as far as the Prince's Rock. What did you do after that?'

'I hung around for half an hour, hoping she'd turn up, but finally I decided I'd missed her and returned to base.'

'By way of the Prince's Path?'

A fractional hesitation, then McNeil said, 'Well, no. I was in no hurry, so I walked round the head of the glen to Loch a Bealach, and back by the Devil's Staircase.'

The same route Nicky had taken the following day, Robb reflected, pleased to find himself able to visualise the lie of the land from his study of the contour model. 'Weren't you afraid you might bump into one of the stalking parties from Glen Buie? With the wind where it was, you must have known they'd be on that beat.'

McNeil shook his head, smiling. 'It was after five by the time I reached the loch. I knew they must be on their way home, if they weren't back already. In fact, I'd seen Fergus's vehicle go down the track with the stag in the trailer, and I knew the other party was ahead of me on the path.'

'Could you see them?'

'No, but I could hear Archie booming away like a foghorn.'

So you slunk along behind them like a wolf, keeping out of sight, thought Robb. No wonder the Hanburys find you an uneasy neighbour. Between half-past two and five o'clock left a lot of afternoon unaccounted for. Aloud he said, 'It's a pity you didn't speak to any of them.'

'Oh, but I did.'

'With Sir Archibald?'

'With Ashy. She must have stopped for a pee, because she was behind, hurrying to catch up. She came running down the path, so I told her not to worry, they were only just ahead. She gave me a bit of a wave, and went steaming on without stopping.'

'Weren't you afraid she'd tell Sir Archibald she'd seen you?'

McNeil grinned. 'Ashy knows when to keep her mouth shut. There's a lot of common sense under all that gush and chatter of hers. Now if *she* was to marry Nicky and take over Glen Buie forest, none of us would complain.'

Chapter Fifteen

SIR ARCHIE WATCHED from the door of the gun-room as Fergus and his party squeezed into the big black Trooper next morning, and bumped away up the glen track.

He was well aware that he had played a low trick on Inspector Robb by going over his head to the Chief Constable, but what was the old boy network for if you didn't pull strings when you needed to? At this stage of the cull, he couldn't afford to lose a single day's stalking, let alone have it indefinitely suspended. Any day now the weather might turn against them: it was essential to shoot all the stags they needed before mist, gales or snow forced them on to the low ground.

On a personal and practical level, he was by no means sorry to have seen the last of Beverley. Nicky had always been easily influenced, and any determined gold-digger could make mincemeat of him. If only, thought his father longingly, he would settle for Ashy, who would give him the kick-start he needed. Then there would be no need to involve Johnny in Glen Buie affairs after all. Though he would never have admitted it to his sister Marjorie, there was something about his elder nephew that set Sir Archie's teeth on edge.

Johnny was shooting today, with Ashy as second rifle, should a second chance present itself. Maya and young Benjamin were in support, together with Robb's sidekick. Sir Archie would have liked to go with them himself, but the Inspector had wanted Sergeant Winter to have a first-hand look at the ground, and any more would have made the party unmanageable. Reluctantly he had stood himself down, resigned to yet another day of frustrating inactivity.

Marjorie had gone fishing, and he thought he might join her later, though after a run of fine days the water was so low that she had little chance of catching anything on a fly.

Gwennie and Lady Priscilla, escorted by Wpc Kenny, had gone to visit Everard in hospital. That's *one* person I shan't be asking here again, thought Sir Archie. If Priscilla wants to come up next year, I'll suggest she brings her son Lucas and leaves Everard to look after her dogs.

Catching sight of the purposeful figure of Inspector Robb heading towards the house, Sir Archie locked the gun-room door and hung the key on its nail hidden between two beams. Then he walked briskly out of the back door and down the path towards the river.

★★★★★

'Cheer up, laddie! It may never happen,' said Donny with a wink as they jolted together in the back seat of the Trooper.

'What may never happen?'

'Whatever's bugging you.'

Ben hunched his head into his shoulders and didn't answer. He wasn't in the mood for Donny's banter, nor would he have come out today if his mother had not insisted. She had opened the door of his top-floor bedroom only minutes after he'd switched on his ghetto-blaster.

'Turn that off at once. I didn't bring you here to skulk in your room listening to that mindless rubbish.'

With a sulky glare, he had obeyed.

'Go downstairs and get your boots on. Quick! The stalkers are leaving in five minutes.'

'But, *Mum* – !'

'Do as you're told and don't argue.'

He knew she would watch to make sure he obeyed. She had

been looking for a way to get at him ever since she found Elspeth lying on the floor with him yesterday evening, giggling over *Phat!*

'What are you doing up here?' she had demanded then, while Elspeth pretended she didn't exist.

'She was lending me some tapes.'

'I should have thought you had enough of your own without scrounging from the servants,' his mother had said in the way that made him cringe. 'Every drawer in your room is stuffed with the wretched things.'

He would have liked to tell her to keep her snoopy nose out of his drawers, but didn't quite dare.

'*Demo* tapes, Mum. Not the kind you buy. I need them for my Band.'

But she had allowed him no time to play through Elspeth's tapes, let alone work on them last night; and this morning Elspeth had caught him in the serving-room during breakfast, and demanded them back.

'What's the rush? I haven't nearly finished with them.'

'I want them back. I'm leaving this afternoon,' she had said jerkily, and he noticed that her eyes were puffy and pink.

'Leaving? Why?'

'Never mind why,' snapped Elspeth. 'Kirsty's giving me a lift to the ferry, and I want those tapes before I go.' She had turned to carry out a stack of plates, but he caught her shoulder.

'Wait! You've got to tell me why you're going, and where I can get hold of you.'

'The old cow has sacked me, that's why,' said Elspeth bitterly. 'She's had her knife into me ever since I was late back that night.'

'Did Ishy tell on you?' He lowered his voice, conscious that Maya was filling her coffee-cup on the other side of the serving-hatch, while Nicky piled his plate with sausages.

'*I* don't know. It was all your fault, but I'm the one gets the blame.' She sniffed and said spitefully, 'And you're going to catch it when Sir Archibald hears what Angus Buchan's got to say.'

'Who's Angus Buchan?'

'One of the crofters. Those were his sheep that you – '

'Oh, God!' said Ben, paling visibly.

'He wants compensation.'

'But can he – does he know it was me?'

'You'll find out when he comes again tonight, won't you? I wouldn't be in your shoes then.'

He had looked at her with a spasm of dislike. Had he been crazy to ask her to sing with his group? She had talent, OK, but those tapes of hers needed a lot of work. Cut out the crummy tracks, sharpen up the backing. It would take him all morning...

He had said, 'What's your dad going to say?'

Elspeth shrugged. 'I don't care. Look, do I get my tapes back or not?'

'Give me a chance. I haven't played them through yet. I'll give them back before you leave, honest.'

She had given him her insolent, upward-slanting look through her fringe, and he thought she was going to be difficult, but she said, 'Meet you at the larder, then, but don't be late. The ferry goes at three, and Kirsty won't wait.'

She had hurried out of the serving-room, and Ben had gone through to the dining-room and wolfed his breakfast, eager to get up to his room and start work, but his mother's intervention had ruined his plan.

You'd think Mum would be glad to see me doing something worthwhile, he thought morosely as the vehicle lurched and jolted. All she cares about is showing Uncle Archie what brilliant sporting sons she has. What's so special about stalking, anyway? Any fool with a rifle can shoot a stag. Even that pompous fart Mr Cooper managed it in the end. I hope to God Mum gives up this grisly idea of making me work here during my gap year. I couldn't bear that.

'I'm sure your uncle can find a use for you,' Marjorie had said, staring at him as if he was some botanical specimen she was planning to re-pot. 'Nicky spent six months here, and it did him the world of good.'

'He loathed every minute of it,' said Ben, much alarmed. 'He nearly died of boredom.'

'Only boring people get bored,' she had said maddeningly. 'You spend far too much time indoors. It's high time you got out to see the real world.'

If the group could see me now, they'd say this is *unreal,* thought Ben rebelliously. Five of us squashed into this rotting tin can, and Fergus driving like a maniac.

Silently Donny offered roll-ups. Maya shook her head, but Ben's hand shot out.

'Thanks.'

He glanced defiantly at his brother as he lit up, but Johnny was too busy gawping at Maya to notice. Wedged between the two boys, back against the rear door-handle and long legs stretched out, she looked elegant and at ease, but as she mulled over the conversation between Ben and Elspeth that she had overheard through the serving-hatch, she remembered the evening Elspeth had been late back on duty: the day Everard Cooper had shot his Royal... the day Beverley had been murdered.

It had also been Mary Grant's day off. Coming wearily into the kitchen in search of a cup of tea, Maya had found Ishy alone there, flurried and furious, trying to do Elspeth's work as well as her own.

'She's awa' tae Tounie, leaving me single-handed,' Ishy had said, tight-lipped. 'She swore she'd be back by six at the latest, but that's Elspeth all over. Give her an inch, and she takes an ell.'

'Let me help,' Maya had offered; and together they had managed to lay the table and dish up before the sacred eight-thirty deadline. Elspeth had not appeared until nearly ten, scuttling in through the boot-room to face the lash of Ishy's tongue as well as the washing-up.

Where had she been all that time? Maya wondered, and why did she blame Ben? He had been back in good time himself, emerging pink and scrubbed from the bath as Maya hurried to her own bedroom to change.

Impossible to ask him now, with his brother listening. She glanced up, caught Johnny's stare, and wished he would stop giving her soulful smiles.

On the bench seat in front, Ashy was talking softly to Fergus, who stared straight ahead, the knuckles of his muscular hands showing white as they gripped the wheel.

'After you'd gone last night, that horrid old schoolmaster tried to chat me up. You know the one I mean.'

'Hector Logie.'

'That's him. He showed me a whole heap of photographs, then told me he'd given better ones to the police. Fergus! You're not listening.'

'It's nothing to me,' he muttered without turning his head.

'But it is!'

'Keep your bloody voice down,' he said, low and harsh, glancing in the mirror.

'Fergus, darling, why won't you listen?'

'Because ye're blethering.'

'I'm trying to *warn* you. It's no use saying you never went near the trout-loch last Tuesday if Logie has a photograph of you there. And Ian McNeil saw you come down to the track looking for Everard's stag.'

'Bloody man! Always where he's least wanted.'

'The police were talking to him last night in Jock Taggart's parlour.' Ashy stole a glance behind her, but the dog-guard and rifle-rack made an effective barrier between front and back seats. 'Will you meet me at the pub tonight?'

'I will not.'

'Because of what I told you? Don't be angry, my angel. I was only trying to help you.'

'A nice mess you've made of it,' said Fergus savagely. 'Ye'd have done better to mind your own business. And don't call me that.'

Ashy's eyes crinkled. She began to sing softly, watching him sideways.

'Tell me he's lazy, tell me he's slow,
Tell me I'm crazy, maybe I know,
Can't help loving that man of mine!'

Fergus said harshly, 'I thought you'd your sights set on Mr Nicky. Two for the price of one, is it, you're wanting?'

The tune changed to *Greensleeves*: *'Alas, my love, you do me wrong,'* sang Ashy, stepping up the volume.

'Will you hold your wheesht?'

'Not unless you meet me tonight. If you're good, I'll buy you a dram.'

'I'll buy my own bloody dram!' exploded Fergus. 'And for Christ's sake take your hands off me. Do you want us in the bloody ditch?'

'Goodness, you are in a bate,' said Ashy, withdrawing her fingers from his pocket. 'Better not let Johnny hear you. Did you know that Archie's thinking of putting him in charge here next season?'

'If he does, he'll do it without me,' said Fergus grimly, and slammed on his brakes.

The others crawled stiffly out of the back. Fergus conferred with Donny, who heaved the massive deer saddle from under the trailer's tarpaulin and went whistling off towards the five-acre horse park where two shaggy ponies were grazing.

'Right, sir,' said Fergus briskly to Johnny. 'We'll take a spy up the face of Sgurr Connuil. If there's nothing there, we'll have a look into Corrie na Fearn. That way the sergeant will see where we were stalking last week, and get the lie of the land.'

'Fine by me,' said Winter. He looked assessingly but without apprehension at the rocky ramparts towering two thousand feet-odd above them. He belonged to a cross-country running club, and thought it unlikely that keeping pace with today's company would give him any problem. The big girl, Ashy, was built for strength rather than speed, and Miss Ethnic Minority looked as if she would feel more at home on a catwalk than a mountain. John Forbes was slope-shouldered and gangling, and his young brother's pinched white face and dark-rimmed eyes might have belonged to any inner-city hophead. If the party's rate of ascent was determined by its slowest member, Winter thought the climb would be a doddle.

Steady rain was falling, but just below the line of cloud that blurred the skyline, half a dozen deer were scattered among the rocks, flecks of brown warmth against chilly grey. Fergus and Johnny studied them carefully through binoculars; then Fergus moved to sit with his back against a boulder, steadying the telescope between knee and stick.

'Aye,' he said at length, clicking the sections shut. 'There's some good beasts there, right enough. We'll go on up the burn and take a look from the head of the corrie. All set?'

'Half a tick,' said Ashy. She took off her waterproof and tied it round her waist by the sleeves. After a momentary hesitation Maya did the same. In single file, with Fergus leading and Benjamin bringing up the rear, they splashed across the pebbly mouth of the burn and begun to climb the dark, narrow gully down which it flowed.

★★★★★

Everard Cooper had activated his medical insurance, and had himself moved to a private room where he lay propped on pillows, looking pink and sleek and remarkably healthy in his blue silk pyjamas with a monogram on the pocket.

'You can't stay holed up here much longer,' said his wife, looking down on him without sympathy. 'There's nothing wrong with you and no doubt they need the bed.'

'Damn it, I'm paying, aren't I?'

'BUPA's paying.'

'Same thing. Look, Priss. I didn't ask you to come and badger me. I've had about as much as I can take from the police. Was it you who sicced them on to Mona Peat?'

'You're paranoid about Mona Peat!' She was puzzled as well

as indignant. 'Why should the police be interested in that?'

'Because that bloody little slut Beverley was trying to blackmail me! You were the only person I told, so how else would the police hear of it?'

Lady Priscilla laughed scornfully. 'My dear old numbskull, since you were the one who pulled her out of the river, it's hardly likely that you would have put her in it. The police aren't that thick.'

For once he was too worried to resent being patronised. 'The theory is that I shot her, and someone else dumped her in the river.'

'Absurd!' She stared at him for a moment, then added with less certainty, 'Isn't it?'

'It's preposterous. That's what I've told them, again and again. I might as well talk to a brick wall.'

'All right,' she challenged. 'Tell me your story. See if I believe it.'

He looked down at the hospital blanket, lower lip thrust forward, and began plucking at a loose thread. 'There'd have been none of this hassle if Archie had allowed me to shoot a decent head,' he muttered.

'What d'you mean?' she said incredulously. 'You had umpteen chances and missed the lot.'

'Only because they all had such miserable little antlers.'

His wife said slowly, 'Are you telling me you've been missing on purpose?'

'Of course. I came up here hoping to bag a couple of good heads for the boardroom. You know we've just had it done up?'

Wordlessly she shook her head, and he said, 'Of course not. You're never interested in how money is made, only in spending it. Well, a couple of sets of good-looking antlers are just what it needs, and I told Archie so when we arrived, but you know what he's like. 'Sorry, old boy. No trophy-hunting here.' So I thought, Right, I'll see if a few quid make Sandy and Fergus a bit more co-operative.'

'Did it?' Her face betrayed nothing but polite interest.

Everard said disgustedly, 'I honestly believe they went out of their way to make sure I didn't get what I wanted. There's no shortage of good beasts, but they made damned sure they didn't give me a chance at one. *However!*' He brightened up and began to speak more quickly, his fingers steadily unravelling the loose thread.

'At about four last Tuesday, I spotted this beautiful Royal lying a little way beyond the hummel which Fergus wanted me to shoot, and I thought, Right, mate: this is for you. I had him in my sights just nicely, and was waiting for him to stand, when suddenly he jumped up and was away almost before I could get off the safety. I had to take a snap shot, and knew I'd hit him, although he kept going. Fergus thought I'd missed, and told me to fire again, but of course he was looking at the wrong stag. I saw my Royal swing downhill, then stop, so I fired again; and blow me if that infernal woman didn't pop up from behind a rock, staring round like a startled rabbit, and then duck back out of sight.'

'You're sure it was Beverley?'

'No question.'

Lady Priscilla sat for a moment in silence, nibbling her lower lip. 'Did Fergus see her?' she said at last.

'I can't tell.' He shook his big head like a baffled and dangerous bull. 'He didn't say anything, but then, of course, he wouldn't.'

'He must have said *something*.'

'Well, yes. Obviously at that point he still thought I was trying to shoot his wretched hummel, and supposed I'd missed again, but I knew bloody well that I'd hit the Royal. I wasn't going to let on until I was sure it was dead, though, so I played dumb, and just said, 'Hang on, Fergus. I think that beast was hit. We'd better go and have a look.' He argued, of course, but I insisted, and eventually he told me to stay where I was, while he went on with the rifle. The minute he was out of sight, I slid down to where I'd last seen the Royal, and there he was, dead as a doornail.'

He grinned at the memory, but Lady Priscilla was in no mood to applaud. 'Where was Beverley?' she said sharply.

'No sign of her.'

'You're quite sure you didn't hit *her* with your second shot?'

'Positive,' he said a shade too quickly. 'By then it was pissing with rain and blowing half a gale, and I was worried that Maya would be frozen stiff where we'd left her. So I shouted for Fergus, and waved him up; and as soon as he came back to where the Royal was lying, I went to collect Maya.'

So that she would act as a curb on Fergus's tongue, thought Lady Priscilla with contempt. 'Did you tell Fergus about seeing Beverley?'

'No.'

He hesitated. 'But while I was waiting for Fergus to come up to me and the stag, I'm almost sure I heard a shot. I did ask him if he'd heard it too, but he said it must have been the other party on Carn Mhor.'

'But that's miles away.'

'Exactly.'

'How much of this have you told the police?'

'Everything, apart from seeing Beverley practically under the feet of my Royal. Why put ideas into their heads?'

She was silent, recognising the unnaturally frank, steady-eyed gaze he adopted when bluffing. 'It's no good expecting me to help you unless you tell me the truth.'

'I *am,*' he insisted. 'The trouble is, it's Fergus's word against mine. As far as the police are concerned, we were both in the right place at the right time, and I had a reason to want her dead, while as far as they know, he hadn't. *As far as they know,*' he repeated with emphasis. 'What you've got to do, my angel, is find out why Fergus should have had it in for her. Do a bit of digging. Talk to the housemaids, or Mary Grant, or even Sandy's old mother. She's the biggest gossip on the place.'

'Why the hell should I do your dirty work?'

'Because you're so good at chatting up the lower orders.'

His smile was malicious. 'Your lovely daughter takes after you, doesn't she?'

'Meaning?' said Lady Priscilla coldly.

'Wasn't there a spot of bother during her last year at school? With one of the gardeners? And that Greek waiter – I heard you had to buy him off: hardly the sort of son-in-law you're looking for. But I can tell you this: unless she stops running after Fergus like a bitch on heat, dear Ashy is going to bugger up her chances of catching Nicky Hanbury on the rebound, that's for sure.'

Lady Priscilla regarded her husband with distaste. How could she have left poor Mikey McLeod – so honourable and oh, so painfully dull! – for this hairy-heeled shyster?

'Leave Ashy out of this,' she snapped.

'How can I, when the wretched girl has landed me in the shit?' he responded angrily. 'Why did she have to interfere? If she had left Beverley where she found her, instead of dumping her in the river – '

'*Ashy* did? Don't be absurd.'

Everard hitched himself higher on the pillows and spoke with new vigour. 'Listen, Priss. Ashy was up at the trout-loch, painting, on Wednesday afternoon when Maya found the body – right?'

She nodded.

'And when Maya didn't come back, Ashy walked up to the head of the loch, looking for her. That's what she told us, didn't she?'

Lady Priscilla said slowly, 'I suppose she *could* have looked under the boat, too...'

'Could? I'm damned sure she did, because she already knew it was there. Why? Because she put it there herself the day before. Remember she was with Archie's party on Carn Mhor, and when the stalkers crawled in for the shot, they left her looking straight across at Carn Beag. I'll lay you any money you like that she saw Fergus run down to the track looking for *my* beast, which would have been his chance to take a snapshot at Beverley before coming back to me. I've been lying here thinking it out, and I'm sure that's what happened.'

He paused, then said casually, 'That Robb fellow came here with a blow-up taken by some bloody twitcher who was in his hide on that cliff above the trout-loch on Wednesday afternoon. It showed a boat just pulling away from the shore at the top. Robb asked me if I recognised who was in it.'

Lady Priscilla caught her breath sharply. 'You didn't say it was Ashy?'

'Do you take me for a fool?' He stared out of the window and said slowly, 'There's no doubt in my mind that Ashy found Beverley's body on Tuesday afternoon, when she stopped for a pee on the way home. It must have been between the track and the loch. She pulled the boat over it to hide it, and reckoned she'd save Fergus a heap of grief if she dumped it in the river in the one pool where no one was likely to find it. So she went back next day, sent Nicky and Maya off in different directions, and when they were well out of sight she did exactly that.'

Lady Priscilla shook her head. 'The Greeting Pool must be nearly a mile from the trout-loch. How could Ashy get the body down there?'

'On the pony, of course. Remember how late Ashy got back that evening? How she said she'd had trouble with the pony? I'll lay you any money you like that what old Rory was objecting to was having a stiff loaded on to his saddle along with the painting gear.'

'I can't – I simply *cannot* believe that Ashy – '

'Well, I can.' He saw her uncertainty and pressed his advantage. 'And if you don't want me to air that particular theory to Inspector Robb –'

'You wouldn't!'

'Care to bet?'

'All right,' she said abruptly. 'I'll dig out any lowdown I can on Fergus. But don't expect –' she broke off as a trim blonde nurse bustled in.

'Time for your bath, Mr Cooper.'

'I'm just off,' said Lady Priscilla, uncoiling herself from the low armchair. 'I'll look in tomorrow if there's time.'

'Don't strain yourself.' Everard winked at the nurse. 'These lovely girls know how to make me comfortable.'

As Lady Priscilla walked away down the shiny corridor, she heard a stifled squeal followed by a slap and, a moment later, her husband's loud chortle.

★★★★

To his surprise, Sergeant Winter was enjoying himself. Though the climb had been stiffer than he expected, and he had soon been obliged to shed both anorak and sweater, the slow, unvarying pace set by Fergus had brought the party up to the heights with very little hardship.

Now, as the mist cleared, he saw for the first time the grand spread of peaks stretching to the limit of vision like a petrified sea of grey crests and ridges, interspersed with deep troughs: a view that car-bound visitors to the Highlands never guessed existed.

Below them, a veil of low cloud hung over the shining thread of the Buie river, with its fringes of green oak, red-berried rowan, and elegantly branched Caledonian pine. Here and there a glimpse of the river track could be seen, winding along the bank above spate-level, with wooden bridges spanning the many small burns rushing down to join the parent stream. As they climbed, the lush, coarse grass of the lower slopes had shaded into this thin, flaxen-tipped sedge and cottongrass, gradually tinting a deeper gold until the vegetation between the outcrops of rock they were now traversing was tipped with ginger and bronze.

Cloud-shadows dappled the heights, and accentuated the dark-blue hollows, while away at the far horizon, hills and sky merged in a grey-blue haze. Winter checked his compass, and noted that the wind, which in the glen had blown steadily from the north, was at this height swirling in from an easterly quarter, and this was dictating Fergus's oblique approach to the group of stags they had seen from below, in order to keep his party constantly downwind of their quarry.

Even more to his surprise, Winter found himself very keen to come up with that quarry.

Twice they had interrupted the climb to rest for a few minutes and observe the deer. The half-dozen big stags that had been visible from the track were now revealed as part of a much larger mixed group of beasts, scattered among the boulders and overhanging cliffs a couple of hundred feet below the summit.

'We won't be able to get above them with the wind as it is,' Johnny had muttered, elbows propped on knees to steady his binoculars, and Fergus grunted assent.

'We'll crawl up under them. There's cover enough so long as some damned old hind doesna spot us and give the alarm. How are ye doing, Mrs Alec?'

'Fine, thanks.' Maya smiled at him, but Ashy's face was turned away. Benjamin, too, stared sullenly into the glen, taking no interest in the stalk. Winter himself would have liked to ask questions, notably how Fergus planned to cross the open ground between them and the next cluster of boulders, and had to remind himself that he was only here to observe. The less attention he drew, the better.

It was cold at this height, and although he had been sweating when they halted, the wind soon began to cut through his shirt. He was glad when they set off again, but before they had climbed more than fifty feet obliquely across the steep, rock-strewn slope, Fergus suddenly froze.

A loud, indignant, sibilant sniff that was almost a bark sounded directly in front of them. Peering over Maya's shoulder, Winter glimpsed an upflung, inquisitorial nose pointing at them, and smelt the warm, rank pungency of a stag.

Crouching, Fergus signalled them back, and the party retreated with ape-like haste, knees bent and fingers to ground, until a shoulder of hill hid them.

'We maun get round that young bugger,' said Fergus, taking the rifle from its sleeve.

'One up the spout?' said Johnny quickly.

'Not just yet awhile, Ready, now?'

He led the way back at a cracking pace, making a big swing that would bring them above the young sentinel. Winter lost count of the times they crossed and recrossed the rocky burn, following the faintest thread of path. As it flattened out in a desolate bowl-like corrie where pools of standing water shone black between tussocks of sedge, he realised he had quite lost his sense of direction.

Before he could consult his compass, they were moving again, crawling forward with deer all about them, outlying hinds and young staggies forming a defensive barrier around the big beasts. Sometimes they hurried, sometimes they crouched or lay flat, faces pressed into the soggy, boggy ground. To his chagrin, Winter discovered that the canvas-panelled hiking-boots which he had chosen from the Tounie emporium gave him little purchase on wet vegetation and none at all on wet rock. Despite his efforts to keep pace with Maya, next up the line, the gap between them constantly widened.

Panting hard, he tumbled down an overhung peat bank into a gully, landing almost on top of Maya, who sat there alone amid a tangle of sticks and coats and haversacks.

'They've gone on,' she whispered; and a moment later, staring over his shoulder, she asked, 'Where's Ben?'

Chapter Sixteen

FEVERISHLY CALCULATING TIMES and distances, Benjamin rattled the Trooper over the stony track with scant regard for its suspension. The trailer bounced and jolted behind.

Ten past twelve now. Twenty minutes to get back to the Lodge. If he allowed himself forty minutes' work on Elspeth's tapes, he should just catch her before she left for her rendezvous with Kirsty at the end of the drive. Then he could drive back and return the Trooper to its parking-place before the stalking-party came off the hill.

He had better top up with Diesel from the yard pump before he went back, and concoct some story to explain why he'd left the stalkers. Tummy trouble...wrenched ankle...didn't want to hold anyone up... He rehearsed excuses, right foot stamping down to the floor as he bucketed over the bumps.

Damned old rattletrap, he brooded. If only Uncle Archie would have this track properly graded and surfaced, they'd be able to drive up and down the glen in half the time. Not that anyone at Glen Buie was much interested in driving, or knew anything about cars. The row of stuffy saloons and medium-range estates parked on the gravel sweep proved that.

Even Nicky's red Caterham had been a disappointment. When he had swerved to avoid a bunch of sheep lying on the tarmac, the little sod had nearly skidded off the road, and Elspeth had such a fright that she'd refused to go any farther with him. Out she had jumped, and insisted on walking the rest of the way back. All her subsequent troubles had stemmed from that.

Reaching the loch road at last, Ben swung through the entrance gates and bumped over the cattle-grid before roaring the last couple of hundred yards to the back door. He parked in the outer courtyard, beside the fuel pump, and hurried into the house through the kitchen passage.

Indoors all was quiet and still. Aunt Gwennie liked the domestic staff to take a long break in the middle of the day, to make up for working early and late. Passing the open kitchen door, Ben paused and looked in. The sink was empty, draining boards bare, and clean cloths hung folded on the Aga rail. Every surface had been cleared of the usual clutter, ready for the evening frenzy of whipping and peeling and chopping, but the loaded double-deck tea-trolley waited near the refrigerator for the first of the returning guests to wheel across the hall to the drawing-room, where the party would gather for a long-drawn-out, plates-on-knees tea.

He lifted the starched white cloth that covered the food, and abstracted a triangular hunk of shortbread and two iced buns. The big chocolate layer-cake with its thick dark frosting tempted him briefly, but a missing slice might invite unwelcome speculation. Reluctantly he left it untouched. As he replaced the cloth, the click of a doorcatch made him glance round nervously, but his straining ears caught no other sound, and after a moment he relaxed..

Now to work. Clutching his cakes, he took the back stairs two at a time, and pushed open the door to his bedroom. Like the rest of the house, it looked unnaturally tidy. His folded clothes lay on a straight-backed chair. He shoved them on to the floor and pulled it up to the dressing-table, on which he had set up his tape-deck. Alternately pressing buttons and wolfing buns, he played the first three tracks at full blast through his earphones, and sighed. Given time, given his synthesizer or, better still, the stereo equipment belonging to Dozo Dawson's father, who worked in sound engineering, he could make these really good. Her voice was great, and the lyrics weren't bad, but the backing was crap, no two ways.

He glanced at his watch. Just over an hour before he was due to meet her. With a backhanded sweep of the sleeve, he flicked the shortcake-crumbs on to the carpet, ran the tape back to the beginning, and switched to *Record*.

★★★★★

Sandy had not troubled himself to seek clearance from the police before taking a bunch of stirks to market on the mainland, as Robb discovered to his annoyance when he finished his paperwork and went in search of the head stalker.

After drawing blank round the buildings, he got back into the borrowed Land Rover and drove the two bumpy miles up the glen track to the Stalker's Cottage, but there was no vehicle outside, and only a big, fluffy tabby and a noisy pack of kennelled terriers responded to his knock.

Robb turned around on the muddy patch of turf by the woodshed, drove back to the junction of tracks, and took the branch that led towards the Greeting Pool and Strathtorran House. Before he reached either, however, he spotted Sir Archie's silver Mercedes parked in a bay scooped out of the bank, and pulled in behind it.

The doors were unlocked, the key in the ignition, and rod-clips open on the roof, but where was the driver?

Robb let his feet follow the narrow path that led obliquely down the heather-covered bank until it merged with what was evidently a well-worn fishermen's trail beside the water. Here the ponticum thickets had been cut back, and eroded sections of the path shored up. Boggy patches were bridged by planks covered in wire netting to prevent slippage. Shafts of sunlight filtered through glossy dark-green foliage, and the peaty, spongy soil produced the sensation of walking on chocolate mousse.

After passing two promising-looking pools at either end of a big S-bend, Robb came on his quarry seated on a tree-stump that leaned over the water, hat wreathed in pipe-smoke, with a black labrador at his feet.

He was squinting into the pool through Polaroid glasses, and calling soft instructions to the bulky, green-veiled figure casting expertly from the far bank.

'Too far. Just a bit more to the left. No, your left. There, you were over him then. Try again.'

The moment he stood still, Robb understood the reason for pipe and veil. Black clouds of midges descended on his face and hands, and he was aware of furtive movement in the hair at the nape of his neck. Slapping and scratching, he asked where Sandy was.

'Gone to market,' said Sir Archie, looking round. 'I told him I'd clear it with you. No point in keeping beasts on once they're fit.'

Robb swallowed his irritation and said that was fine. He still had other people to interview.

'Well done, Inspector. Keep up the good work.' Sir Archie turned back to more interesting matters. 'Not so far, Sis. He's only halfway between me and the roots of that willow.'

Robb ran his fingers over his neck and pinched sharply, capturing a struggling, many-legged insect. 'When do you expect Sandy back, sir?'

'No idea. Depends if they make their reserve in the ring or if he sells privately.' He thought for a moment, then said, 'Hang on, I can tell you who *will* know, and that's Catriona McNichol, at the gate-house. Sandy's mother, eighty-six and sharp as a knife. She part-owns the beasts, and Sandy always drops in to give her the crack before he goes home.'

'Thank you, sir.' For nothing, Robb added to himself as he retraced his steps along the peaty mousse. *Sis.* So the veiled figure had been Marjorie Forbes – well, you could have fooled him. Bulked out in waders, he had taken her for a man. Or had Sir Archibald said, 'Priss.' No, because Lady Priscilla had gone to visit her old man in hospital, and she at least had had the civility to clear it with him first. What a job it was keeping track of these people! They drifted about as they pleased, and made it clear enough that they thought his investigation not only a bore but a waste of time as well. Beverley Tanner was no loss, as far as they were concerned, and they would have been happy enough to let sleeping dogs lie and forget she ever existed.

Frustrated and suddenly hungry, he drove on until he found room to turn, then made his way through the high deer-gate and down the back drive, stopping by the two little pepperpot towers with an archway between them that constituted the Glen Buie Lodge gate-house.

★★★★★

Visitors were the breath of life to Catriona McNichol, imprisoned by age and arthritis in her armchair between the two windows of the room above the gate-arch. One overlooked the front drive, which curled right-handed into the gravel sweep before the front door, while the left-hand fork vanished into the dark shrubbery flanking the back drive.

On the other side of her living-room, a matching window commanded the shore road and gentle slope leading eventually to the harbour where, even now, the 1.30 pm ferryboat was chugging out beyond the breakwater on its way to Tounie.

'You certainly have a fine view,' observed Robb, when the cracked old voice invited him to come up the stairs since she couldn't get down to him.

'Aye, 'tis grand, right enough, and Sir Archie's very good. He's had the double-glazing put in so I can sit here summer and winter, too. There's no one goes up to the Lodge without me seeing them,' she said with a twinkle that told him she was well aware of the purpose of his visit.

Better than any watchdog, he thought, remembering the unlocked doors.

She was a squat, solidly-built old woman, with white hair waving strongly back from a broad, lined forehead, a ski-jump nose and hooded, rheumy, pale-blue eyes that nevertheless sparked with curiosity. Her worn hands were knotted with arthritis, and the stick-thin legs planted firmly apart, their feet in sheepskin slippers, looked too brittle to support her body. Clearly she spent most of her waking hours in this position. To her right was a large television and VCR. On the table to her left, within easy reach, were an automatic tea-maker and biscuit caddy, an untidy heap of magazines, and a pair of 8 x 30 Zeiss binoculars.

'Can you remember who came and went last Tuesday?' Robb asked.

'The day yon puir lassie was kilt? I mind it fine, sir,' she said with a briskness that seemed incongruous in someone so old and immobile. 'I have little to do but look through the window all day long. I have it written down for ye. Wait, now, while I put my hand on it.'

She shuffled a pile of papers and picked out a sheet of lined foolscap. Date, names, times, vehicles – all set out in the elegant schoolroom copperplate hand of yesteryear. Robb received it almost reverently.

'Take a look at that, and if there's aught not plain, ye have only to ask,' she smiled, and leaned back in her chair. With close attention, Robb began to read the record of Tuesday, September 22nd, as seen from the gate-house window.

Mrs McNichol had taken up her station at 8 am, when the red post van delivered letters and newspapers. She had noted the departure of the two stalking-parties to Carn Mhor and Carn Beag at 9.10 and 9.15 respectively.

At 9.30 Nicky and Benjamin had driven off in the red Caterham, fishing-rods sticking through the passenger window.

At 10.10, Donny had led the white pony, wearing the stag-saddle, up the back drive towards the Carn Mhor pony-path.

Nothing had happened then until 11 o'clock, when Duncan the gardener had gone off to the harbour on his motorbike, and Mary Grant and Ishy had left the house in Mary's blue station-wagon.

Robb looked up. 'What about the other girl? Elspeth?'

'Yon thrawn lassie!' Mrs McNichol chuckled, half-admiring, half-censorious. 'Och, she had other fish to fry. I saw her come flying out the house close on noon, with her hair all tangled like a bush full of snakes. She'd a shining gold jacket, and nothing on her hinder parts but a skirt as long as a pie-frill. Surely to God, I thought, she can't be going on the bus in that rig? But go she did, for I never saw her return. Yon's no' one to fret over what folk think, though if her auntie had seen her then, she'd have lost her place sooner than she did. She's a hard woman, is Mary Grant.'

'When did Elspeth return?'

The lined brow crinkled. 'As to that, I canna say for certain, but it must have been after dark, for I'd Ishy on the phone soon after six, in a rare taking because Elspeth wasna there to help with the vegetables, and Mary away to visit her sister on the Black Isle.'

Robb rubbed his jaw and read on.

At three o'clock Donny, John Forbes, and the white pony carrying a dead stag had passed under the arch on their way to the game larder. Soon after, the game-dealer's refrigerated van paid its weekly call, departing twenty minutes later.

At 5.15, Ishy had returned in her own car, and simultaneously Lady Hanbury and Lady Priscilla had appeared with their fishing-rods from the direction of the trout-loch. Ten minutes later, Marjorie Forbes and her dog had arrived tired and hot at the gate-house. They had come straight up the stairs to share a pot of tea with Catriona.

'Miss Marjorie was aye a kind lassie, and loved the hill,' said the old woman affectionately, 'but it's only since her husband the minister died that she's come here again, bringing her lads with her.'

She leaned forward confidentially. 'She was after telling me that Sir Archie is minded to put young Mr Johnny in charge here, now poor Mr Alec's dead and gone.'

At 5.30, the rest of Sandy's party had returned from Carn Mhor, and repaired to the gun-room for a dram.

An hour later, Fergus's Trooper had driven under the gate-house, with the Royal in the trailer and Mrs Alec in the front seat, while Mr Cooper had to make do with the back.

Just as the light was fading, Nicky's red sports car had roared in and skidded to a stop, 'which is no way to treat Duncan's gravel, as Mr Nicky knows full well,' said the old woman severely, 'and they with hardly time left to dress before the gong. Her leddyship canna abide the guests to keep dinner waiting on them.'

Soon after that the yard lights had been extinguished, and Mrs McNichol had drawn her own curtains, switched on the TV, and turned her attention to supper.

With her permission, Robb folded the paper and put it in his pocket. He felt depressed. What had seemed at the outset a neat, self-contained crime had begun to spread outwards like fungus, blurring its parameters.

Too many people going in different directions. Too many guns and people who knew how to handle them. For all their law-abiding demeanour, these people were the devil to deal with, he thought. Not only were they on first-name terms with the Chief Constable, but young and old, male and female, they belonged to a circle for whom killing large mammals was a normal activity. People accustomed to deciding whether or not a stag was 'better off the hill' might with no great mental or moral adjustment apply the same criterium to their own species. Most of them hardly bothered to conceal their conviction that Beverley was better off the hill. A dangerous outsider. A threat to the sport they loved. One of them might well have decided to get rid of her in the same spirit as he or she would have disposed of a fox or mink, or any other destructive vermin.

It was perfectly possible, too, he thought gloomily, that several of them knew who had taken that decision and, approving of it, would do what they could to foil his own efforts to get at the truth. And if he did succeed in nailing the villain, it was Lombard Street to a china orange that the Chief Constable would be furious.

Time for a pork pie, a pint, and a Mars bar to banish such thoughts. Without Winter's calorie-conscious eye on him, he might even enjoy them. He thanked Mrs McNichol, and rose to leave.

'You'll no' take a cup of tea before you go?' Clearly she was disappointed to lose him so soon.

'Thank you, but no. I don't suppose you spoke to Miss Tanner yourself?' he added as an afterthought.

'Indeed I did.' The old woman brightened. 'She was aye dropping in here, asking questions about the old days. A nosy body, right enough. Many an hour she spent looking through the old albums from Strathtorran, and she'd a wheen questions that were none of her business, but there! The young folks have no manners today.'

Robb bade farewell to the Mars bar, and resumed his seat. 'What did she want to know?'

'Och, about the auld laird's troubles, and how Lady Helen was drowned, but I saw no cause to go raking over old sorrows for that one's edification.'

'No, indeed. But it might help us.'

'Maybe.' The old eyes considered him. 'And then again, maybe not.'

'Who told her you had the photographs from Strathtorran?'

'That would have been Kirsty, sir.'

'Your son's wife?'

'In a manner of speaking, aye. 'Tis my belief she sent that one to me to keep her away from the Stalker's Cottage. She's been as jumpy as a cat ever since Miss Tanner went up there without so much as a by-your-leave, and told Kirsty she was wasting her life in such a godforsaken hovel.'

Mrs McNichol's eyes sparked danger.

'I tell you, sir, if she'd said that in my hearing, I'd have given her a piece of my mind.'

'I should think so. Why would she want to upset Kirsty like that?'

Mrs McNichol pursed her lips until the whistle-lines looked more like pin-tucks. Robb did not press her, and after a while she sighed and said, 'The Dear knows, that puzzled me too, but now I see it was all part of her politicking ways. She couldna abide a body that was contented with her lot, and she was aye ettling to change the social order here at Glen Buie. Well, I'm an old woman, sir, and able enough for the likes of her, but wee Kirsty's no' in a very strong position. Ye'll have heard how my son took her in when she ran from home?'

Robb made a noncommittal noise, and she went on with grim humour, 'She's not the first choice I'd have made for him, nor yet the second, but she's a good wee thing, for all she canna cook nor sew. It would break Sandy's heart to lose her now.'

'I'm told she looks very like Lady Helen McNeil,' said Robb, and she gave him a sharp glance.

'You shouldna pay too much heed to Miss Ashy's blether. That one can spin tales from cobwebs, just as young Mrs Ian would.'

'You mean Eliza McNeil?'

'Who else? Many's the time she's sat where you are sitting now, and told tales that would make my flesh creep if the half were true.'

'How long did she live over at Strathtorran House?'

'Four winter months,' said Mrs McNichol heavily. 'September to Hogmanay, and if there were two days together it didn't rain, I never saw them. Such a wet year's end as never was known, and Strathtorran is a lonesome place for a lassie when she's nae sight of her husband for weeks on end.'

'Where was he?'

'Off with the Army hardly a year after they married. Poor Mrs Ian! Running a salmon farm was never the life for her. Small wonder it wasna long before she went looking for mischief.'

'What kind of mischief?'

'Breeks,' said Mrs McNichol, with a tremendous roll of the r. 'And none too choosy who wore them, forbye.'

'Did Lady Strathtorran know?'

'That I canna say, sir. Her leddyship was busy at the house, and she's one that willna abide idle hands. It was "Eliza, do this, and do that," until she'd ride her bicycle here to see me, just to get away. "What's the news, Catty?" she'd ask; and then, "Does nothing *ever* happen in this dump?" Och, I can hear her now.'

'It must be very quiet here in the winter.'

'A grave would be noisier,' she agreed.

'The Hanburys weren't at the Lodge, then?'

'No, sir. The big house is aye shut up at the end of the season, and if any of the gentlemen come to shoot hinds, they take their meals with Mary Grant and sleep in the bothy. The winter you're speaking of, Mary had Mr Nicky to cook for as well as the ghillies, for he'd failed in his examinations and Sir Archibald's orders were that he must live here and study to make up the work.' She chuckled. 'Before he'd been here a week, Mrs Ian had him running her errands. Well I mind the day I came in to find the pair of them puffing those nasty French cigarettes of hers, turn and turn about. I tell you, sir, the smell was enough to make you sick. I opened the window and told Mr Nicky he should be ashamed. "What would your father say if he saw you now?" I asked. "I'd tell him Eliza's leading me astray," he said, and they both laughed, but I made him throw it on the fire for all that. She was a woman grown and could do as she pleased, but I didna want Sir Archibald saying I had encouraged him.'

'How old was Nicholas then?'

'Eighteen, I'd say,' she answered after a moment's consideration, 'but young for his age. All that money! It's no' chancy for a boy to ken he can buy the moon if he chooses, though his father was aye strict with him – too strict, some would say.'

'Can't be too strict,' said Robb heartily, and rose. 'I must have a word with Kirsty. Will she be at home now?'

'The bairn's due at the clinic at four, and she'll go over on the three o'clock ferry,' said Mrs McNichol. 'Ye'll likely catch her at the house if you hurry.' She shot him a conspiratorial glance.

'Ye'll no' be telling her you were talking to me, now?'

'Mum's the word.'

As he drove away, he glanced up at the big window over the archway, and saw she had resumed her self-imposed vigil. On impulse he sounded his horn, and glimpsed the white blur of a waving hand.

★★★★★

The larder in which the dead stags were hung, headless but still in their skins, to await collection by the game-merchant's van, stood at the junction of front and back drives, screened from the main house by a thicket of laurel and ramping ponticum. To the left of the larder's door, the refrigeration plant's motor throbbed in its weldmesh cage. To the right, was a wooden bench on which the stalkers would prop antlers with identifying labels for guests who wanted to take them home.

It was a gloomy, dank spot, from which no amount of hosing and sweeping could entirely banish flies. The smell of blood and corruption lingered about the drain grilles, together with scraps of hair and splinters of bone. But as a rendezvous, it had the merit of being equidistant from the Lodge and Mary's cottage, yet hidden from both. It was also private. Apart from the flurry of activity at the end of each day's stalking, when stags were unloaded and hung up for weighing, no one had any reason to linger there.

'Elspeth?' Ben called softly as, clutching a plastic bag full of tapes, he hurried down the cinder path that wound through the leafy jungle. 'Sorry I'm late, but – '

He stopped abruptly, realising that the shape on the wooden bench was an overflowing black polythene sack full of severed heads and legs awaiting disposal in the offal pit. Of Elspeth there was no sign.

He walked all round the larder and returned to the door.

'Elspeth?'

It surprised him that the door was ajar. Usually the stalkers were careful to lock it, though the key's hiding-place was known to everyone. He pushed it a little further, and thought he heard a rustle and gasp of indrawn breath, like stifled laughter. It would be just Elspeth's idea of a joke to hide behind the door and jump out at him. She could be quite childish at times.

At least that would mean she had cheered up since breakfast. He grinned: all right, he'd play it her way. He stepped quickly through the door and moved into the dank, meaty-smelling gloom, where the afternoon light filtered dimly through windows set near the roof.

'I know you're here.'

No answer. Inside the larder, the beat of the refrigeration plant was muffled to a soft, steady thrumming. Gimbals and pulleys, empty now, hung from the beams, and a large spring-balance, the dial calibrated to 200 kg, was suspended over the long butcher's table, V-shaped to support a carcase belly-upward, and criss-crossed with cleaver scars.

Along one wall stretched a stainless steel refrigerated cabinet with a heavily-flanged door at either end. This was where the carcases awaiting collection were stored in the chilled hygienic conditions demanded by Brussels. Gone were the days when dead stags could be towed down the loch behind the outboard, then hung a week or more in the open larder.

Now the stags were weighed, their heads and lower legs removed, and then the gimbal with each carcase would be slotted on to electrically-operated rails at one end of the chiller. A push of a button moved it farther along as the next one was loaded in, so that the dealer's men could carry out the stiff bodies from another door at the far end, which opened on to the drive. This ensured that the carcases were collected in strict rotation, with no need for the collectors to enter the larder itself.

Where was Elspeth hiding? Ben pressed the light-switch just inside the door. As soon as the twin fluorescent tubes flooded the larder with flat light, his eye was drawn to a scrap of bright material, incongruous against the grey concrete floor.

He picked it up and fingered it , puzzled, a little disturbed, recognising it as one of the elasticated chiffon rings with which Elspeth tied back her long red hair. Shocking pink, electric blue or dayglo yellow, they made a strong contrast with her dark uniform dresses, defiantly declaring that she was only *pretending* to be a skivvy.

She must have pulled it off deliberately. It couldn't just fall off, and without it her thick, crinkly tresses got in the way of everything she did. Why had she left it here? It had the look of bait...a clue that she was close at hand, but where? Surely even Elspeth would not be so reckless as to hide in the chiller?

Suddenly anxious, he tugged at the sprung handle, and the heavy door swung outward. He hooked it back and peered into the shiny, sterile interior. Icy vapour plumed out to meet the warmer air, and when the miasma cleared he glimpsed the stiff, truncated, hairy bodies silvered with frost as they hung from the rail. Wedged between two of them was another shape.

Behind him he heard a footstep and turned quickly, anxiety dissolving into relief. 'Oh, hi! I'm looking for -'

Then he gasped, and his voice rose sharply to a shout, a choking terrified roar: ' Hey! Don't do that! Stop it! Let go! What are you − ?'

★★★★★

Moments later, the larder door swung shut, and its key grated. The grim little building resumed its usual secretive stillness, broken only by the buzzing of bluebottles around the grilles of the drains.

Chapter Seventeen

KIRSTY STOPPED THE battered Volvo a hundred yards short of the gate-house, and looked anxiously towards the house to see if Elspeth was coming. It was 2.45 already, and she had been due to pick her up five minutes earlier. Dougie had dropped off to sleep in his padded seat as she bumped down the track from the Stalker's Cottage, but the moment she switched off he woke and began to grizzle.

Hastily she re-started the engine and let it idle, watching the child in the rear-view mirror. His crying stopped, but she knew it was only a temporary reprieve, and willed Elspeth to hurry. Though clumps of shrubs hid the car from the gate-house, she knew that inquisitive old Catriona must have seen her drive down the track, and would soon wonder why the car had not emerged on to the shore road.

Just knowing Sandy's mother was watching made Kirsty nervous. She drummed her fingers against the wheel, tension building inside her. Stupid girl! Why couldn't she be punctual? By offering a lift, Kirsty was saving her the cost of a taxi: you'd think she'd make an effort to get here on time.

Five minutes crawled past, while Kirsty watched the toddler and the temperature gauge with equal anxiety. She dared not switch off, but the ancient engine was getting dangerously hot.

At nine minutes to three, her patience gave out and she put the car in gear. Elspeth would have to shift for herself. If Dougie missed his appointment he wouldn't get another for a week, and she couldn't bear seven more days of wondering what was wrong with him. As it was, she was cutting the ferry finer than she liked.

With a final glance up the deserted drive, she shrugged and let in the clutch. 'Won't be long now, bairnie,' she crooned to Dougie, and drove as fast as she could towards the harbour.

★★★★★

Sunday's taped-off areas and police signs had been removed, but still the sandy head and well-filled uniform of Constable McTavish maintained a lonely vigil on the bridge across the Greeting Pool, ready and waiting to repel the world's press should it choose to descend on his patch.

He had been leaning over the parapet, jaws moving rhythmically, but as Robb approached he straightened, pulling down his tunic.

'Not the first body that's been pulled from this pool,' said Robb by way of greeting.

McTavish's larynx moved convulsively and his toffee slid on its way. 'Indeed it's not, sir, and I doubt it will be the last,' he said with ghoulish relish. ''Twas here that poor Lady Helen drowned, and young Mistress McNeil, forbye. 'Tis an unchancy spot.'

Even the late gleam of sunlight that often ends a wet day could not dispel the sinister air of the Greeting Pool. If anything, thought Robb, adopting McTavish's position at the parapet, the ruddy glow emphasised the oily blackness of the water, the sinuous strength of the current sucking round the bridge's pillars, swirling in eddies and whirlpools over submerged rocks, and washing a yellowish froth into backwaters.

'Is it true what they're saying, sir, that the lassie was kilt on the hill and her body put in the river later awhile?'

'That's the way it looks,' Robb nodded. 'Shot first, and dumped in the water next day.'

'If she was shot, sir, it would have tae be one of the stalkers. There's no one else here with a rifle.'

'You're not troubled by poachers, then?' Robb saw the leap

of apprehension in McTavish's eyes and relented. 'No, you're right. It looks like the work of a stalker, but the question is, which one? Pro or Am? There's half a dozen rifles in the gun-room at the Lodge, all licenced and above board, and close on a dozen people used to handling them. Male and female. Young and old.'

'Aye. They say Miss Ashy's a grand shot, and her leddyship, too.' McTavish pushed back his cap and deftly intercepted a ked about to take refuge in his sandy curls. 'And there's Ian McNeil has the auld laird's .300 Magnum over at Strathtorran, the one they call Mons Meg. Did ye no' find a bullet, sir?'

The question brought Ashy's artless prattle to mind. Robb leaned farther over the parapet, scanning to right and left. He said, 'Go and stand on the bank below and look back at the bridge. Tell me if you can see a stone missing below the parapet.'

With a mystified air, McTavish complied, and presently called back that there was a stone out at the top of the central pillar. Guided by his shouts, Robb moved a few paces to his left, and soon his searching fingers located the cavity. It went back further than he expected.

Heaving himself ponderously on to the coping, he balanced on his stomach and wriggled forward as far as he dared, feeling both absurd and insecure as he groped within the hole. What was he expecting to find? Sweets for the wee folk? An indignant toad?

At first he thought it was empty. Then his questing fingers closed on the damp smoothness of paper – an envelope – and with a grunt of satisfaction he tried to wriggle backwards. A gust of wind buffeted him between the shoulders, and his feet waved helplessly like a stranded crab. Too much of his heavy body was hanging over the edge. He could get no purchase on the smooth parapet to push himself to safety. For a moment his head swam as he stared into the swirling black water far below; then a hand like a ham grasped him by the collar.

'Have a care, sir!' Puffing and alarmed, Constable McTavish heaved him on to firm ground. 'Losh, man, I thought ye'd fall! What have ye there?'

'Got a knife?'

The plain buff envelope was clean, though damp. It had not been in the hole long. Holding it by one corner, Robb slit the top and extracted a folded postcard headed: *D. L. Paish, Studio 12, TRL Films (UK) Ltd.*

The message was brief and to the point. *No chance last night, but will try again. Enclosed brings us up to date. Regards, DLP.* Clipped to the postcard were ten £10 notes, crisp from the ATM.

★★★★★

'That's odd,' said Ashy, as she and Maya, with Sergeant Winter close on their heels, slid down the last forestry bank and reached the Trooper. They had been on the hill for eight hours and were chilled, sodden, and exhausted.

'What is?' asked Winter.

'The Trooper's moved. Fergus parked over there, by the ash tree, don't you remember?'

'So he did,' said Winter, examining tyre tracks, 'and look, the key's in the ignition. Fergus hid it inside the front bumper.'

'Let's g-g-get in out of the wind,' said Maya, too cold and tired to be interested. The soles of her feet felt raw, and she longed to strip off her wet clothes and flop into a hot bath.

'You're frozen.' Ashy bundled her into the front seat and switched on the engine. The heater blew a little warmth into the cab as they huddled together, willing the two hunched figures dragging the dead stag between them to hurry down the last few hundred feet. It seemed an age before the limp body had been heaved into the trailer and Fergus swung the Trooper round.

'Home, James, and don't spare the horses,' said Ashy through chattering teeth.

It was not until they had bumped a mile down the track with the heater roaring full blast that Johnny said aggressively, 'I told you we'd catch up with those stags in the end, didn't I?'

No one answered. It had been a very long day. As the

vehicle lurched over the potholes, Ashy sighed and laid her blonde head gently on Winter's shoulder. After a startled glance at her oblivious face, he shifted to make her more comfortable, and wedged himself against the door-frame to protect her from the bumps.

★★★★★

'Where's Ben?' said Maya, looking round, as the party assembled for drinks before the drawing-room fire.

Ashy made a warning face. 'Don't ask,' she murmured. 'He's not back yet, and his dear Mamma is hopping mad. She thinks he ratted on the stalking so that he could sneak off to another rave-up on the mainland.'

'Ah.' So that was what those teenagers had been planning in the serving-room. Maya wondered whether to repeat the conversation she had heard, but Nicky was approaching, bottle in hand, and Ashy turned to hold out her glass.

'What were you up to today?' she asked.

He pulled a face. 'Kicking my heels in Tounie while the mechanic messed about with my car. There's something rattling underneath, and sorting it out took forever.'

'That car's more trouble than it's worth, though I must admit I wouldn't mind getting my hands on it!' laughed Ashy.

In response to her mother's gesture, she moved away and Nicky said shyly to Maya, 'What were you saying about Ben?'

'Oh, we were wondering if he'd gone to another of his rock concerts. I heard him make a date with Elspeth this morning, so I guess that's where they've gone.'

'Don't tell anyone else,' said Nicky anxiously. 'Poor Ben's in enough trouble as it is for sliding off from stalking. My aunt's furious.'

'Don't worry – I won't give him away,' promised Maya. 'I remember what it was like when everything you ever wanted to do was off limits.'

She was rewarded with his rare flash of smile, but before he could say more his father's voice boomed, 'Come on, Nicky! Keep that bottle moving,' and he hurried on his rounds.

To her surprise he was back in a few moments, saying hesitantly, 'I thought about you up there on Ben Shallachan while I was in the garage. I hoped you weren't getting frozen in those hailstorms.'

'It sure was kinda cold.' Standing before a blazing fire, drapes drawn, glass in hand, dinner coming up, the memory of this afternoon's knifing wind and sleet seemed unreal. And this was early autumn! What could it be like on the high tops in midwinter? 'There was as much water coming out of my boots as going in,' she added in the hope of another smile. He was a little like a deer himself, she thought: no wonder Alec had felt an urge to protect him.

'Will you go with the stalkers again tomorrow?' he asked after a pause.

'Are you kidding?'

'Come fishing with me instead. The river's rising, so there'll be a good chance of a salmon.'

She found his eagerness flattering, and hated to disappoint him. 'I'm sorry, Nicky. I already told Johnny I'd go fish with him.'

His face fell. 'Come with me instead,' he persisted.

'Oh, Nicky, I'd like to, but I can't. I'm sorry. Why don't you join us?'

'No, thanks.'

Maya felt irrationally guilty. The deer had come trustingly to feed from her hand, and she had struck it. 'Some other time, hmm?' she said hopefully, but he turned away without answering.

✶✶✶✶✶✶

'All right,' growled Sandy, glaring at Robb like an embattled badger in the mouth of his sett. Badger-like, too, was the smell of imperfectly washed socks drying on the Rayburn's rail, and the debris associated with a small child looked all the more squalid without wee Dougie there to give it relevance. 'I don't deny it,' he went on. 'Yon pool's never fished, so where's the harm? I sent Mr Paish and his team tae the young laird, but he would have none o' it; so when they persisted, I gave them permission maself.'

'And pocketed the fee.'

Sandy blinked rapidly and lowered his head. 'For God's sake, man! It was nothing tae them – *nothing!* They told me themselves it would cost them four times as much tae swim with the fish in an English river.'

'You're telling me that's all they wanted to do? To swim with the fish? They didn't take a few home with them?'

'Och, they werena in the business of killing fish!' Sandy laughed scornfully. 'Saving them, more like. A behavioural study of wild salmon, Mr Paish was making, and I was proud to help him. Aye, proud! I've never liked the cages.'

Light dawned. 'So Mr Paish was filming fish in their natural habitat – why? To show the shortcomings of intensive salmon farming? Was that the reason for secrecy?'

'Aye. If the lads from the fish farm heard of it, they'd have smashed his cameras and run him off the place. They're a rough lot when their jobs are at risk, Inspector, and the laird's ain brother is roughest of them all.'

'Does he own the salmon farm?'

'They call him the manager, though it's little enough managing they do beyond pumping the fish with antibiotics and spraying OPs on the poor creatures,' said Sandy with contempt.

'OPs?'

'Organo-phosphates tae kill the lice. The salmon is a grand fish, and it's a sair sight tae see them packed so tight in the cage they maun swim upright or drown.'

'How long had Mr Paish been filming here?'

Off and on for two years, it appeared. The team visited the Greeting Pool at irregular intervals, and avoided contacting Sandy directly. Generally Mr Paish stayed at Fas Buie with Hector Logie, and his blonde assistant posed as a hiker.

'Hector Logie has a key to the deer-gate?'

'Aye, so he has. Sir Archibald permits him to go where he pleases.'

From time to time, on his return from the Strathtorran Arms at night, Sandy would see signs that Paish and his team had been at work, and would find his fee under the parapet. Recent police activity round the Greeting Pool had made it difficult to check the cavity.

'How did ye come tae look there?' asked Sandy with a sharp glance.

'Routine investigation.' Robb pushed away the memory of the black, swirling water drawing him closer. 'More to the point, who told Beverley Tanner where to look?'

Sandy thought the sneaking, snooping little skellum might have watched him extract his last payment. 'She was aye hanging about the river path. About ma house, too, telling Kirsty that hers was no life for a bonny lass.'

He rose and filled the kettle. 'Ye'll take a cup of tea?'

'Thanks. Did you speak to Beverley about that?'

'I did, too. I told her tae leave Kirsty and the bairn alone, and if I found her at the house again, I'd make a complaint to Sir Archibald.'

'What did she say to that?'

A spasm crossed the weatherbeaten face. 'She said I should be ashamed tae let such a bonny lass rot in a godforsaken hole like this, and I shouldna be surprised tae come home one day and find her gone.'

'Anything else?'

'She said she knew things that would cost me my place, but I paid no heed. I've but a year wanting tae my pension: nothing she said would harm me. Kirsty and I have a croft built down the strath that's waiting on us now, and the school bus passes the door.'

That rosy vision would turn to dust should Kirsty be drawn to the bright lights. Robb understood Sandy's anxiety very well.

'Was that the last time you spoke to Beverley?'

'It was.'

'But not the last time you saw her? She was walking down the track towards Loch a Bealach just after Sir Archibald shot his stag on Carn Mhor.'

'He told you that?' Sandy looked betrayed. 'Well, that's a matter of opinion. Sir Archibald's eyes are not what they were, and for myself, I was more concerned with the gralloch than staring round at the scenery.'

'Miss Macleod was with you. Didn't she tell you it was Beverley Tanner?'

Sandy stared at him with a baffled air, plainly wishing he knew what the others had said. 'We'd left Miss Ashy a wee bit back,' he admitted cautiously. 'By the time she came up with us, the hiker was out of sight.'

'How long was it before Miss Macleod joined you? Did one of you go back to fetch her?'

A long pause while Sandy considered. 'I told ye,' he said at last, 'I was at the gralloch. Sir Archibald went back up the hill and waved her down himself.'

'Leaving Sandy with the rifle, one dead stag, and Beverley walking along the track a hundred and fifty yards away. Did he succumb to temptation? Was that the extra shot?' mused Robb aloud as he and Winter sat that evening in the spartan tartan sitting-room at the hostel. 'Sandy's a territorial animal, and used to acting on his own initiative.'

'He'd have had to be quick to shoot her and hide the body before the others joined him.'

'He knew where the boat was, because he'd given Logie permission to use it for his photographic equipment.'

Winter said slowly, 'She could just as easily have been shot from Carn Beag.'

'All I'm saying is that Sandy had both motive and opportunity.'

'So did Fergus,' said Winter doggedly. 'He got into trouble

at his last place for selling venison on his own account. John Forbes was only too happy to give chapter and verse.'

'Implying he's been up to the same tricks here?'

'Different ones. John Forbes says Fergus has been having it off with Sandy's girlfriend. And guess who told Forbes that?'

'Beverley,' said Robb resignedly.

'So Fergus had a good reason for wanting her out of the way.' Winter eased his muscles deeper into the hard little armchair. He felt very well exercised, face tingling, and though his collarbone was sore from the pulling-rope, a general glow of satisfaction pervaded his body. The memory of Ashy's blonde head on his shoulder was not disagreeable, either.

Robb, in contrast, felt edgy and dissatisfied, unable to rid himself of resentment that while Winter had been disporting himself among the high tops, he had been plodding through boring, inescapable, routine questioning, during which he had been bitten by midges, and patronised – and probably lied to as well – by toffee-nosed nobs. Too many weapons, too many people with reason to want to be rid of Beverley Tanner.

It made no difference that Winter had gone stalking reluctantly. He had returned in so exalted a mood that it was plain his scruples about taking part in blood sports had evaporated. To Robb's half-jocular question on whether he had enjoyed his day, he had simply replied that it had not been what he expected, not at all. Since then his main contribution to the murder investigation had been to raise objections to every theory Robb put forward.

He also appeared to be dropping off to sleep just when the time had come for constructive thought.

'Wake up!' barked Robb, and observed with satisfaction his subordinate's startled jump.

'Sorry, sir.'

'Let's have a look at that timetable. The track past Loch a Bealach must have been like Piccadilly Circus, with all the coming and going, yet someone was there alone long enough to spot Beverley, shoot her, and hide the body, and vanish unseen.

We should be able to work out who had that opportunity. Now, the last *admitted* sighting was – when?'

Winter considered, stifling a yawn, hoping this wasn't going to be a long session. He was a morning man himself, brain fizzing at 6 am, whereas Robb liked to burn the midnight oil. 'Lady Priscilla thought she saw her at about lunchtime – say 1.15 – but she wasn't sure. Then old Logie saw her while he was waiting for the ladies to leave the boat for him. Say 2 o'clock or thereabouts. She must have been wandering about the area for an hour or more.'

'Perhaps she went as far as the Prince's Rock, took some pix, and cut across the hill to get back to the track. They said she refused to stick to the paths.' Robb frowned at the map. 'Those boys – Benjamin and Nicholas. They were on the river.' Robb frowned at the paper. 'She must have walked right past them. Did either of them mention seeing her?'

Winter shook his head. They had been over this ground before, and he wanted his bed. 'At the time she was shot, Nicky and Benjamin were over at Tounie,' he pointed out. 'They only got back just before dinner.'

'Which is odd, when you come to think of it,' said Robb, now studying the ferry sailings. 'The concert ended at 5.30 so that the fans could catch their ferries home, right? The last sailing for Strathtorran harbour leaves Tounie at 6pm – right? – and docks at 6.45. How far from harbour to Lodge? Three miles? Four?'

'The dressing-bell is rung at 7.30.' Winter roused from his torpor.

'So why where they late? Was the ferry delayed? Easy enough to find out. Did they spend half an hour admiring the sunset? Even if they did, they should have had plenty of time.' His finger traced the road along the sea-loch, and stopped at a dotted line just beyond the fish farm's little bay. 'What's this? Another crossing?'

'That's just a foot ferry,' said Winter, looking over his shoulder at the map. 'Mostly used by shoppers and school children. It doesn't take vehicles.'

'Find out how often it runs.'

'Will do,' said Winter and suppressed another yawn.

To his relief, Robb glanced at the clock. 'All right, Jim, we'll pack it in for now. Tomorrow I'm going to take a look at the fish farm while you check out the ferries. Then we'd both better have a chat with Lady Strathtorran. I've a notion there's a good deal more she can tell us.'

The early evening depression had left him. He felt clear-headed now, and optimistic of sorting out this mess in short order. The sequence of events leading to Beverley's murder was complete in his mind; tomorrow he must return to the contour map and blu-tac blobs. Stare at those groupings long enough, look through the pattern to the image within, and like a magic-eye postcard, the blur would resolve into a focused picture.

That, at least, was the theory.

Chapter Eighteen

AS USUAL, GWENNIE breakfasted off a tray in her room, and when she came downstairs just after ten next morning, the big house was quiet, with only the distant clatter of crockery and hum of the hoover to break its stillness.

In the dining-room, she was surprised to find her sister-in-law still sitting amid the remains of breakfast, hands clasped about a cooling cup of coffee, gaze abstracted. She had an untidy, rumpled look, as if she had slept badly.

'No sign of him?' asked Gwennie at once.

Marjorie shook her head and gave a sigh so deep it was almost a groan. Last night's anger had turned into acute anxiety. 'He's never done this before. Not for so long. I – I can't decide what to do. If I make a fuss and then find that he's simply dossed down in Tounie – '

'Children are the devil,' said Gwennie. She stood behind her sister-in-law's chair, patting her shoulder as she might have soothed a horse. 'Poor Marjie... What is it, Mary?' she asked as the cook's head appeared through the serving-hatch. 'Do the girls want to clear?'

'It's no' that, my lady.' The rest of Mary appeared in the serving-room doorway, plainly agitated. 'My brother Malcolm just phoned from Selkirk. He says Elspeth's no' come home.'

'Elspeth!'

'Aye. He went tae meet her at the bus station, but she wasna on the overnight, nor yet the morning coach.'

Gwennie's brow creased. She glanced at Marjorie, murmuring, 'Could they have gone off together?'

'Oh, surely not.' Marjorie looked agonised.

'Did Ben have any money on him? I know Elspeth had, because I'd just given her a month's wages.'

'A month!' exclaimed Mary, scandalised.

'Yes, well, you know, in lieu of notice,' admitted Gwennie a trifle guiltily.

'Benjamin never has any money.' His mother's hands trembled as she put down her coffee cup. 'There's nothing for it. We'll have to call the police.'

'Oh, lord,' said Gwennie wearily. 'I suppose you're right, but I do so hate them poking about, asking questions...'

She broke off and glanced out of the window as a big white van turned in through the archway and swung down the back drive towards the stag larder.

'There's McIntyre's man now,' said Mary.

'But he doesn't collect today.'

'They're a man short, so they've changed the schedules, my lady. I maun tell him there's two beasts from Strathtorran along with ours.' Mary hurried out of the room.

The others sat silent, locked in their own thoughts.

Ought I to warn her? Gwennie worried. It's all very well for Archie to pay Angus Buchan to keep mum, but these things have a nasty way of escalating. Next time it might be a child.

If only I hadn't chased him off to go stalking, thought Marjorie. I knew he was tired, but then he's always tired when I want him to do anything. How can he prefer to lie on his bed listening to these hideous dirges when he could be on the hill?

From the back of the house a medley of unaccustomed noises broke into their reflections. Commotion in the courtyard. Running feet. Slamming doors. A dog barking hysterically.

'What's up?' Gwennie rose hastily.

Together they hurried down the passage and through the swing door. In the kitchen, Ishy was standing with her back to the sink, rubber-gloved hands clutched to her face. On a straight-backed chair drawn up to the kitchen table, a burly, shaven-headed young man in a white overall sat doubled up, retching into a plastic bowl, while Mary bent over him, supporting his head.

'What's the matter? Is he ill?' demanded Gwennie.

'Oh – oh my lady! It's terrible. Terrible!' keened Ishy.

'Pull yourself together, girl! Stop that noise at once. Now! Tell me what's wrong.'

Nobody spoke until Mary allowed the young man to straighten. 'There, lad. Ye'll do now.'

Heavy features still white and shiny with shock, he stared vacantly before him as she sloshed cooking brandy into a tumbler and pushed it into his hand. 'Go on, Geordie, drink that and tell her leddyship.'

He gulped convulsively. 'I was after taking beasts frae the chiller,' he said hoarsely, 'when the one jammed on the rail and wouldna budge. I switchit off the power and went tae pull it out by hand, and there by ma feet – ' he swallowed hard – 'I saw two bodies, dead as stanes.'

'*Bodies?*'

At her side, Gwennie heard Marjorie's shocked intake of breath.

'Ane atop the ither. A lassie and a young lad.'

'Benjamin!' Marjorie's legs buckled and she slid to the floor.

'What's going on?' asked Sir Archie, appearing in the doorway. His wife turned to him, white to the lips.

'An accident. A terrible accident. We must get the police.'

★★★★★

Autumn had turned the chestnut avenue leading up to Strathtorran House into a gold-and-ginger tunnel as Robb and Winter bumped up it slowly, avoiding the worst potholes. Though the door to the hostel was unlocked and Janie's yellow VW Estate parked in front of it, the building was deserted. Continuing along the weedy gravel towards the big house, they spotted a slight figure in a boilersuit perched on the rungs of a ladder laid across the steeply-pitched slates above the great hall. A grappling-hook secured one end of the ladder to the roof-ridge, while the other was wedged into the top rung of a second ladder propped against the gutter. The whole apparatus looked ramshackle and insecure.

'Lady Strathtorran!' called Robb, who wouldn't have liked to see his own wife thus employed.

'What is it? Can't it wait?' she shouted over her shoulder.

'We'd like a word with you.'

'OK. Half a tick.'

'To your right, my lady,' called the rheumy-eyed, red-nosed old man in a long tweed overcoat belted with bindertwine, who stood with his boot on the ladder's lowest rung. 'There's anither agley.'

Janie crouched to her task, a slender green monkey on the vast expanse of slates. 'Hold the ladder steady, Jock. I'm coming down.'

'Here, give over.' Winter stepped forward authoritatively, but Jock glared at him like a pugnacious terrier and refused to yield. The laird's wife backed carefully down the two ladders and turned to face them, pink with exertion.

'This roof! Every gale brings down a few more slates. We ought to have it re-done from scratch, but that would cost a fortune.' She wiped her hands down her thighs and said, 'That'll do for now, Jock. Leave the ladders and we'll finish later. Come in, Inspector – or was it my husband you wanted to see?'

Without waiting for an answer, she pushed the ancient studded door, and they followed her into the panelled gloom of the old hall, where a dozen mounted stags' heads surveyed them glassily. Halfway along one wall, a cabinet housed a stuffed blackcock in full display, and in another glass case an immense trout, mean-eyed and lantern-jawed, hung suspended in lonely majesty.

Robb peered at the inscription: *Greeting Pool, May 10, 1911. 9lbs 6oz. Bloody Butcher. Hon Eleanor Arbuthnot.*

'How can I help you?' Janie's impatience was contained but discernible.

Robb said in his most reassuring rumble that he was sorry to interrupt her busy morning, but wondered if she could account for Beverley Tanner's wish to buy Strathtorran? On the face of it she seemed ill-suited to life here, more of a townie, from what he had heard.

'Of course she was,' snapped Janie; and then in an obvious attempt to be more helpful, 'but after all, so was I when I first came here. I had no idea what a slog we were going to have – any more than she would have if I'd pointed it out to her.'

'Didn't you point it out to her?'

Janie shook her head. 'Believe me, it wouldn't have made any difference. I've seen it happen time and again: people come here and fall in love with the scenery just as irrationally as they fall in love with unsuitable people.'

'Did she discuss her plans with Lord Strathtorran?'

A pause while the blood mounted from Janie's cheeks to her forehead. 'Not directly, no,' she said at last. 'I thought it would be better if I raised the subject with him myself. I – I was waiting for the right moment. I didn't want a knee-jerk reaction. I thought if we talked it over quietly, just the two of us – '

'What happened when you did bring it up?'

'Happened?' she said uncertainly.

'What was his reaction?'

'He wouldn't listen.' Now there was no mistaking the bitterness in her tone, no further attempt to pretend all was rosy between her and Torquil.

'Did that surprise you?'

'Of course.' But a moment later her shoulders slumped a trifle and she said despondently, 'Actually, I suppose I should have known he wouldn't even talk about plans for the future unless his brother Ian was there to shove his oar in, and that was just what

I didn't want. I might possibly have persuaded Torquil, but my brother-in-law is incredibly pig-headed, and I knew he'd be dead against selling Strathtorran, particularly if it was my idea.'

'So you felt that if push came to shove, your husband was liable to side with his brother?'

Janie nodded. 'He always takes his cue from Ian. Always has, and I suppose always will.'

'Does Mr McNeil have a financial interest in Strathtorran?'

'Not really. Their father left everything to Torquil – lock, stock, and barrel. We pay Ian to manage the salmon farm, so that's the full extent of his financial interest, though from the way he behaves, you'd think he owns the place.'

'So you and your husband had a row,' said Winter in his flat, short-circuiting way, and Janie blinked.

'I don't go in for *rows,* Sergeant,' she corrected with a tight little smile. 'I'm not good at them.'

'An argument, then.'

'Hardly. It's not easy to argue with Torquil.'

'Not something to complain about,' commented Robb, who saw too much domestic violence in his job.

'I'm not *complaining,* for heaven's sake!' Exasperation was near the surface. 'Just trying to explain.' She drew a deep breath and went on more calmly. 'My husband was born with a malfunctioning liver, and was in and out of hospital most of his childhood. No one really expected him to live. He had one operation after another, and finally a transplant, and touch wood – ' She left the sentence in mid-air and continued, 'It's not surprising that he's fatalistic about money, success, all the things we materialists worry about; but it can be difficult to live with.'

'It must be,' rumbled Robb, and she gave him a grateful glance.

'Ian's always had a lot of influence with Torquil. He talked him into coming to live here after their father died, and I went along with it, especially since in a physical sense it seems to have done him good. But mentally, of course, we stagnate.'

'Don't you go away sometimes?'

'Can't afford it. Ever since we came here, we've been sliding deeper into debt, and Torquil simply ignores the figures. I can't do that. Kim – I mean Beverley's offer seemed to be the lifeline I'd almost given up hope of, and I couldn't let it slip through our fingers. I spelled it out to him: if we don't grab this chance, we're done for, and in trying to make him face reality, I said all sorts of things I didn't mean – or at least didn't mean him to know. So *stupid* of me,' she said fiercely, pushing her hair back as if thinking about it made her head ache. 'I said all the things I'd bottled up for months, and when I finally ran out of steam, Torquil said – I remember his words exactly – he said, "My poor darling! I never realised. I simply hadn't the foggiest. The last thing in the world I want is to make you unhappy."

'So I said, "Do you really mean you'll accept Kim's offer?" and he said, "Good lord, no. I'll do anything you like, my love, but you can't expect me to sell Strathtorran. Not when it's been in our family for three hundred years." And then... ' – her voice wobbled suddenly – 'he just walked out of the room, and things have been strained between us ever since. The maddening thing is that it was all for nothing. Neither of us ever saw Kim again, so I'll never know if her offer was genuine, or if she was just a Hanbury stooge.'

'Would Sir Archibald want Strathtorran as well as Glen Buie?'

'Of course he would.'

'Even though he's been told to stop stalking himself?'

'What difference does that make? If the whole forest was reunited, he could sell it for twice the price. There's nothing the Hanburys would like better than to see us scuttle back South with our tails between our legs.'

'Yet you seem – '

'Friendly enough?' Her laugh had a bitter ring. 'There's only one difficult Commandment, Inspector, and that applies just as much here as in the suburbs.'

Love thy neighbour, thought Robb, but already she was hurrying on, as if Torquil's absence had unfettered her tongue. 'When we moved here, we were determined to get off on the right foot with the Hanburys. We knew a hostel wasn't something they'd normally welcome, but damn it, we've got to live. We thought we could work things out together. After all, they're only summer raiders. They couldn't dictate how we live all year round.'

'Did they – do they – try to?'

She hesitated. 'The old guard are still pretty starchy. Gwennie, for instance, and Lady Priscilla, and that frightful Everard Cooper...'

'What about the younger generation?'

'Oh, Ashy's as much our friend as theirs. No problem with her. Who else? The Forbes boys I hardly know; Nicky was here one winter, poor kid, banished to the wilds by his father with orders to study for his A-level retakes. Some hope! We got to know him a bit then, but we haven't seen much of him since.'

'Was that the winter your brother-in-law's wife died? Will you tell us how that happened? Just after Christmas, wasn't it?'

Janie bit her lip and nodded. 'After Hogmanay. January 3rd. We were all feeling a bit flat – not to say hungover. The party was breaking up and most of our visitors were leaving. Alec Forrester was due to fly off to the States at the end of the week to take up his new job – that was before he was married, of course. We were all sad to see him go. Actually, that was the last time we ever saw him.'

She sighed. 'If he hadn't gone – if he had taken over from Archie – if, if, if! Where was I?'

'January 3rd,' supplied Winter.

'Yes. Pouring with rain as usual, and Eliza said she was feeling ghastly, so Torquil took Ian to the ferry. He was due to rejoin his regiment in Ulster after catching the night boat from Stranraer.'

'Did he and Eliza part on good terms?'

Janie made a curious little noise in her throat, which seemed to indicate equal reluctance to tell tales or lies. 'Not all that,' she said eventually. 'It crossed my mind that they'd had a – a disagreement. A bit of teeth-gritting over the goodbyes.'

'Go on.'

'Well, I'm ashamed to say that after they all left, I went straight back to bed, and I thought Eliza would do the same. When I woke up it was already starting to get dark, and I was alone in the house.'

'What time was that?'

'Oh, three-ish. Then the dogs came scratching at the door, wanting their dinner, and that's when I began worrying, because Eliza's Jack Russell was very much her dog, and simply never left her. I fed them, and little Tigger began whining to go out again, and I was sure something was wrong, so I rang around, but no one knew where she was. As soon as Torquil came back from Stranraer we got together everyone who was even half sober, and set out to search, but of course it was hopeless in the dark.'

'Did the stalkers from Glen Buie help search?'

'Oh, yes. And even Nicky, though he'd been in bed with 'flu and Mary Grant tried to stop him going out. It was a pig of a night. Everyone joined in...' She cocked her head, listening. 'Hullo! Listen to that. Davie McTavish is in a hurry.'

Seconds later both Robb and Winter heard the distant wail of a siren.

'Check the R/T,' snapped Robb, and Winter sprinted across the gravel to where the Land Rover was parked. Below the dashboard, a red light was flashing.

By the time Robb rounded the corner of the building, Winter had turned the vehicle in its own length and shoved open the passenger door. 'Trouble at the Lodge,' he said as Robb eased his stiff leg aboard.

'Quick as you like, then.' Robb's hand sought automatically for the seat-belt he knew wasn't functional as the vehicle swung out of the chestnut tunnel and between tall stone pillars, then headed up the track towards Glen Buie.

★★★★★

Old hands that they were at coping with crises, Gwennie and Mary Grant had restored a semblance of calm in their respective domains before the police car swept under the gate-arch, with Robb's Land Rover close behind. They found that Marjorie had been coaxed into bed with Valium and hotwater bottles, Ishy slapped out of hysterics, and Sir Archie was trying, like a worried sheepdog, to round up his scattered flock. In twenty minutes he had aged ten years.

'Ashy and her mother went up to the trout-loch, so I've sent a ghillie to fetch them back,' he told Robb. 'John Forbes has taken Maya off to fish the river – without a word to me, naturally. They could be anywhere on six miles of river. It drives me *mad,*' he said with suppressed fury, 'the way people drift off without leaving word of where they're going. Johnny knows that perfectly well, but does he care? Does he pay any attention to what I say?'

'They can't be far, darling. They've only been gone an hour.' Gwennie took his arm in a comforting grip, but he shook her off as if his nerves were strung too tight to bear her touch.

'All this bloody week,' he muttered. 'One ghastly thing after another.'

'Who else is missing, sir?'

Gwennie said, 'Nicky may have gone into Tounie. Mary asked him to get some crayfish, and if he can't buy them at the harbour, he'll have taken the ferry across.'

Silently Robb endorsed the complaint about drifters, but there was no point in voicing it now. If backed into a corner, Sir Archie would be on the blower to old Blood-and-Guts before you could say knife, and at this point the less interference from above the better.

'Everyone else accounted for?' They nodded. 'Why didn't you tell me that Benjamin was missing?'

Sir Archie groaned. 'Don't rub it in. We thought he'd sloped off to another of those concerts, and when he didn't show at dinner, we supposed he was afraid of getting a rocket from his mother. He knew she'd be furious because he'd sneaked away from the stalking-party, and I daresay he'd got wind of the fact that I had a bone to pick with him, too.'

'What bone was that, sir?'

Sir Archie beckoned him into the study and waved him to a chair. 'No reason not to tell you, now the poor boy's dead,' he said after a moment's thought. 'The fact is, young Ben was crazy about cars. Obsessed with them. Couldn't keep his hands off them. He'd been in trouble at school for pinching a master's car and driving it off the road. My sister paid him off, and we managed to keep it out of the papers. It gave Ben a fright, and we hoped he'd learned his lesson, but – '

'Was he doing it again? Joyriding?'

'Listen,' said Sir Archie heavily. 'Yesterday morning one of the crofters asked to see me. Name of Buchan. Angus Buchan. One of his Blackface rams had gone AWOL and he'd been searching for it for days. Eventually he found it dead below the bank on that sharp bend in the loch-road just a couple of miles from here. It had obviously been hit by a car. Then Mrs Buchan remembered seeing a red sports car skid badly there last Tuesday evening.'

'Your son's car?'

'There aren't many red sports cars around here. But from her description the driver sounded like Ben.'

'Have you spoken to your son about it?'

'He's off running errands for the cook,' said Sir Archie with a return of the pent-up exasperation, 'though why she can't get Duncan or one of the boys to fetch her bloody crayfish is beyond me.'

'The game dealer usually comes on Friday, right? Who, besides yourself, knew the collection day had been altered?' asked Robb after a few minutes' consideration.

'Mary knew. And Ashy – I remember mentioning it to her.'

'Sandy? Fergus?'

'I doubt it. The collection day doesn't make much difference as far as they're concerned. That chiller can take twenty stags, and we never get that many in a week. Top of the range model. I put it in last year. I wasn't having bloody Brussels saying our hygiene wasn't up to scratch.'

'You don't keep it locked?'

'Of course we do.'

'Who knows where the keys are kept?'

'Everyone,' said Sir Archie, and rubbed his eyes wearily. 'Whoever unlocked that chiller yesterday has to be one of us.'

★★★★★

Mary Grant folded her hands in her lap and placed her well-shaped calves decorously sideways. 'She was no' a bad lassie, but she hadna been brought up tae service,' she said judiciously, when asked the reason for Elspeth's dismissal. 'She didna take kindly tae orders.'

'It must be difficult to get girls to work here,' suggested Robb, and she gave a scornful snort.

'That one didna know the meaning of work!' Her constraint in speaking ill of the dead rapidly evaporated as she continued with mounting indignation, 'Always wanting time off and blethering about unsocial hours – oh, she'd a grand idea of her rights, and none at all of her duties. But what could ye expect, brought up the way she'd been? It was wasting breath tae try tae change her, as I told her leddyship right out.'

'You complained about your niece? To Lady Hanbury?'

'And why not? I never asked for her in my kitchen, not that she spent a wheen time there. Too busy playing her tapes wi' young Ben tae fash if vegetables were peeled or no. She'd no training, and little respect, and if I raised a hand to her she'd threaten me with the Social. Her leddyship turned a blind eye as long as she could, even when Elspeth left Ishy tae serve dinner alone, but she had tae heed me in the end.'

'She left Ishy alone on your day off last Tuesday?' Robb remembered old Catriona's description of Elspeth dressed for the concert, and felt things were falling into place at last.

'I'd have sacked her then and good riddance,' said Mary Grant, the hard woman. 'Her leddyship's too soft – doesna like trouble among the staff. She gave her warning: one more complaint from me, and that was it. "Nosy old besom," says Elspeth, with her leddyship hardly out of the room. "She can't boss me around." "You'll keep a civil tongue in your head," I told her. "One more peep from you and your feet willna touch the ground." After that, she minded me, but when Miss Marjie caught her in Benjamin's bedroom after dinner, the fat was in the fire and her leddyship told her to pack her bag.'

'Was Elspeth upset? Angry?'

Mary considered. 'More angry, I'd say, sir, though her leddyship gave her four weeks' pay instead of notice. Nothing was ever her own fault, not with Elspeth.' Belatedly she recollected the circumstances of her niece's death and added with a nod at convention, 'Well, she's paid for her folly now, poor wean; but what in the world were the pair of them at, there in the larder where they'd no business to be?'

'That,' said Robb, 'is a question we'd all like answered.'

Chapter Nineteen

'ROUND UP EVERYONE who was here when Eliza McNeil died, and make them account for themselves between noon and three o'clock yesterday,' snapped Robb, harassed now, and deeply worried. He was also keenly aware of living on borrowed time. The long-drawn-out and, from his point of view, most welcome armed siege in Kilmarnock had ended peacefully, and the ravening media pack, cheated of drama there, was likely to turn its attention here. Brash reporters would demand a press conference where they could trip him up and tie him in knots in order to fabricate sensational headlines: *Killer Stalks Blood Mountain. Teens in Freezer Tragedy.*

'Concentrate on the men. Find out if anyone went near the larder after the stalking party left yesterday, but first make sure of everyone's whereabouts. I want the whole lot together under one roof, Strathtorrans included. No one, repeat no one, is to go anywhere without my permission. Got that?'

Winter nodded at McTavish, and they hurried from the study. Robb tapped his biro against his teeth, staring down at the contour model, then ran his forefinger lightly over the thread of path that ran from the back of Strathtorran House, over the shoulder of Ben Shallachan, and down to the sheltered bay in which the salmon-cages were tethered. Beside the tiny matchstick pier lay a minuscule ferryboat half the size of a walnut, with a wisp of cottonwool above the funnel and a scrap of flag emblazoned *Island Maid*.

That's the way he came back, he thought. Too far on foot, impossible by car, but a mountain biker could get from the salmon farm to Loch a Bealach in less than an hour. The car-crazy teenager, the long bag of golf clubs: it all fitted.

He got up restlessly and stared out of the window at the sea-loch whipped to a creamy foam by the incoming westerly breeze. Winter's voice close behind made him start: did he have to creep about like a bloody panther?

'McNeil brought two stags from Strathtorran and hung them in the larder between noon and one o'clock, according to Duncan,' reported Winter. 'He was in his garden, and McNeil shouted to him that the beasts were weighed and labelled. "For once," Duncan said.'

'Where is he now?'

'Still trying to trace him, sir. He hasn't been at the fish-farm today. The lads there think he's off on his mountain bike because it's missing from its shed behind the office.'

Bingo! thought Robb, but his sense of pressure increased. There would be time enough to sift and slot together evidence when all were safely gathered in. Until then...

'Looks like Donny's found one of the strays,' said Winter, recognising the red woollen cap. 'Now, which – ?'

It was John Forbes, panting, white-faced, visibly distressed. Before they could move to intercept him, Gwennie ran out from the french window and hurried across the lawn. They watched her speaking earnestly, shaking her head. Eventually she put an arm round his shoulders and led him indoors.

'I'm sorry, sir, but I couldna keep it from him,' said the young ghillie defensively, following Sir Archie into the study. His gaze flickered uneasily over the leather-bound books, the high-backed wing chairs and the rugs worn bald by generations of recumbent dogs. 'He'd a fish on the line when I found him, and didna wish tae leave the water.'

'Never mind that,' said Robb. 'Where's Mrs Forrester? Wasn't she with him?'

'No, sir. She was gone from the pool where Mr Johnny left her, but there's still a mile of bank canna be seen from the track. Will I take another look for ye?'

Robb hesitated, glancing at the map. From the bridge spanning the Greeting Pool, the Glen Buie fishing extended three miles down- and three upstream before losing its identity in the maze of small burns and lochans that formed the spawning pools.

'How long would it take you to walk the length of the river?'

'Look here,' broke in Sir Archie with authority, 'we'd better take my car to the bridge and split our forces. 'I'll go one way and Donny can go the other. That'll be quickest.'

'Just a moment, sir.' Further investigation would become impossible if people rushed hither and thither on ill-defined missions. 'Sergeant Winter will go with one of you, and Constable McTavish with the other. Tell me just where Mrs Forrester was last seen, Donald.'

'By here.' The boy's bitten nail scratched a dent in the map about a mile above the Greeting Pool. Robb bent close to peer at the tiny print.

ALT NA CHORAIN, MAIDEN POOL; FALLS; TIGHTROPE.

'Come on, we're wasting time,' urged Sir Archie, and Robb nodded, understanding his need for action, however futile; and wished that he, too, could stride up or down the river bank instead of waiting passively here for the next disaster to strike.

For a few minutes after the searchers drove away, he went on staring at the map, thinking of accidents that could have been murder; of times and distances and bodies in deep black pools. A rap on the door disturbed his musing.

'See who that is, Peg.'

Voices murmured in the passage. Wpc Kenny returned. 'It's Lady Priscilla, sir, and Miss Macleod, wondering if you'd spare a minute.'

Lady Priscilla's long horse-face was pale and purposeful,

and all the bounce had gone out of Ashy.

'So sorry to barge in, Inspector, but my daughter has something to tell you,' she said with controlled anger. 'Go on, Ashy.'

'Not with you here.' Ashy was subdued but defiant.

'Very well. I'll leave you to it, but no running out, mind! If you don't come clean, I'll tell him myself.'

'*Go away, Mummy!* Don't talk to me about *omerta*,' she said bitterly as the door closed. 'My mother doesn't know the meaning of the word. And if you tell me the road to hell is paved with good intentions, I'll – '

'Miss Macleod, this is a murder enquiry,' Robb cut in harshly. 'If you have something relevant to tell me, please do it now and don't waste my time.'

The edge to his voice startled her as he had intended. She blinked, gulped, and almost visibly took herself in hand.

'Oh, God,' she said unevenly, 'I've done something really stupid. Criminal, I think. And now Maya's missing... All I can say is that it seemed a good idea at the time.'

★★★★★

Johnny will be wondering where I am, thought Maya, flicking her line into the deep, dark water and waiting for the current to carry the fly across the narrow rocky pool. She felt a twinge of guilt at slipping away without a word to him.

'I've come to rescue you,' Nicky had smiled, appearing unexpectedly on the river bank while she was struggling to unravel a snarl of Gordian complexity without attracting an offer of help from Johnny. 'Where's the guru?' he added. 'I thought he was teaching you to cast.'

Maya had put her finger to her lips and pointed to the slender tip of a rod projecting from the bank some forty yards downstream. An hour's instruction by Johnny had been every bit as tedious as she had anticipated.

'Come with me. I know a much better place than this,' said Nicky, eyes dancing with mischief.

Maya was glad enough to be rescued. 'OK, but just hang on a tick while I tell Johnny.'

'Do you really want him tagging along? He will, you know.'

'Well – ' Maya had hesitated – 'maybe not...' and she had followed Nicky along the bank and out of sight while Johnny fished on, oblivious.

'Let me carry the rod. This is where we cross,' said Nicky leading her towards a triangle of cables stretched from one bank of the river to the other; but Maya took one look at the perilous drop beneath the wires and shook her head firmly.

'No way. It gives me vertigo just to see it.'

'Oh, come on! It's not as bad as it looks, honestly.'

'Can't I cross some place else?'

'Well, there's the ford, but I'm afraid it'll go over your boots.'

'I can take them off,' said Maya, and she had crossed the shallow, fast-running stream barefooted, with her boots in one hand and clinging to Nicky with the other, glad of his support because although the water was no more than knee-deep, its force was quite enough to sweep her off her feet. On the farther bank she had dried them as best she could, and replaced socks and boots. Now, under Nicky's instructions, she was trying to catch one of the big silver salmon she could see cruising among the rocks, while he sat smoking and watching twenty yards away, with his anorak hood pulled over his head and his back against a rock.

'You try,' she said at last, joining him under the sheltering ledge as the long-threatening rain began in earnest.

'No, no, keep at it. You're doing fine. This is just what we want to freshen up the pool. As soon as the water rises the fish will start to take.'

'Don't you think we should be getting back?' She stifled a yawn. 'Sorry! I didn't sleep much last night.'

'Something on your mind?'

'I was thinking about your aunt Marjorie. It seems kinda

mean to let her go on worrying where Ben has gotten to.'

'I know.' Nicky threw his stub into the water; his expression was serious now, even sombre. 'You heard what they were saying in the serving-room yesterday morning, didn't you?'

'I heard them fix a meeting at the larder, so that he could give back her tapes.'

Nicky smiled, his mood lightening. 'Look, Maya, my advice – for what it's worth – is to let sleeping dogs lie. Ben will turn up in his own good time, and quite honestly I think Aunt Marjorie would worry even more if she knew he'd gone off somewhere with Elspeth.'

'Maybe so.' Unconvinced, she got up and bent her head forward to let the water drain from her hat-brim. 'I guess I'll go on back now, just the same.'

'Wait!' He laid a thin hand on her arm, drawing her back under the rock. 'There's something I want to – '

Abruptly he broke off, and following his gaze she saw a kammo-clad figure moving along the path on the other side of the river. *Slinking,* she thought, though she would have found it hard to say exactly what it was about that steady, stealthy gait that immediately suggested furtiveness, a wish to remain unseen.

'Who's that?' she asked in a low voice, although the noise of water would have covered anything less than a shout.

'Ian McNeil, after our salmon again.'

'Why would he want to do that?'

'Because they're ours, of course.' His lips tightened. 'I'm going over to have a word with him. Wait here.'

It didn't make sense to Maya. Why would a man who raised captive salmon for a living want to poach yet more fish from his neighbour's river? Wet and tired as she was, she dreaded the idea of confrontation, the inevitable delay in getting back to the Lodge.

'I'll come with you,' she said quickly, hoping that if she was there to act as a buffer, they might feel obliged to stay civilised, but Nicky simply shook his head.

'Won't be long,' he said tersely, and was gone before she

could protest.

Damn, damn, damn! she thought, watching him swing rapidly across the wire bridge and hurry up the bank to the path. Now I'm stuck here until he comes back.

There could be no doubt that the river was rapidly rising; rocks upon which water had broken in white spray when she began fishing were now submerged, and the lazy swirls of current had straightened out to form an urgent, tumbling torrent as feeder burns high up in the hills delivered fresh rainwater to the main stream. Remembering the unexpected force of water against her legs as she clung to Nicky's hand, she doubted very much that she could cross even the ford alone now. That left two equally disagreeable options: either she faced a wet wait of indeterminate length, or she must tackle the wire bridge.

★★★★★

'Let me get this straight,' said Robb. 'You hid Beverley's body beneath the boat because you thought she had been shot by Fergus?'

'It seemed absolutely obvious,' said Ashy with exaggerated patience. 'She was dead, but only very recently, and from where I was sitting on Carn Mhor, I had seen Fergus fairly hurtling down the shoulder of Carn Beag, nearly as far as the path; and then a few minutes later climbing up again, still carrying the rifle.'

'Had you heard a shot?'

'No, but that doesn't prove anything. When our own party got down to the path, I said I wanted a pee and dropped behind Sandy and Archie, and there I found her, right down by the loch. It looked as if Fergus must have shot her.'

'And when did you begin to doubt that?'

'Not soon enough,' said Ashy. 'I'm sorry now that I even tried to cover up for him, but at the time I was so shocked that I simply wasn't thinking straight. I just pulled the boat over the top of her to give myself time to work out what to do next, and spent the rest of that day and most of the night wondering how on earth I was going to make sure no one else put two and two together.'

She looked defiantly at Robb. 'OK, yes; I went back to the trout-loch next day, saying I wanted to sketch it. Then I sent Maya off to fish from the bank, while Nicky walked up to the Prince's Rock, and when I was sure they were out of sight, I nipped over to where I'd left the boat, heaved poor old Bev into it, and brought her down to the jetty. Then I loaded her on the pony — that was a struggle, I can tell you — and down the hill to the river path. I tied a good big rock to her legs, and dumped her in the Greeting Pool where, apart from that interfering ass of a stepfather of mine — '

'Please confine yourself to the facts,' said Robb coldly.

'Oh, OK. Well, once she was in the river, I thought that was that. But of course I didn't know that Maya had already looked under the boat.'

'You didn't telephone the hostel to say that Beverley had cut short her holiday?'

'Good lord, no. And I was amazed when Gwennie said one of the maids had taken a message from Bev on Stornoway, but Elspeth is such a scatterbrain, I thought — ' She stopped and bit her lip.

'Go on,' said Robb brutally. The less opportunity she had for digression, the more likely he was to hear the truth.

'Well, of course I was horrified when my stepfather went and fished Bev's body out of the water. As soon as I could, I got Fergus to meet me at the pub — you saw us there the other evening, didn't you? — and told him what I had done and why.'

'How did he react?'

'He wasn't in the least grateful,' she said indignantly. 'In fact, he called me an interfering you-know-what, and when I tried to make him see sense, he walked out on me. The end of a beautiful friendship,' said Ashy, pulling a face, 'and all I was trying to do was help him.'

'But why did you think Fergus should have wanted to shoot her? Had he a special reason to want to get rid of her?'

Silence from Ashy. Robb tried again. 'Was she threatening him in some way?'

'Fergus is the sort of man who hates being pinned down.' She gave him a sideways glance.

'Was Beverley trying to?'

She shook her blonde head. 'Not Bev, but Eliza McNeil. Ian's late wife.'

'Who drowned in the Greeting Pool nearly three years ago?'

Ashy nodded sombrely. 'She and Bev were mates, you know. They ran a catering business together. I thought Bev might have known that Fergus had been Eliza's lover…and…and… You know she was pregnant when she drowned?'

'Ah,' said Robb, as a chunk of jigsaw clicked into place. 'So you envisaged a sequence of events in which – correct me if I'm wrong – he wanted to break off the relationship and she didn't – right? And she tried to pin him down, as you put it, by threatening to tell her husband – right? And she persuaded him to meet her at the Greeting Pool to sort it out on January 3rd three years ago, and somehow or other Eliza ended up in the river? Is that what you thought?'

'It all fitted,' said Ashy defensively. 'But when I suggested it to Fergus, he hit the roof and said he wouldn't have slept with Eliza McNeil if she'd been the last woman on earth. He called her a bloody cradle-snatcher who'd got more than she bargained for, and if she was pregnant it was certainly not by him.'

'And you believed him?'

'Oddly enough, yes; but that makes no difference because he doesn't give a damn what I think. He's hardly spoken to me since.'

In his mind, Robb caught an echo of old Catriona's verdict. '*Breeks!*' That was the mischief Eliza McNeil indulged in when her man was away. And what had she added? '*None too choosy who wore them, forbye.*' He had assumed she meant Eliza preferred a bit of rough, but for Fergus to call her a cradle-snatcher gave

Catriona's assessment a very different complexion. How old had Nicky been that wet, dreary winter? Studying for A-level retakes – say seventeen or eighteen? It was by no means impossible.

Putting that thought aside for the moment, he said, 'What makes you so sure the baby wasn't her husband's?'

'Morag heard her tell him so,' said Ashy simply. 'She was in the kitchen with her ears flapping while they were yelling at each other just next door. When Eliza said she was in love with this other man, Morag assumed she meant Fergus, because she's not only his great-aunt, but his greatest fan as well. But of course if said lover-boy was *Alec,* it all makes much more sense, because it was when Alec left for America that Eliza got so down in the dumps.'

'You're surely not suggesting that Alec Forrester killed her? I thought he left for America two days before she died?'

'Shock, horror! Not Alec! Oh, heavens, no! But suppose,' said Ashy quickly, 'suppose Eliza had told Ian that she was pregnant with Alec's baby? Suppose she'd asked for a divorce so that she could marry *Alec?'*

'I'm not in the business of supposing,' Robb told her curtly. 'Now if that's all you've –'

'Ian could have shot Bev,' said Ashy, ignoring the hint. 'Don't forget I met him coming down the path by Loch a Bealach just after I'd pulled the boat over the body. And, of course, Ian was the only person at Strathtorran who knew who Bev really was, and where she had come from.'

Personal as well as professional experience told Robb that she would go on fabricating her fantasies and twisting facts to accommodate them until he booted her out of the study; knew, too, that this sudden excess of helpfulness was designed to cover her own misdemeanours so deep that they escaped scrutiny, a strategy dear to his own middle daughter.

'I'll bear it in mind,' he said, rising to end the interview, but Ashy still lingered with her hand on the door-handle.

'Duncan told me that Ian put some stags in the chiller yesterday.'

'Yes, we heard about that.'

'And he's always prowling about the river.' She shivered. 'I wish I knew where Maya was.'

Not half as much as I do, thought Robb.

Chapter Twenty

SERGEANT WINTER'S SINEWY legs set a cracking pace up the river path, with Donny on his heels and Sir Archie labouring a hundred yards behind. After the younger men had waited several times with ill-concealed impatience for him to catch up, he finally acknowledged that he would have to let them go on without him. Donny was a sensible lad. He'd keep the cop on course and bring him safe back.

'Sorry. I'm holding you up too much,' he said as he collapsed, panting, on a rock to get his wind. 'Go on at your own pace, and I'll meet you back at the car.'

For a moment Winter looked as if he would object, but Donny said firmly, 'Verra good, sir,' and set off without a backward glance.

Irritated and dejected by this further proof that he was cracking up, Sir Archie watched them power-walk away, and sought consolation in the right-hand pocket of his Barbour.

'Damn and blast it,' he muttered, fingers encountering unfamiliar shapes and textures. Someone else's coat had been hung on his peg; further examination of the contents revealed lipsalve, a half-eaten bar of Kendal mint cake, and several plastic bags, unattractively greasy inside, and a small bottle of insect repellent. The long, tubular shape he had hoped was his pipe turned out to be a nine-inch section of antler, hollowed and filled with lead, the hand-made 'priest' for giving a salmon the *coup de grace* which he remembered Sandy presenting to his sister for her seventeenth birthday.

Marjorie's coat, then. Why the hell couldn't she use her own peg? Mint cake was no substitute for tobacco, but he shared the half-bar with his labrador, then turned back along the river path, giving the dog permission to range ahead. Presently she left him, and vanished through the roots of an alder towards the water.

'Here, girl!' he called after a couple of minutes' wait. He whistled, and she appeared farther along the path, carrying with careful pride a shining silver salmon balanced in her black velvet mouth.

'Thank you.' He took it from her with pats and praise and no little astonishment. A beautiful fresh-run fish, still iridescent, with a couple of sea-lice clinging, and a good six pounds in weight.

The labrador watched, eyes laughing, ears expectantly cocked. He knew that expression well.

'Hey-lorst!' he encouraged, and she dived down the bank again. Sir Archie followed just in time to see her draw an almost identical fish from under a tree-root. Further investigation revealed a third, and his astonishment turned to outrage.

'This is the outside of enough. This is just too bloody much!' he exclaimed aloud.

He examined the fish minutely. Above each tail-fluke, faint but discernible, was the mark of a wire. There was not much doubt in his mind whose work this was, and he couldn't be far away. Those fish hadn't been out of the water more than fifteen minutes. If he went quietly down to the wire bridge, there was an excellent chance of nabbing him red-handed.

'Good girl. Clever girl!' He made much of Linnhe and called her to heel. Cautiously he began to work his way through the rocks and scrubby trees that lined the riverbank, eyes alert for any clue to the poacher's whereabouts. *Getting warm,* he thought, spotting a branch bent back, and his heart-rate quickened. *Softlee softlee catchee monkee...*

He was still hidden in the trees some fifty yards from the wire bridge when a scream pierced through the steady roar of water. High, thin, terrified.

Maya! he thought with sick, familiar dread. Slipping and stumbling on the rough ground, he ran as fast as he could towards the sound, with the black dog bounding ahead.

★★★★★

Two steps into the swollen brown waters of the ford had been enough to convince Maya that she could not cross there alone. The formerly clear shallows in which every pebble shone distinctly had been transformed by the downpour into a gurgling torrent the colour of milky coffee, and hardly had her right foot gropingly joined her left under its heaving surface, than the borrowed rod was plucked from her grasp and whirled downstream with no hope of recovery. Indeed, her attempt to save it was nearly her undoing. For a long, horrible moment she fought to keep her balance against the relentless thrust of water, and when she managed to splash and stagger the few feet to the bank she was frightened as well as very wet. Archie had called this place 'untamed,' and now she saw exactly what he meant.

That left only the wire bridge.

With water squelching from her boots, she clambered over rocks and up the shaley bank until she reached the stout tree round which the lower wire was looped, with a hook-and-eye tension adjustment a couple of feet from the trunk. A large metal peg of the kind used to guy marquees secured the upper wires to the rock-face. They felt reassuringly taut when grasped in both hands, and without giving herself time to think what would happen if she slipped, Maya placed both feet sideways on the lower wire and forced herself to slide away from the bank, as she had seen Nicky do.

Keep breathing, she told herself. Keep moving, *don't look down!*

Five yards, ten yards, fifteen...right foot sideways, left up to join it, right foot out again; body bent against the wind, hand-wires braced apart for maximum stability. She was doing fine, nearing the middle, no wobbles, no vertigo...

A tremor ran through the left hand-wire, but she ignored it, sliding her feet in carefully co-ordinated rhythm to minimise bounce, careful not to hurry. Again the wire vibrated, and this time she flicked a glance sideways – just a glimpse from the corner of an eye – and through the veil of rain she saw a man on the bank.

Nicky! In the swamping rush of relief, she was tempted to wave, but this was the slackest, most perilous part of the crossing, demanding all her concentration. Hard though she tried not to look down, she was well aware how close the bottom wire hung over the turbulent brown torrent.

Whoops! A gust of wind threatened her balance. For a sickening instant she swung to and fro, feeling fresh tremors in the hand-wire, while the racing, spray-capped water drew her gaze with magnetic force. Dragging her eyes away, she looked full at Nicky, and saw with a shock of disbelief that the vibration came from the hacksaw he was rasping across the wire. As in a nightmare, she saw him seize it in both hands, shaking it as the strands parted, his expression absorbed and intent.

'Cut it out!' she screamed. 'Stop it, Nicky. What are you doing?'

Dumb question. There was no doubt what he was doing, or that he would soon succeed. For ten, fifteen seconds she clung desperately, screaming for help; then just before the wire snapped, she launched herself in a shallow dive, aiming for the slack, scum-topped water beyond the reach of the current.

The shock of the icy torrent nearly stopped her heart. Down she went, tumbling over and over, and when her head broke the surface at last she was forty yards below the bridge and travelling fast, with her trailing clothes so tangled about her arms that they seemed certain to drag her under.

'*Don't fight it,*' rumbled her father's deep, warm bass inside her head, just as he had after she tumbled into the river in Colorado when she was eight years old. '*Lie on your back, arms out to the side, and pretty soon the current will wash you to the bank.*'

But this wasn't Abner's Creek on a blazing afternoon in June. A snow-fed Scottish spate river could chill a body into numb helplessness in just a few minutes. If she didn't get out of the water before that, her chances of survival were slim. Nevertheless, she struggled into the classic cross position, head back and arms stretched so wide that her fingers scraped the water-slick walls of the gorge, but there was nothing she could do to arrest her progress.

Near the bottom of the gorge the cliffs leaned so close together that an athlete could have leapt from one side to the other, and she saw with horror that Nicky was kneeling there, waiting for her to float past. He must have sprinted across the point, and positioned himself directly above the swirling black water. As in slow motion, she saw him manoeuvre a boulder the size of a case of wine to the lip of the cliff, waiting poised like a cat at a mousehole until she was right beneath him, and then, in the last second before he heaved it over the edge, she glimpsed a black dog bound from the trees and rush up to him, planting paws on his shoulders from behind as it licked at his face.

Then the boulder was falling, falling, blotting out the light, and a tidal wave of white water swamped her.

She must have blacked out briefly, because when she regained her senses, choking and spluttering, she was clear of the gorge and cliffs, being borne rapidly between the sedgy banks of the Falls Pool towards the foaming, rock-strewn cataract. She struggled weakly, trying to edge out of the mainstream, but her limbs were heavy and helpless against the powerful suck of the current.

'Oh, God!' she moaned weakly. 'What'll I do?'

With an enormous effort, she managed to turn on her side and there, in direct answer to prayer, she saw the kammo-clad figure of Ian McNeil bounding along the river path, trying to get downstream of her. She had no time to wonder at his reappearance before he plunged waist-deep in the water, pulled out the hook of an extending gaff, and struck it hard into her trailing oilskin slicker.

For a long, agonising moment, it was a toss-up which of them would prove the heavier. McNeil had nothing to hold on to, and the weight of water together with Maya's momentum threatened to drag him over the falls with her.

'Don't move!' he yelled above the water's roar and, terrified that the slicker would rip, she lay like a log while he struggled unavailingly to pull her to safety.

'Catch hold of that, man!' Donny's pulling-rope was thrust into Ian's free hand; and suddenly the empty riverbank became a scene of shouting, splashing and confusion, as three strong men hauled Maya clear of the water and laid her gently on the bank.

Chapter Twenty-One

'IT WAS AFTER I told him I'd heard Ben and Elspeth fixing up a date at the stag larder that Nicky began pressuring me to go fish with him,' said Maya in her husky drawl. 'I was talking to Ashy before dinner, and Nicky was filling glasses. I remember telling him I planned on fishing with Johnny, and he tried to persuade me to go with him instead.' She paused, shaking her head. 'You know, I was surprised – but maybe kinda flattered, too – because up till then he hadn't had a lot to say to me. I thought he might be mad at me.'

'Why?' asked Robb.

'You know Alec left me his share of Glen Buie? Well, I thought Nicky might not be happy about that.' She smiled wanly, and laced her fingers through Ian McNeil's as he perched behind her on the back of the sofa's faded gold brocade. 'I guess I was right, too.'

Warmed through and through at last, Maya had regained her glowing colour and most of her composure, yet Robb sensed strain and kept his questions low-key.

'You say he cut the wire bridge while you were crossing?'

She swallowed convulsively and moved her head, eyes closing, still scarcely believing that shy, hesitant Nicky could have done his best to drown her. 'I thought at first he was playing some dumb kind of joke, but when I saw it was for real, I jumped before it snapped. I mean, that wire could have whipped round me. Taken my head off.'

McNeil's hand tightened on hers. 'Don't think about it.'

'I tell you, I can't stop thinking about it. I see it over and over.'

'Go on,' rumbled Robb. 'You'll find it helps to talk it through.'

'You sound like a shrink.' The teasing smile was a shadow of its former self. 'OK, so there I was in the water, and the next I saw he was rolling this big chunk of rock up to the edge of the cliff. He was planning on dropping it right on top of me.'

'But instead he fell in himself? I suppose he missed his footing – ?'

'Or maybe the dog caught him off-balance,' said Maya.

There was a moment's silence, then Robb said quietly, 'What dog?'

'I'm not sure. I just got a quick sight of it running down the slope and jumping up at Nicky.'

'Jumping up?'

'As if it was glad to see him. You know, the way dogs do.'

'Big dog? Small dog?'

'Kind of chunky. Dark.' She glanced at McNeil. 'You didn't see it?'

'Can't say I did.'

Too late she caught his warning frown and breathed in sharply. 'I'm sorry. Maybe I just imagined it.'

'Makes no odds,' said McNeil easily; but of course it did. All the difference between *Did he fall?* and *Was he pushed?* The difference between accident and murder. At Glen Buie, dogs did not wander about on their own, and as the police surgeon had already pointed out, the torpedo-shaped contusion above Nicky's left ear was hardly consistent with a fall into water.

Pushing the matter of the dog into the mental file marked 'Pending', Robb took Maya through the rest of what she had overheard by the serving-hatch the previous morning, and she told him how Elspeth had blamed Ben for getting her sacked, and warned him he was in for trouble himself when Angus Buchan talked to his uncle.

'Ah, yes.' Robb nodded. Time for another word with Sir Archibald, he thought.

Thanking Maya, he left the drawing-room, and followed Gwennie's directions down a long, dimly-lit passage lined with mounted stags' heads to a small, square work-room adjoining the scullery where, under the glare of an Anglepoise lamp, Sir Archie sat at a carpenter's bench equipped with a miniature vice. Thread, glue, tweezers, hooks, coloured feathers and fluff in various shades were laid out neatly to hand. In a hinged box beside him, row upon row of home-dressed salmon and trout flies were ranged by size along the underside of the lid.

A peat fire smouldered in a small basket grate, with grey-muzzled Linnhe's back pressed so hard against it that she looked in danger of scorching her thick black coat. Even with the shutters closed, the curtains fluttered, and a background roar of surf gave notice that winter was on its way.

'That you, Robb? Come in if you're coming and close the bloody door,' barked Sir Archie without looking round; and if he had added *And you can keep your bloody sympathy to yourself* the message could hardly have been clearer.

'Sorry to disturb you, sir.' Robb squeezed past the bench and stood by the fire.

'You're not disturbing me, for Christ's sake! God knows how long I've been waiting for you to come and have the courtesy to tell me what the hell's going on.' The square face lifted, eyes challenging, defences in place. 'I gather you're packing it in? Not looking for anyone else, according to Ashy.'

Thank you, Miss Macleod, thought Robb. 'We've a few loose ends to tie up, sir, but that's about the size of it,' he said equably.

'So it *was* Nicky.' A statement, not a question.

'When did you realise, sir?'

In the silence that followed, Robb waited, watching the averted profile as Sir Archie's blunt, capable fingers wound strands of yellow floss tightly round the shank of his fly and secured it with a dab of glue. At last he sighed, removed his half-moons, and turned.

'I didn't want to see what was staring me in the face,' he growled. 'You hear of parents shopping their delinquent children to the police when they find they can't cope any more, but it's not something I could bring myself to do. Besides,' he added bitterly, 'I thought I *could* cope. If it had been only Beverley, I'd have kept my mouth shut and dealt with my conscience alone, but when we found those children – ' he paused, closed his eyes momentarily, and went on harshly – 'I thought: that's it. This can't go on.'

About time too, thought Robb. Though his expression did not change, Sir Archie caught the thought and said irritably, 'Sit down, man. Don't hover over me like a damned hen-harrier. Blood's thicker than water, as you know very well.'

Robb took a chair as the grumbling voice went on, 'I blame myself, of course. I should have known better than to send a boy of eighteen up here to work on his own, out of season; but I was angry with him for messing up his exams though sheer bloody idleness, and I thought it might concentrate his mind to see how the other half lives. Wrong! Instead of getting down to his books, what must he do but fall head over ears for Ian McNeil's wife, Eliza. Ian was in Ulster. Eliza was lonely and bored. Nicky was bored and lonely... Work it out for yourself.'

A simple equation. Robb said, 'So...?'

'Old Catriona McNichol's as sharp as a knife. She saw what the form was and made no bones about letting me know, but like a fool I told her not to worry. It would blow over.'

'Do you think your son and Mrs McNeil were lovers?'

Sir Archie shrugged. 'That's more Ashy's territory than mine. She's always full of theories. In my view, Eliza was just amusing herself while Ian was away. I doubt if Nicky meant much to her, but that doesn't mean she wasn't above making use of him – or of his money. She still owned half that catering business she ran with that bloody woman.'

'*Gentlemen's Relish?*'

'That's right. It was in low water at the time, but Eliza got Nicky to bail it out, so they could sell it as a going concern. He never had any sense about money.'

'So that was how he met Beverley Tanner?'

'Initially, yes. But of course once she had her hooks well in, poor Nicky was sunk. Good causes, bad causes, downright frauds – whatever she wanted money for, he was expected to ante up. Once you pay the danegeld, you never get rid of the Dane.'

Abruptly he rose and went to open a cupboard. 'Hark at that wind! Time for us summer raiders to be going home. Come on, man, have a dram and don't give me any bullshit about being on duty.'

A glass in the hand would make it no more difficult to listen, and probably easier for Hanbury to talk, thought Robb, accepting the heavy tumbler.

'So – where were we? Beverley,' said Sir Archie with revulsion. 'She was soaking Nicky for all she was worth. I could see that the moment I set eyes on her. But Gwennie and I completely misread the situation. It never occurred to us that he hated her more than we did. She'd trapped him into marrying her –'

'You knew that, sir?'

'Ashy told me – but only after they'd pulled Beverley from the river. No: during the week she spent here, we were at our wits' end trying to keep Nicky in the family fold without appearing to freeze her out. Ironic, really, because according to Ashy *he* was breaking his brains trying to work out how to get rid of her.'

'Why did he bring her here in the first place?'

Sir Archie said sombrely, 'I suppose he reckoned that it's easier to set up an accident in a wild, empty place like this than it would be in SW1. He'd be on his own patch. He's been coming here every summer since he was eight years old, and he knew the forest like the back of his hand.'

'And she came because she thought she could make money out of it?'

'She thought he'd bankroll her plans to turn the whole

peninsula into a theme park,' said Sir Archie with bitter scorn. 'Of course, Nicky knew that was a complete non-starter. Torquil Strathtorran may be struggling, but he'd never sell the land.'

'Yet Lady Strathtorran was interested, I understand?'

'If wishes were horses, beggars would ride. Poor girl!' he added unexpectedly. 'I don't suppose she had much say in the matter, but if she *did* encourage Beverley to think she was in with a chance of buying Strathtorran, she played straight into Nicky's hands.'

'So – let me get this straight – in the event of your death, Nicholas would have inherited Glen Buie? What about Mrs Forrester's share?'

'I expect he thought she'd be glad enough to let him buy her out, or – ' a spasm crossed Sir Archie's face – 'maybe today's accident didn't happen on the spur of the moment. We'll never know. Maya has only a life interest in Glen Buie, you see. On her death Alec's property reverts to his mother, my wife –'

'So Nicholas could expect to inherit that as well?'

Sir Archie nodded, and said wearily, 'Beverley must have thought she'd got Glen Buie in the bag, but she still needed Strathtorran. As I see it, Nicky encouraged her to go and stay with them, and check in to report to him what she was doing each day. He must have set up that RV at the Prince's Rock on Tuesday, and shot her when she walked back to see why he wasn't waiting there. Of course, he was gambling that we'd be so relieved to be rid of her that we wouldn't give a damn where she'd gone or what she was up to.'

He brought his fist down on his knee in a gesture of exasperation. 'And that's precisely what would have happened if Ashy and Everard – blast them – hadn't fouled up his plans.'

He took a swig from his tumbler and leaned forward. 'But when Everard fished her out of the river, I did begin to wonder...' His voice died away with the sentence incomplete.

'Wonder what, sir?' prompted Robb.

'Who felt threatened enough to bump her off. As we've

all been telling you, she had made herself thoroughly disliked in the short time she'd been here, but your pathologist chap insisted she'd been killed last *Tuesday,* and that put most of this party's marksmen in the clear.' He ticked them off on his fingers. 'Gwennie and Priscilla were together all day, and Marjorie joined them in the afternoon. I could vouch for Johnny, Sandy, and Ashy. Everard and Fergus cancelled one another out, so who did that leave? Answer: Nicky. And where was he? Allegedly giving young Benjamin a lift into Tounie.'

'You mean he didn't take him there?'

'I mean he *took* him there, but he didn't bring him back.'

'You think Benjamin drove himself back? A boy of what – fourteen? Fifteen? Surely the ferrymen would have noticed?'

'Not if he drove back round the end of the sea-loch,' said Sir Archie. 'It's all of thirty miles as opposed to three from the ferry terminal, but as I said, Ben was always mad about cars. The longer the drive the better, from his point of view.'

Robb nodded slowly. 'So what you're suggesting is that he and Nicky went across together on the car-ferry, but returned separately?'

'I can't prove it, ' said Sir Archie heavily, 'but that's how it looks to me. Why would Nicky want to kick his heels in Tounie all afternoon? No: I guess he gave Benjamin the car-keys, and came back himself on the foot-ferry, which docks just behind the fish-farm.'

Carrying his rifle concealed in his golfing bag, thought Robb. Yes, it was feasible. Sheds at the fish farm were unlikely to be locked. He probably knew that Ian McNeil kept a mountain bike behind the office. Then two miles up the road to the forestry track, leave the bike at the junction with the Prince's Path, and Nicky could have been lying in wait on the shoulder of Ben Shallachan when Beverley popped up like a startled rabbit at the sound of Everard's shot.

He'd have to get Winter to check it out, but it felt right to him.

'And Elspeth?' he prompted, tying up loose ends. ' She was at the concert, too. I know she was late back that night.'

'She was indeed. According to Angus Buchan's wife, watching from her sick-bed, after the sports car skidded, a red-haired lassie jumped out. She said they stood in the road, arguing, then the young lad drove off and left her to walk. Chivalry!'

'And the car is a two-seater.' Robb nodded. That clinched it for him. While the wind soughed in the chimney and the labrador whined and paddled in her sleep, he visualised Nicky shouldering his rifle and climbing the Prince's Path, each long stride diminishing the distance between him and his quarry. To a marksman accustomed to stalk wild and wary deer, an unsuspecting human – a townie, at that – was a laughably easy target. How long had he followed her? How many times had he taken aim then decided to wait for an even better chance?

Everard Cooper had had four misses that day before shooting his Royal, and Nicky could have used any one of those shots to camouflage the sound of his own. Ashy had discovered the body still warm, still wearing an expression of outraged surprise. Had Beverley recognised her killer?

Unprofitable speculation: no hard evidence, nothing to convince a jury, and now with the murderer himself in the Tounie mortuary, no need to make a case against him. What did it matter that he, Robb, was privately certain that Nicky had died by his father's hand? Sergeant Winter was a natural bureaucrat who would feel duty bound to dot the i's and cross the t's, but as a pragmatist Robb knew that in police work more than many other areas of life it sometimes made better sense to play the Advantage Rule.

Now that he had completed the jigsaw to his own satisfaction, he felt inclined to let matters rest.

Sir Archie took out his pipe, knocked it against the grate, then returned it to his pocket. With his tweezers he picked up a tiny barred hackle, measured it against the shank of the salmon-fly under construction in the vice, and delicately bound in the quill with thread, expertly using hands and teeth to secure the ends before finishing off with a blob of varnish.

'There!' He removed it from the vice, blew on the varnish, examined the fly minutely through his half-moons, and held it out for Robb's inspection. 'What do you think?'

'I'm no judge, but it looks good enough to kill a few fish, sir.'

'Keep it.' A moment's pause, then he went on evenly, 'I expect you know the medic's told me to stop stalking? I've asked young McNeil to take charge here until I can sort out something permanent. Turn the poacher into gamekeeper, eh? It's what I meant to do after my stepson Alec died, but my wife insisted it would be wrong to bypass Nicky. I wish I hadn't let myself be persuaded.'

'Hindsight's a wonderful thing, sir,' said Robb bracingly; but if he hoped to forestall further confidences, he was disappointed.

'Nothing to do with hindsight, Inspector. I've known for a long time now that my son would never come up to scratch. Animals have more sense than we do. If there's a wrong 'un in the litter, out it goes and there's an end to it. Nature may be red in tooth and claw, but it's more merciful than human justice, when all's said and done.'

Why must these people pretend they don't give a damn? thought Robb, studying the rigidly-controlled features. '*Boys mustn't cry,*' his parents probably said to little Archibald as they abandoned him at prep school. Part of his trouble might be that he still believed them.

'Was Nicholas a wrong 'un?'

The wide mouth tightened, as if the teeth behind were clenched, but Sir Archie's tone was almost casual as he replied, 'My wife and I – both my wives and I – tried to treat him like any other child, but yes. He was never really *right*. People sensed it, made excuses for him, tempered the wind, you know? "Poor Nicky," they would say. They could tell there was something wrong. Something... missing.'

With an air of finality he rose and poked the sullen fire, showering the labrador with grey ash. 'Well, old lady, if you must lie there... How about a refill, Robb? A parting glass?'

Recognising the dismissal, Robb made his excuses and left, muttering about paperwork, though Winter and Peg would deal with most of that. There was no need to fill them in on the past half-hour. In days gone by his superiors had done the same to him, and now it was his turn to chest his cards if he pleased. Winter could like it or lump it.

Squeezing behind the Land Rover's wheel, he drove under Catriona McNichol's curtained window, feeling the wind rock the vehicle as he turned along the track bordering the sea-loch, past the Glen Buie boat-house, and on to the headland. As he switched off the engine and doused the lights, the sky still looked pale, with a high, hazy moon. Ragged black clouds were flying south-east to merge with the dark bulk of hills behind the lighted windows of the Lodge.

Forty minutes passed. An hour, and Robb got out, shivering, reaching into the back for his Barbour. Presently he began to walk back the way he had come, treading softly.

As he neared the boat-house, a deep voice said, 'Buck up, old lady. Come on, if you're coming,' and he heard the scrabble of claws on wood. A moment later he made out the dark outline of a boat gliding backwards out of the building's shadow, bobbing as it met choppy water beyond the slipway. Nose to wind, tail outstretched, the silhouette of a dog in the bows formed a figurehead. In the stern, a bulky figure bent over the outboard.

I ought to stop him, thought Robb, but he did not move.

Twice the engine choked and died; then it caught, and settled into a steady putter. The boat swung round and headed down the path of the moon, black against shining pewter, steadily diminishing. As it reached open water, the dog left the bows and moved to sit on the stern thwart beside her master.

Was it to this craggy headland vantage-point that the shawled, barefoot women and ragged bearded men would creep to watch the Viking longships set sail into the wind-whipped autumn waves? Robb strained his eyes into the salt-laden gloom until he could no longer make out that moving black dot. Almost unconsciously he raised a hand in salute. The last of the summer raiders was going to his long home.

Buttoning his collar and digging icy fingers deep in his pockets, he turned away from the sea and trudged back to the car.

THE END

ACKNOWLEDGEMENTS

Foremost among those I would like to thank for encouragement, support, and expert advice are my husband Duff, and my problem-solving sister Miranda Lindsay; my editor Karen McCall, for her boundless enthusiasm and keen eye for detail, and Merlin Unwin, my publisher, who also created the detailed map of the Strathtorran Peninsula, thereby giving apparent reality to an imaginary landscape.

I am also very grateful to my nephew Rory Lindsay for permission to use his photograph of stalkers on the high tops at Conaglen for the jacket illustration.